Like Breathing

a novel by Ricc Rollins

An Ishai Book

Published by The Ishai Creative Group, Inc.
709 East Caracas Street • Tampa, Florida 33603-2328

This book is a work of fiction. Any references to real people, events, establishments, organizations or locales are intended to give this workof fiction a sense of reality and authenticity. Other names, characters and incidents are either the product of the author's imagination or used fictitiously,as are those fictionalized events and incidents that involve real persons and did not occur or are set in the future.

Library of Congress ard Catalog No.: 98-941-96
ISBN # 1892096331

Author's Photo: Robert Sargent, CPP*
Cover Photo: Photography Wil Adams *
Cover Design: Billianna Austin *
Covel Model: Casio *

A portion of the proceeds from the sales of "Like Breathing" will be donated to the People of Color AIDS Coalition in St. Petersburg, Florida.

PRINTED IN THE UNITED STATES OF AMERICA
FIRST ISHAI CREATIVE GROUP, INC. EDITION: December 1998

Dedication

This book is dedicated to
the people that I love
like breathing...
First and foremost to my
Heavenly Father who loves me
for me and gives me breath.
Next, to my "pops"
there isn't a day that goes by
that I don't miss you.
To my mother, my daughter
and son, my partner, 'Z'
and the many friends who
have kept me encouraged
on the journey.
Thanks to you all
for your love, support
and prayers. Know that
with each breath I take,
I love you more.

Acknowledgements

To my heavenly Father, I thank you God for the use of your gift; I pray that I have used it in a way that gives you the glory and honor that you so rightfully deserve. To my father in heaven, "Pops," I miss you! Thank you for showing me how to be a man by being one. To my mother, best friend and diva, Allie McEady Rollins, thank you for loving me just as I am and teaching me to love myself. To my partner, friend and companion, Lorenzo, thank you for your love, honesty and support, it's been a journey, but well worth the trip. Thank you for two years that get better with every breath and for the poem that captures the book's essence. To "my greatest creation," Jessica Ryan, thank you for just being daddy's little girl. To my son, Akiem, know that I love you and will always be grateful for your love. To my sisters, Aurson and Yolanda, thank you for just being you.

To my editing team, Dr. Deborah Austin, Anne Marie Huggins, Lorenzo C. Robertson, Marta Borges, and Billianna & Steven Austin, thank you for making sure that all of the t's were crossed and the i's dotted; I couldn't have done this without you, nor would I have wanted to. Know that I am eternally in your gratitude for making me look so good. You are each angels; your halos are on the way.

To my support team, Dr. Trevy McDonald, Maurice J. Jackson, Lisa R. Campbell, Diana Fitzgerald, Eric Grate, Chris Miller, Gwendolyn Evans Rollins, William Forde, Alonzo DuPree, Gregory Williams, Ellen Fiss, Denise White, Clarence Reynolds, Darrell Evans, Tony Turner, Keith Boykin, Carl DeVine, Gregory Taylor, Mac Arthur Flournoy and Glenn Alexander; I thank each of you for being there when I needed you. Just knowing that you were there helped me continue when I thought there were no more words. A special thanks to: Pat and the folks at A & A Printing; Patti at For Any Occasion and Brian from NPC, *"You make me look good."* And to E. Lynn Harris, thank you for your encouragement and friendship.

To my advance team: Anne Blunte, Lori Bassett-Sharrieff, Cloe Cabrera, Judy Candis, Katherine Carey, Felecia Wintons, Maurice Jackson, Bryant Haith, Dallas Manuel and Donald West; thank you for your support and your honesty.

And lastly, to the booksellers and readers, thank you for believing in me enough to buy my first book. Hopefully, you'll love reading it as much as I loved writing it.

Like Breathing

one with himself

love washed over him like a gentle spring rain
cooling waters purged his soul and freed his brain
he was at peace with himself

devotion to his God was pure, innocent and effortless
essence of God pierced his body the sensation was painless
he was in harmony with Him

reverence anointed him like early morning dew
soothing mist cleansed his spirit and made him anew
he was at peace with himself

adoration to his beloved was simple genuine and miraculous
fragrance of his beloved seared his spirit and it was tremendous
he was in harmony with him

lorenzo robertson

One

The microwave sounded, letting Zander know that his fat-free entree was done. He knew that his mother would have a fit if she knew that he wasn't eating regular food. She hated microwave dinners and microwaves for that matter. While he wasn't a fan of them either, it was quick, easy and most importantly, not fast or junk food; or at least this was his rationale. He hadn't been to a gym in weeks and work, not working out, was all that he had time for. He had never been fat, but he wanted to insure that he would maintain his toned physique until he could hit the gym again, so the fat-free dinners were his insurance. He placed it on the oven mitt and made his way to his home office, which was really the third bedroom in the house. He settled into his black leather high back chair, clicking the icon to his online service. The familiar welcome prompt came on at rocket speed. He smiled reassuringly to himself. The new high powered modem was an investment after all. He had lamented about buying another computer gadget, wondering if it would end up in the closet with the all the rest of his "toys."

The voice prompt informed him that he had email. His mail box was filled with the usual invitations to visit porno sites and start a home business; he hit the delete button almost at reflex. He frowned at the invitation from"Jasmine and Jill" to watch them play. He laughed to himself thinking that if"Big Brotha" really was watching then he should know better. He sorted through the rest of his email, a daily note from his mother and one from Desmond Lowe, his best friend from college and fraternity brother.

He looked forward to the notes from his mother. They kept him updated on what was going on. While she wouldn't admit it, Zander knew it was also his mother's way of saving money on long distance calls. He read his mother's latest email and smiled. She was telling him that she had met a new"friend" online in the widow's chat room and that she was meeting him for Sunday dinner at her favorite buffet styled restaurant. He replied to her message, warning her to exercise caution and not move too quickly. He reminded her that things were different back in the day and that she had to be very careful. He closed out the message with his usual closing,"with love from your greatest creation." His mother had called him that for as long as he could remember. With the click of the mouse the message was transmitted to"Big Mama." He always had to laugh at his mother's screen name because Henrietta Eady was not big by any stretch of the imagination, she was just the opposite."Rita," a name that she gave herself as a teen because she hated her real name, was, in her son's opinion, one of the most beautiful women this side of heaven. She had shoulder length black and silver hair, beautiful copper colored skin, big brown eyes and a shape that would rival women half her age. Zander loved his mother like no other woman on this earth, in fact, she was the only woman he had ever loved.

He then read Desmond's email notifying him of the annual fraternity convention in DC and of course the latest update on his online conquests. In the email message from"DLowe247" Desmond had written:

<< 'Z' I am on my way to see this guy that I met in the CharlotteM4M chat room. He is hotter than hell and twice as red. (see pic attached) His name is Ty and his screen name is 'FlyBoyee'... he's a flight attendant, on lay over. Says that he's a bottom with a cute bubble butt that needs tending to! Here are his stats: '5'9", 150lbs., green eyes (exotic heaven) light brown skin, curly salt/pep hair with a fade, hairy chest and a body by God. Speaking of, when you see the pic I think you'll agree, I've died an gone to heaven. AND yes Z baby he's negative. Give you all the dirt when I get I back. Love u ;-) >>

Desmond knew how Zander worried about him meeting perfect strangers and"hooking-up" with them without knowing much about them. He clicked on the icon to download the pic, putting it in the file, 'D'sBoyz,' a file he created to keep up with Desmond and his many men as a precaution in case anything bad ever happened to his friend. He looked at the pic as it revealed itself on the screen. He thought that the guy was attractive and that he did have pretty green eyes, but Zander wondered to himself if they were real. He said a quick prayer of protection for Desmond and clicked the box, removing the pic from the screen.

Desmond told Zander that he picked the name"DLowe247," because he was on the"DL" or"down-low" meaning that he was discreet about his sexual orientation every day all day. Zander always thought that it should have been"DNile" because he truly was in denial.

They had been best friends from day one. They met during their freshman year at college and Zander said that he knew Desmond was"family" at first glance. And if he knew, others did too; a fact that Desmond denies to this day. That aside, he admired Desmond's zest for life and he loved his best friend like a brother. In fact, he considered him the brother he never had. And people always thought that they were brothers. They did look alike, but not that much so they always thought. Zander always thought that Desmond was the better looking of the two.

Everyone that met Zander and Desmond always admired the duo's modelesque looks and sculptured bodies; but Desmond was the type of guy that even straight guys looked at. He had naturally wavy hair atop his perfectly oval shaped head. He had the most perfect teeth that Zander had ever seen; they were the perfect accent to his warm smile. Desmond always thanked his orthodontist and his parents for those"perfect teeth." His eyes changed from light to dark depending on his mood and they had a slight slant that made him look unique.

Zander always commented that his best friend put the"s" in style. Desmond could put on a pair of old jeans and a t-shirt and people would comment on how good he looked. He was the only person that Zander knew who never worked out and looked like he did. However, Zander was the more muscular of the two and Desmond was an inch or two shorter. But Desmond always reminded him that he had the bigger muscle in another area. Zander was the darker of the two, his caramel colored skin exuded a warmth that suited his personality. He had big brown eyes much like his mother and he had his father's crooked smile, along with his cleft chin. He had a solid body. People were always asking Zander if he worked out, even before he started doing so. While Desmond's hair was curly, Zander's was silky, wavy and curly. Rita called it"wash and wear hair," and now it was starting to gray ever so slightly, a trait of all the Eady men.

The chime informed him that he had an incoming message. A"quick note from OnePhineBM" appeared. He was one of the guys that Zander had befriended online in the BlackMen4Men chat room. He greeted him with his usual"wassup." Zander responded and they proceeded to exchange cordialities. He really wasn't in the mood to talk, but he didn't want to be rude, so he did. He continued his online conversation while flipping through the channels with the remote looking for something to watch on television. Nothing worth watching was on, so he returned to his attention to his online conversation."OnePhineBM" had messaged him again with"hello, hello" when he didn't get a response to his question. He really wasn't paying attention and told him that he would holla at him later. He thought about going out, but opted to stay in and play online.

He clicked on the bookmark for his favorite chat room, the local Blk M4M room. He perused its audience, scrolling down to see if any of the names looked familiar or if there was anything or anyone of interest online. In between reading profiles and talking back to the screen, he took a couple of quick bites of his now lukewarm dinner, making a face as he put the meal back on the corner of his desk. He refocused his attention to the profiles, wiping the marinara sauce from his mouth and swallowing the bite that remained in his mouth. He read some of the preferences, the phallic bragging and the personal quotes of the men in the chat room and thought to himself that this was a real waste of his time. He didn't want to meet any of the guys, he just wanted to talk. He had to admit that as much as he loved his home, he was lonely and that sometimes his house seemed so big and empty.

He hadn't been online in a while because he was so swamped at work. He began feeling guilty about playing online and told himself that instead of reading profiles he should be going over his notes for tomorrow's presentation, but he didn't want to overdo it. He looked on the desk at Keith Boykin's book *One More River to Cross* and thought about starting it. He had been waiting to read it for so long, but wanted to do so when he could really concentrate and enjoy it. He told himself that this was just the mindless diversion that he needed.

As he continued to read the profiles he saw one that seemed very familiar, but he couldn't quite put his finger on why. Not only was it familiar; it was uncomfortably familiar. He read and reread the profile trying to see if this person was someone he knew. The screen name didn't ring a bell, but the verbiage did. He repeated the screen name"Phine9Bro" over and over as if chanting the name would conjure up an image of who this was. He read the profile again, this time outloud imitating a television announcer's voice:"*GBM, 6'2" 185... Good looks and looking good...UB2...workout regularly..Former slave, mandingo warrior...*" Reading the mystery man's description made Zander chuckle. He continued..."*Looking for brothers who can dish the big 'D' as well as take it! No Fats or Fems need reply. If I'm online, I need someone to service my nine.*" And a poet too, Zander thought to himself, laughing at the last line. Zander couldn't help but wonder if Mister Phine9 was telling the truth or embellishing in the endowment category as so many people were known to do online.

He thought back to some of these guys at an online Party he had attended at Club Eclectic, one of his favorite hangouts. From that night on he had a new rule of thumb-guys that talked about being handsome, cute, VGL (very good looking) or phine were normally creeps, full of it or themselves or most likely looked nothing at all like the descriptions in their profiles. Even when they sent a picture it was normally not them. He walked around the room looking at name tags and trying to remember the pictures that he had received online. Most of them didn't match.

He continued to read the profile but couldn't figure out who this person was..."This is going to nag at me all night long," he thought to himself."This guy is someone that I know, but who?", he whispered. This really had him puzzled.

Zander sighed and stroked his chin, imitating the detective from some movie he had watched the night before on the Classic Movie Channel. He decided that the only way to find out was to quick message Phine9Bro. He typed"wassup" in the message box and was about to send it when his inner voice said"NO!" and it was never wrong. He canceled the message and began to sign off. Still perplexed, he decided to read the profile one last time. Maybe he had missed something, a clue, a phrase, anything that would solve the mystery. He looked at the birth date...nothing... then he read the quote."*Looking for brothers who can dish the big 'D' as well as take it...*" and then it clicked. This was someone from his past that he didn't want in his present or his future. A sick and sinking feeling took residence in his stomach."What was he doing in town?" Zander asked himself. He quickly clicked off the profile and put his face in his hands, peeping through the separation of his fingers at the half eaten entree. Suddenly he wasn't hungry anymore. He needed a drink. Normally he didn't drink on a work night, but tonight he would make an exception."Why? Why! WHY?" He screamed silently. Maybe he was wrong, maybe this wasn't him at all. It had to be him! The profile reeked of Gage Gregory,"*dish the big 'D' as well as take it!*""He's still using that line. Some people!" he thought out loud.

This had to be some bad dream. He told himself that he would wake up and this blast from the past would fizzle like a wet firecracker. He poured a drink and downed it in one gulp. It burned going down but it didn't hurt any worse than the memories that were about to surface.

Two

"Why is he here?" That lone question caused Zander to toss and turn, while he kept telling himself that he needed to get some sleep. This was the big one; this could make or break his career. He needed to be as sharp as a tack, but work was the last thing on his mind. He tried counting sheep, reading, even a little stroking of his manhood. The latter always put him to sleep, but nothing worked. The thought of Gage Garrison Gregory a/k/a"Phine9Bro" being in the same city robbed him of sleep just like he had robbed him of his happiness and his heart five years ago when they lived in Orlando. Desmond called Gage the"thief of hearts." He laid there listening to the sounds of the night, thinking about the fact that somewhere out there in the same city, his city, was Gage. It was going to be a long night.

Zander hadn't thought about Gage in ages. He actually had managed to put the past behind him. It wasn't like this was his first love, but this was love like he had never known it before. Gage swept him off his feet and it was a long time before he ever touched the ground again. He was the only man who got Zander to let his hair down and have some fun without thinking of the consequences. He taught him how to throw caution to the wind and let it all hang out and just happen. For Zander, loving Gage was like breathing. It was easy, without effort or thought, he just did. He and Gage were inseparable. Those in their circle called them everything from the dynamic duo to the poster children for Black Gay Love. The latter was Desmond's contribution. If you saw one, you saw the other. They did everything together. Some even speculated that they probably used the bathroom together.

Gage was the new kid in town when they met at *Secrets*, the local hangout. It was a hot summer night and the club was packed as usual. The dance version of Mariah Carey's *Dream Lover* was playing as Gage made his entrance. When he entered the club, Zander thought that Moses was parting the Red Sea all over again. People actually moved to make way for him as he made his way to the dance floor. Even the club kids who never stop dancing took five to look at this Black Adonis. He was an MIB (man in black) long before Will Smith ever thought about becoming one. He was wearing a pair of black Calvins that seemed to be molded to fit his fine behind and highlight his more than generous serving of manhood. His black t-shirt hugged his pecs and actually indicated that there was a six pack that would make Budweiser proud underneath. He wore a pair of black-ostrich skinned cowboy boots and a funky belt of the same. He had the most beautiful blemish-free caramel colored skin which glowed even in the dim lighting of the club. He wore his hair closely cropped and faded on the sides. He sported a neatly trimmed goatee and the most intriguing light brown eyes Zander had ever seen. You know the kind, when the person stares it's like he's reading your mind or looking right through you. In a word, he was gorgeous.

Zander was engaged in conversation with his boys when he turned to see what all the fuss was about and wham, he landed smack dab in Gage's body-by-God chest. Talk about knocking somebody off their feet! Zander began to fall back as Gage caught him and the rest, as they say, was history.

Zander just laid there. How could this be happening now? Why not last week, last month, last year!"How about never!!!" he yelled internally. He tried again to put him out of his mind, but no go. He thought about emailing Gage and asking him why he was in town. He was sure some of their mutual friends had told Gage that Zander lived there; the kind of"friends" who can't hold water. Probably some hopeless romantic who wanted to see them get back together or some treacherous drama queen who just wanted to start some trouble. Okay. Then why hadn't he called, why no messages on the voicemail, no email...no nothing? All of a sudden Zander found himself ticked at Gage for not trying to contact him. Knowing that SOB, this was all a game. He was messing with his head, after all he had already broken his heart. Zander was pissed. This was so like Gage."Some people never change," he thought."I can't handle this," he said to himself.

"Where is the phone," he mumbled as he sprung out of the bed. He reached for the cordless and hit the speed dial. A sleepy"hello" and a throat clearing greeted him on the other end of the phone; he felt bad about calling in the middle of the night but he had to talk to somebody.

"You'll never guess who is in town," he said without even as much as a hello."C'mon guess, GUESS!"

"Chile, have you lost your mind? You my bristah (it was a compound word of brother and sistah that Desmond created) and all, but a diva needs his rest." Desmond rarely punked, but when he did, watch out! Zander apologized for calling so late and proceeded to tell Desmond about his online dilemma.

"D... how could he do this to me, why would he do this to me? Why?"

He began to ramble and Desmond sensed that his friend was really hurting.

"Hey, hey , HEY! Z, Zbaby, calm down! First thing you need to do is chill...Mistah Man ain't worth it! You know this, I know this AND HE KNOWS THIS..." Desmond screeched. Zander had to laugh.

"Thanks 'D' you're right, but he's here...what am I gonna do if he calls me, what am I gonna say? Oh - my - God!"

"What chile? What?" Desmond said, thinking something had happened.

"And what if he wants to see me, do I see him?"

"He ain't called yet, so what makes you think that he's gonna call? Why conjure up trouble? If Mister Wunnerful knows what's good for him he'll stay away. I'll be on my broom in a hot second in full Endora drag... HE DOES NOT! I REPEAT, DOES NOT, want a piece of me...well actually he does... but then again, what man doesn't."

They both laughed and Desmond reassured him that everything would be okay. He reminded him that his presentation was the most important thing now. He also reminded him that things always have a way of working themselves out and that this too would pass.

"But seriously D..." Zander began,"what am I going to do if I have to see him?"

"Aaaagh! Z! Why you asking for trouble?"

"I'm not asking for trouble, I am a realist! If it is him and he is in town, you know that he's going to try to see me!"

"Yes, he is predictable!"

"D! C'mon voice of experience... speak to me!"

"Chile! Blink like Jeannie and banish the bastard!"

"Okay, I see that you are not going to help me here. I guess I'll let you get back to your beauty rest...God knows you need it."

"Oh no you didn't!"

"Yes, I did and what you gonna do about it?"

"Hocus, Pocus, Snap, Snap, Snap...." Desmond began his incantation.

"What are you doing?"

"Eye of trade, weave of Ms. Ross..."

"You are one sick man!"

"Show Zander who is boss!" Zander just laughed at Desmond's feeble attempt at sorcery.

"Okay Marilyn the Magician, sorceress of the sissies..."

"No you didn't...that's Endora to you thang-a-lang!"

"I'll let you go, since you ain't gonna be no help! Any last words of wisdom?"

"Maybe if you put in a tape and handle yo' biz..."

"Anyway..." They both laughed at Desmond's suggestion.

"You one sick brotha, just can't be serious." Desmond cleared his throat trying to regain his composure.

"Okay, Z baby, go take a warm shower, go over your notes and get some rest, Now who loves you?" Desmond said trying to be both serious and sincere. Zander replied with a flip tone,"My mama."

"Very funny, Z, very funny! I'll let that one slide."

They laughed louder and harder, said good night and this time Zander told Desmond that he loved him. Zander breathed a cleansing breath as he placed the phone back on the cradle, laughing to himself and shaking his head at Desmond. It then dawned on him that he was so consumed with his problems that he forgot to ask Desmond about his tryst with"FlyBoyee." He thought to himself that it couldn't have been that great if Desmond answered the phone on the first ring. Oh well, he knew that he would hear all of the details sooner or later. He always did.

For the moment he even managed to forget about Gage. He began to think about the presentation and wanted to go over everything insuring that this day would go off without a hitch. He walked to the closet and pulled out the suit bag from the men's shop where he bought all of his suits. He unzipped the bag and removed the new suit. He took the lint brush and stroked the suit's jacket, removing stray threads and lint from the navy, chalked striped, three button suit. He special ordered it just for this presentation. He went to the other side of his walk-in closet, pulled a freshly laundered white shirt from the rack and placed it beneath the jacket, adding one of his favorite ties to the ensemble. He stood back giving himself a thumbs up. He was going to knock them dead. He pulled out his new black Cole Haan's and wiped them with the shoe cloth housed in their box. He had spent a little more than he wanted on the shoes, but he knew that it would be worth it. He had to be the spitting image of success. The shoes glistened as he set them by the wooden valet that occupied the corner of his bedroom. He arranged everything on the valet and stood back looking at his attire for the big day. He was the man. If he could have reached, he would have pat himself on the back; instead he gave himself a congratulatory high five.

He picked up his brief case and removed his notes for the presentation to review them, one last time. As he settled in, the phone rang, his heart raced. He looked towards heaven and mouthed,"Please no!" He answered the phone"Hell-ll-o?!?" It was a wrong number. "That's okay, no problem. Good-bye," he said smiling as he disconnected. Once again he looked toward heaven and mouthed"Thank you!" He told himself that he had to put this out of his mind. He wasn't going to do this to himself every time the phone rang. He wasn't about to let the past mess up his future, no way, no how.

An hour passed as he reviewed the notes for the presentation. He made mental notes of his points of emphasis and rehearsed his closing. He neatly tucked his notes back in the leather folder that housed them. Clicking the flap of his brief case shut, he placed it back beside the valet and stretched, feeling good about himself. He was as ready as he could be.

It had been a long day and an even longer night. He decided to take D's advice and take a shower. Once he had finished, he grabbed the towel off the hook and began to dry himself. He found a pair of silk boxers and slipped into them. He was ready for sleep and sleep was ready for him.

Three

Zander rolled over to adjust the volume on the radio as it blasted. He laid there for a moment rubbing his eyes and thinking about the day ahead. He slipped out of bed on to his knees as he took a moment to whisper his morning prayers. He thanked God for another day and for his many blessings. He asked God to dispatch an angel of protection around his family and friends. He also prayed for those who had been infected with and affected by H.I.V. and AIDS; this had become a constant in his prayers since he had lost so many friends and a couple of family members to AIDS. As he was about to finish his prayers he remembered his mother's directions and closed his prayers asking that God's will be done in his life. He then added a special request asking for God's guidance as he delivered his presentation later this morning."Amen," he whispered as he sat up on the side of the bed. As he reflected on the day ahead he sat experiencing the peace and solitude of the moment. He said nothing, did nothing and thought nothing. He just...sat. The thud of the newspaper hitting the front door summoned him back to this plane. He felt better and the day seemed to be filled with potential. Zander took a deep breath and stretched. This was the day that he had been waiting on since his first day at the firm. Today, if he had anything to do with it, he would become a partner.

As Zander prepared to get ready, he stopped and listened to the crew from the *Tom Joyner Morning Show.* As usual Tom, Sybil and Jay were going at it. Zander chuckled at their antics as he laid his suit on the bed and proceeded to get ready. He looked at the shirt and decided to change it. He thought that white was predictable and that it looked as if he were begging for the client. He wanted to say that he was in charge. He knew just the shirt. He opened the door to the walk-in closet and pulled one of his favorites from the cedar rod that housed them. He selected a Perry Ellis blue French-cuff shirt from a sea of freshly laundered and heavily starched shirts. He then moved on to the revolving tie rack housed in the pine armoire that served as both a wardrobe and entertainment center. He selected several ties, holding each of them up to the shirt. He was looking for the perfect match, one that would accentuate the look that he wanted to achieve. He finally selected a silk electric blue solid. Zander loved the monochromatic look and it loved him; he always received compliments when he did that look. He lived by the motto,"when you look good, you feel good." There was only one thing missing. He rummaged through the jewelry tray looking for his favorite pair of cuff links."Finally," he said as he located a pair of antique cuff links. He had loved those diamond and gold studs since he was a child. He remembered how he would marvel at them when his"Gramps" or his"Pops" wore them. He would ask if he could wear them when he grew up; to him they were magic. So his mother gave them to him as a graduation present. He wore the cuff links only on special occasions and today was indeed special. They were his good luck charm.

As he clutched the links, his thoughts shifted to his Dad and Gramps; the two men who he looked to for strength, even after their passing. They would be so proud of him today, he thought to himself. He would give anything to talk to his dad right about now. Zander thought his father to be one of the greatest men on Earth; life seemed so simple when his dad was alive. His dad always had a way of making even the toughest situation seem simple. A slight frown replaced his reminiscent smile as he became saddened by a sense of loss. A quiet sigh reaffirmed that loss and the tear parked in the corner of his eye echoed how much he really missed those men.

He looked at his new choices and assured himself that this was even better than what he selected the night before. He yelled at the top of his lungs"who da man? I'm da man!" He added a little dance to it and repeated the mantra several more times until he had worked up a sweat. Since he was already sweaty he decided to do some push ups and crunches, something he hadn't done in a while because his schedule hadn't allowed regular trips to the gym. He finished his mini workout and prepared to take his shower. His body glistened with the rewards of his workout. He stood stretching to cool down. As he approached the dressing area of the master bath he looked in the mirror, patting his flat stomach and winking in acknowledgment that he was still looking good. He needed to stay that way, he thought to himself as he removed the silk boxers.

He flicked on the lights in the master bath and turned on the shower, adjusting the water until the temperature was just right. The steam began to rise and Zander stepped into the shower. The water met and caressed his toned bronze body as he was seduced by its warmth. He stood perfectly still, marrying the steady, sultry stream as he became one with it. Zander loved water, maybe that was the Pisces in him. He lathered the loofah and started to rub it against his body. He seemed entranced as the texture of the loofah massaged his skin. As if magically, he was taken back to a time when Gage would massage him in the shower as they prepared for work or when they would soak and sip wine by candlelight in the evening. As much as he didn't want to, he had to admit to himself that he missed those moments together. He remembered the moments of contact when Gage would touch him, hold him or kiss him; he remembered how Gage made him tremble and shudder. Thinking of Gage consumed him with melancholy. Before he knew it, his manhood throbbed, reflecting the pleasure of his thoughts. He was consumed by the memories when the phone rang, disturbing his erotic interlude. He reached out of the shower for the cordless.

"Hello?" he answered still somewhat dazed.

"Hey boyee! Wassup?" It was Desmond,"how you feeling?"

"Fine..." He answered half-heartedly. He knew that if he told Desmond what he was thinking about prior to his call he would read him until kingdom come.

"Okay, now tell me the truth!" Desmond said.

"...what?" Zander answered in a boyish tone laced with fake innocence."Evan Zander Eady, the fourth" Desmond stated firmly,"boy, don't bs the king of bs... you thinking about Gage ain't you?"

"NO!" Zander snapped, as he asked himself "how did he know-was I that obvious?".

"You lie like a cheap hooker in a sleazy hotel! Thing tell me the truth!"

"Okay! Yes I was thinking about him, so sue me... what do you want anyway?"Zander snapped, feeling really bad about his last statement, but Desmond had it coming. Zander tried to rationalize his anger to himself,"Who did Desmond think he was, an out of work psychic from Dionne's hot line?."

"Hold up bitch! Forgive me for caring about your sorry ass! If you would rather, I can save these coins to call someone who cares! I don't have to call long distance to be insulted!" Desmond retorted.

"D, c'mon bro! I'm sorry; you know it's my time of the month!" He said chuckling trying to ease the tension that he created. But Desmond wasn't biting.

"Don't try it!" Desmond replied. Zander knew he had his work cut out, but he didn't have time to smooth his ruffled feathers."D, don't be mad, pleaaaaseee!" he said sweetly.

"Why shouldn't I?" Desmond snapped as the opening line of what was to be a rather lengthy reading with Desmond calling him everything but a child of God. Zander tried to get a word in edgewise but knew that it wasn't going to be an easy feat.

He managed to maneuver his way around in the shower and finish while half listening to Desmond. He stepped out of the shower and placed the phone on the cradle after pressing the speaker button. Desmond was in rare form and Zander decided to just let him vent, after all he asked for it. He listened as he finished his grooming routine and began getting dressed.

"Yes, D! I'm sorry D! I know"he would answer as Desmond would make statements that required answers.

He made his way back to the full length cheval mirror as he tied his tie for the third time trying to get the knot just right. He adjusted the tie and looked in the mirror he was finally pleased.

"D! D! D!" Zander called out,"I need to get out of here, I'm really sorry that I snapped at you and for hurting your feelings but it's 7:45 and I have to get out of here, k?"

"Okay, but you know that this ain't ovah!" Desmond replied.

"I know D and you know that I love you! I'll call you tonight, aiight?"

Desmond was noncommittal, but he did wish Zander luck and they hung up. Zander grabbed his briefcase and took a deep breath as he closed the door behind him.

Four

Zander loved his job, he had been working there for three years now. As he drove into the office he reminisced about how he came to work at The PRDesign Group.

He had been recruited by the president of the firm, Elle (pronounced L) Paige, a former award winning news anchor and radio personality who grew tired of the radio biz. She started what was now one of the fastest growing public relations and advertising agencies in the country.

While in Orlando meeting with one of the city's major amusement entities, Elle called Zander to meet with her. She told him to pick a restaurant, so he suggested one of downtown's more popular restaurants, The Orange Quarter. Zander was already at the restaurant when Elle arrived. As she approached the table he couldn't help but notice how stunning she was. She wasn't tall and she wasn't short. At the time Elle wore her hair braided and in a French twist. She was a mocha beauty. Her eyes dazzled when she talked, her smile made you smile and her laugh was infectious. He could tell that she was proud of her shape by the outfit she was wearing, while professional, it really accentuated her well maintained body.

During lunch, she informed him that his reputation was quite impressive, that his leadership skills were known throughout the advertising industry and that there was a place for him at her firm. As they discussed business philosophy and trends, he knew that Elle was using her old interviewing skills on him. She wanted to see if he was all talk, or if he had real brains and talent. For dessert she offered him a vice presidency with the firm. She had the waiter bring the contract on a silver platter with a Monte Blanc pen for him to sign with and keys to a brand new bronzit BMW 525ie. She informed him that all of her VP's were given a car when they signed. Zander knew that he wasn't going anywhere with the firm he was with so there was nothing to think about. He took the pen and signed his name to a five year contract. Within three weeks he moved, leaving Orlando behind and the memories that came with it.

From his first day there, Zander knew that he wanted to be a partner at PRDG. As he pulled into the parking lot on his first day the marquee read:

The PRDesign Group
welcomes
Zander Evan Eady, IV
VP, New Client Acquisitions

Zander almost hit his reserved parking space sign looking at the marquee. He had to get a picture of it to send to his mother. Once again he wished that his father could share in this moment. When he got off the elevator, his executive administrative assistant, Asia, a beautiful sistah with long legs, a short curly fro and a body that wouldn't wait, was there to greet him. They exchanged pleasantries and she escorted him to his office, a corner with a view of the city to die for. When she opened the door, he was floored; the office was decorated in Biedermeir and leather. Elle had her designer and best friend, Dimitri, make the office over especially for Zander. As he stepped into the office he scanned the room in amazement; he had never seen anything like this. On the corner of his desk was a Lalique crystal vase with three dozen white roses and a card that read: *"Welcome aboard, your future is crystal clear with a sweet smell of success."* It was signed by Elle, and the rest of the office staff names were neatly typed underneath her sprawling, but artistic signature. He smiled and placed the card back in the wire holder. Asia asked if he needed anything and he politely declined. She smiled and told him to buzz her if he did. As she leaned to show him how the system worked his nose was teased by the aroma of her perfume. He couldn't help but notice how beautiful she was and thought to himself,"if I wasn't gay..."

But he was and so he didn't even go there. Asia excused herself, but not before once again reaffirming how glad PRDG was to have him join their little family. As he settled in, he noticed that there was a memo from Elle announcing his arrival and an itinerary including a meeting with all of the VP's and the rest of the firm's staff. He noticed the nameplate on his desk. It was a glass slab with his name etched alongside the PRDG logo. Also on the desk was a box of business cards and his own letterhead. He picked up one of the cards and read it out loud,"Zander Evan Eady, the fourth, Vice-president, new client acquisitions." He smiled and whispered,"thank you God."

The past three years had been great. Elle never failed to make him aware of how pleased she was with his contributions to the company. Not only did she voice her satisfaction, she exemplified it with bonuses and other incentives. Her latest offering was something that he had dreamed of but didn't know when or if it would ever materialize.

Elle had called him into her office, a beautiful suite that was nestled in the center of the building. Zander always thought this to be appropriate; after all she was the nucleus of PRDG. Her executive suite had its own 25-seat conference room, media room and dressing room complete with full shower. The office walls were lined with original art and the wall behind her desk was adorned with photographs of Elle and her celebrity pals: everyone one from President Clinton to Quincy Jones. His favorite was the picture of Elle and Oprah. Zander also loved going to Elle's office because she always had some baked goodies that her housekeeper, Essie, had prepared and Elle was more than happy to share with her staff.

Zander arrived at Elle's office and was directed by her assistant, Joy to go right in. He walked in and found Elle on the phone, she motioned for him to sit, he obliged and waited for her to conclude her conversation. Once the call was finished she apologized for keeping him waiting. She was smiling as she shared the news that her alma mater was giving her an honorary doctorates. He stood up and gave her a congratulatory hug and kiss on the cheek. She was radiant, not that she wasn't always, but this day she was absolutely brilliant.

"Enough about me, let's talk about you!" she started with a matter of fact tone."You know that I've always told you that one of the best decisions I ever made regarding PRDG was hiring you..."

He thanked her."But I've had to make another decision...one that affects your position with the company." A chill ran up Zander's spine."We have a very important client coming in..." She reminded him of the memo she had sent out regarding the television syndicators that she was courting." He nodded."They want to meet with us and I want you to handle it!"

Zander didn't know whether to kiss Elle or take her temperature.

"Are you sure? If we get them do you realize what this will do for PRDG; we'll be international!"

"Last time I checked I was still in charge."

"I'm sorry, I don't mean to question your decisions but..."

"But what, when I was away at that syndicators convention I left you in charge and you handled the day to day operations while doing your job too... and you didn't loose the company..." Elle laughed and assured him that she knew what she was doing. Zander took another breath and thanked her.

"Oh and by the way, if you land this... we'll be changing your title from VP to partner." She winked and stood up to escort him to the door rubbing his back."Not a word to anyone about this... I don't want anyone to know what's going on! I think you understand , you've been here the shortest amount of time, but your contributions have helped put this company miles ahead of the competition. So Zander, I'm counting on you!"

He squeezed her hand, both to reassure her and to thank her. He floated back to his office. He instructed Asia that he was not to be disturbed. He closed the door behind him and dropped to his knees and let out a silent scream. That night he called Desmond and his mother to tell them the news, swearing them to secrecy.

"Please don't tell anyone, you could ruin this for me if you do, Maybe I shouldn't have told you guys, but I had to tell someone or I was gonna burst. Keep me in your prayers, I'm gonna need them." They both assured him that his secret was safe and that they would keep him in their prayers.

For the next couple of weeks, he reported directly to Elle updating her on his progress and running ideas and proposals by her. She assured him that it wasn't necessary and she trusted him. He was grateful, but he knew that he owed her that much. After all she was the boss. Two weeks and four days later, Zander's presentation was ready. The clients were sending a representative to hear what PRDG had to offer them. The night before the final presentation, he received an interoffice email from Elle. It simply read: *"Not that you need it, but good luck tomorrow... partner."* Zander smiled and replied, *"We'll see, PRAY!"*

As Zander pulled into his spot he looked up to see if the marquee had been changed. It had. He took a deep breath and got out of the car. He opened the back door, removed his jacket from the hanger and put it on. He grabbed his brief case from the back seat, shut the door, locked it with the remote housed on his key chain and made his way to the elevator. He exchanged smiles and small talk with the occupants of the elevator. When it arrived at his floor he bid them all good day.

He stood outside of the glass double doors of PRDG for a brief second and called on everything within himself for strength. He took one last cleansing breath and opened the door.

Five

Elle was waiting in the reception area for Zander. She too was in her power suit, a black chalk striped six-button pant suit with a platinum silk pocket square neatly placed in her breast pocket and a sterling silver stick pen penetrating the lapel. Zander beamed with pride because he had given her the pin on their professional anniversary. To him this was a good luck sign that everything was going to be all right.

"Don't you look sharp! New suit?"

"Yes ma'am! Bought it just for today. And you're looking awfully sharp yourself, love the pin."

"Thank you kind sir, a good friend of mine gave it to me."

"Your friend has good taste..." Zander chuckled and winked.

"Yes, he does! Especially in bosses..." Elle quipped.

"Touche' diva, touche."

Elle escorted Zander to his office with her arm locked in his. They discussed Zander's outline of the presentation and the notes that he had sent Elle. He asked her for her thoughts and any concerns.

"Well... there is one..."

"What.." Zander asked,"what's wrong?"

"Zander, it's about your presentation..."

"What about the presentation?" Zander asked nervously.

"It's a piece of...how can I put this..." Elle paused.

"Elle, just tell me, please..."

"It's... one of the most well written and concise presentations that I've ever read and the video demo is superb." Zander took a deep breath partnered with a sigh of relief. He smiled at Elle and shook his finger in a playful manner.

He was spending fourteen hour days and most weekends writing and rewriting the proposal. Then there was the thirty six hours straight in editing. He would be the first in the office and the last to leave, if he left at all. He often slept on the sofa in his office and showered there too. By the end of the project, Zander was running on pure adrenaline. Rita and Desmond both began to worry that he was going to work himself into the ground. Their email went unanswered and their voicemail not returned, this was not like Zander.

"Zander, you have a call on line one" the intercom buzzed as Elle left his office.

"Asia, who is it, I'm really busy here!" He snapped.

"It's your mom?"

"Tell her I'll call her back." He hit the release button disconnecting the call and returned to the demographic study that he was reviewing. The phone rang again. He punched the speaker button frustrated at his orders not being followed

"Asia, didn't I..." the voice interrupted,"My name isn't Asia and I think you need to change your tone young man, right about now! I raised you better than that." It was his mother, she obviously had talked Asia into putting her through.

"Oh! Hey ma, listen can I..."

Rita interrupted,"don't you hey ma, me, and no you cannot call me back. We're going to talk now young man."

"Ma, this really isn't a good time, I'm right in the middle of..."

"I know you haven't lost your mind. Were you about to tell me that you're too busy to talk with me. Too busy to talk to the woman who gave you life and might I remind you who will take it way if you don't straighten up and fly right."

"Ma!" He said trying to get a word in edge wise.

"Zander, I am worried about..."

"Ma! Look I'm sorry that I haven't called but this is really important!" He snapped,"so I'm going to have to talk with you later..."

"Zander Evan Eady, the fourth... you shut your high powered, mister corporate executive, Hugo Boss suit wearing mouth right now! You didn't know if I was dead or alive and I'm beginning to wonder if you cared."

He realized that he had hurt his mother's feelings and that was the last thing that he ever wanted to do, but he was busy. His future with PRDG depended on the success or failure of this project. If he failed he didn't know if Elle would ever give him another chance.

"I'm sorry ma, what's wrong?"

"Thats what I should be asking you. Are you okay? I haven't heard from you in weeks. I know you're computer ain't broke, what about your dialing finger? Or have you just lost your mind?"

Zander had to laugh."No ma! Just extremely busy."

"Busy, hmmph... too busy for me?"

"I didn't say that... you know you're my one and only!"

"You better recognize!" They both laughed at his mother's attempt at being hip.

"Ma! I love you! Thanks for calling me! and thanks for understanding!"

"Oh no mister Z you aren't getting off that easily! Have you been eating?"

"Yes ma'am." He was lying through his teeth.

"Z, now you wouldn't lie to me would you son? Let me talk to Asia, she'll tell me the truth..."

"Ma! I am a grown man..."

"And you said that to say..."she interrupted."Zander, are you eating real food? Not that TV dinner fat free mess,... ain't nothing healthy about that."

"I know ma! I am eating..." He mouthed"Lord forgive me..." He hated lying to his mother, but he knew that his mother would be on the next plane if she knew that his dinners consisted of vending machine cuisine and juice.

The last time she came out for a visit she cooked enough for him and about twenty other people, freezing it and labeling it with warming instructions. Rita said no child of hers would be deprived of good home cooking as long as there was breath in her body.

"Okay, I'll let you get back to your lil' project. Who loves you?"

"You do ma! And I love you more."

"You better, before someone else does!" Rita winked as if Zander could see her."Bye Mr. Vice President...ooops I mean Mr. Partner..."

"Ma, keep me in your prayers, okay... this is real important. I want this in the worst way!"

"Son, when I wake up and before I go to bed, you're on the top of my prayer list. Have faith in God and let his will be done, okay?"

"Okay, talk with you before the week is out..." he paused,"I promise!" He blew Rita a kiss and she sent one back and said goodbye. He asked himself how she knew that he needed to hear from her. He could hear Rita:"..Mothers always know when their babies need them." He smiled and returned to the work before him.

Zander decided to read over his notes once more when Asia stuck her head into the office to announce that the client had arrived and that they were waiting in the main conference room. Zander's heart raced. The moment that he was waiting for was finally here. It wasn't about becoming a partner anymore, it was proving to himself that he had what it took to successfully complete this task. Elle seemed confident that he could do this, but he had to know it. He believed that he could, but knowing it was a totally different story. It was now or never. He took a deep breath and looked at Elle, she winked. He smiled nervously.

"Are you ready Mr. Eady, your future awaits!" Elle asked.

"When you put it like that I guess I'd better be..." Zander said taking a deep breath.

"You have nothing to worry about, you've worked harder than anyone else around here. You brought in business when the industry said there was none. So this is like breathing for you." she said as she rubbed his back reassuringly to bring the point home.

"Elle, before we go, I just want you to know that this project has been one that dreams are made of..." he paused choking back the evidence of what he was feeling."I just want to thank you one last time for believing in me. No one else has ever given me an opportunity like this and no matter what happens, please know that I am eternally grateful." he said smiling at Elle.

Zander was not one to show physical emotion in the office especially with the president of the company, but he reached out and hugged Elle. It surprised both of them.

"Okay, enough with the mushy stuff! Let's do this."Elle said trying to keep from crying. She did believe in Zander or she wouldn't have given him this once in a life time opportunity.

"Ain't nothin to it, but to do it!" he said trying to convince himself. Zander gestured for Elle to lead the way. She nodded as she exited the office and he followed. As they approached the main conference room he took a deep breath and said a quick prayer. Like Elle said, his future was waiting.

Six

Zander watched the elevator doors close, the client was his. He now knew that because of his determination and hard work he could do anything that he set his mind to. The PRDesign Group would now represent the world's most prominent syndicator, all of their existing projects and new ventures. This acquisition would take PRDG to the top. He took a cleansing breath and made his way back to Elle's office. When he arrived Joy directed him to the conference room. As he entered he saw Elle, the other VP's and management seated around the conference table.

"Zander, would you join me up here please? Today PRDG acquired it's biggest client to date. As most of you know we have been looking forward to this day from day one..." With that said the moment that Zander had waited for was finally here. "This momentous day at The PRDesign Group is a direct result of the hard work of our Vice President of New Client Acquisitions, Zander Eady. For the past three weeks he has given his all to ensuring that this day would become a reality."

The room burst into thunderous applause and evolved into a standing ovation with people giving Zander the thumbs up.

"...and..." Elle continued,"this is the reason that I now introduce you to PRDG's new co-owner and partner, Evan Zander Eady, the fourth."

The room burst into thunderous applause again. Elle hugged Zander and whispered how proud she was of him and that she couldn't think of anyone else she would rather share the partnership with.

"Speech, speech, speech" the room chanted, by this time other members of the staff had come into the room. Asia caught Zander's eye giving him the thumbs up as she wiped a tear with her other hand. Elle motioned for him to take center stage at the podium. He obliged, signaling them to quiet down.

"First and foremost, I must thank two people here at PRDG who believed in me when I began to doubt myself... the one and only Elle Renee Paige..." the applause started up again amid whistling and barking,"and... my right hand Asia Rutledge." Asia was both stunned and honored that Zander mentioned her. With that said, Zander also thanked the other members of his team.

"To each of you, know that you share in this accomplishment. We worked as a team, we succeeded as a team. When I say that I couldn't have done it without you, these are not mere words, it is high praise for some of the most talented people in this industry." He then called the team that worked on the project up to the podium one by one, starting with Asia, and give them each tokens of appreciation that he had custom ordered. Lastly he called Elle to the podium. She was shocked.

"Elle, don't think that I've forgotten you!" He signaled Asia to have the delivery guy bring in a large object draped in black velvet. He motioned for Elle to unveil it and she screeched with joy. It was an original painting by her favorite artist, Sinjaro. Zander and Elle discovered him last year at the city's Black Arts Festival and she said that his work made her heart sing. Remembering this, Zander commissioned him to do a portrait of Elle as his way of thanking her. The room was awestruck, you could have heard a pin drop. Elle gazed at the portrait. She was speechless, this was a first. She hugged Zander and returned to her seat, never taking her eyes off this very special and meaningful gift.

Zander concluded his comments and took his place appropriately at Elle's right hand. The room rose to its feet to embrace their new leader and the partnership. Zander took Elle's hand and raised it in victory as they stood.

Later on, as Zander thought back on the days happenings, he smiled at what had transpired just hours before. He looked up towards the heavens and whispered,"Thank you, God! I owe you one!" He was still on a high from the events of the day. He wasn't sure if it was a natural high or the champagne that they had to celebrate. He picked up the phone and hit the speed dial,"Hello," Rita answered in a melodious voice.

"Hey Ma! How are you?"

"Fine baby, I was just thinking about you. Your meeting over?"

"Yes, ma'am..." Zander decided to have a little fun with Rita and hold off on giving her the good news.

"Boy, don't lie to me... I know you like a book."

"It's just been a long day..."

"So what happened in your meeting?"

"It was just a meeting..."

"Evan Zander..." He knew that he was in trouble now, his mother only used his full name when she was angry with him or he was in trouble.

"Ma! Okay, I'll tell you..."

"Yes."

"You're talking to the new partner and co-owner of The PRDesign Group."

"Thank...you... Jesus!"

"I already did ma! I already did!"

"Son, I am so proud of you!" Rita's voice began to tremble

"Ma, what's wrong?"

"Nothing baby, I'm just happy and sad at the same time..." Zander understood exactly what his mother meant."You're thinking about Pop and Gramps aren't you?"

"They would be so proud of you. They are so proud of you! I'm sure they're in heaven shouting for joy right now."

"I hope so ma! You know when I would feel like giving up I would think of the two of them and I kept plugging. I wore the cuff links today for good luck."

"I thought so! That's why I gave them to you as a reminder of what your namesakes went through to make sure that a day like this one would be possible."

"And I cherish you and them mama for that very reason; you always have my back."

"Baby, your father and I created that back." Zander and Rita shared a very hearty laugh together.

"I love you ma!"

"You better!"

"And I always will!"

They said their good-byes but not before Rita reminded him that she was due a visit from her son; he promised that he was going to visit soon.

Elle had faxed a press release announcing the changes at PRDG to all of their clients, media and other related associates; once the news hit, Zander was bombarded by flowers and other congratulatory presents. It was a bit overwhelming, but he liked it. He was like a kid at Christmas. By the end of the day Zander hardly had room to walk. He instructed Asia to distribute the flowers and the edibles around the office because there was no way he could get them all home. He told her to keep some of the better ones for the herself and one or two for the office. He boxed up the nonperishable items and had them put in the trunk of his car. When Asia returned from making her deliveries Zander told her to take the next couple of days off.

"You deserve it!"

"I was just doing my job.."

"You went above and beyond the call of duty..."

"You've thanked me enough, the lovely gift and then you shared your goodies and flowers with everyone; you've been more than generous. I appreciate the offer, but it's not necessary."

"Asia, we have worked together for three years and I have come to count on you. You have been my right hand, my rock and my friend."

"Zander, you have been a dream boss, you made coming to work challenging and interesting. You've taught me so much. That's been reward enough; I wasn't just an administrative assistant to you, I was given responsibilities and I learned so much. I've done things, been places and met people that I wouldn't have if you didn't include me, but you did. You made me feel like I mattered... that's thanks enough."

"No, its not! You earned my respect and trust. You proved yourself and stepped up to every challenge, especially this last assignment. I couldn't have done it without you. So that's why I want you to get some rest before you start your new assignment."

"I don't need..." Asia stopped mid sentence,"what did you say?"

"What... oh... that the days off aren't thanks enough..."

"No, after that.."

"You need to get some rest?"

"After that..."

"Oh...." Zander smiled,"you mean the part about starting your new assignment."

"Yes, what new assignment? I just thought that I would just continue to work for your replacement or become your executive assistant."

"Asia, you can never be anyone's assistant again. Starting next Monday, you will become PRDG's new Director of Special Projects..."

"You're kidding!"

"Does this look like the face of someone kidding," he said trying not to laugh,"Well?"

"Well, no!"

"Then its settled! I discussed it with Elle and she agrees wholeheartedly. We both agree that you've got what it takes!" Asia thanked him again and assured him that he wouldn't be sorry. She hugged Zander and kissed him on the cheek. The both of them blushed and smiled nervously as Asia left his office.

Zander was preparing to leave the office as the delivery guy from another florist brought in a bouquet of lavender roses with one white rose in the center. The sight of them unsettled Zander. He nervously signed for them, tipped the delivery guy and closed the door behind him. They couldn't be from *him*. He put the roses on his desk and looked at the card.

It read:

"We need to talk. Give me a call!"

Zander looked at the number, put the card in his organizer, gathered his belongings and walked to the elevator. After the doors closed behind him he leaned against the wall and sighed. Talk about the end to a perfect day.

Seven

As the elevator doors opened Zander walked off in a daze. He couldn't believe that his worst fears were true. Zander pulled out of his parking space at PRDG and headed home. He wanted to be happy, but his heart wouldn't let him. It ached as he looked at the card that accompanied the flowers.

He didn't have to guess who the flowers were from. After all, Gage was in town. He swore that if he ever found out who told him where he was living or worked he would kill them...dead.

Today was supposed to be perfect, it was just like him to ruin the day. A day that didn't include him, a day that didn't concern him, a day that wasn't about him. He had to do it! At least he was consistent,"Damn him!" Zander thought.

"Typical," Zander whispered as he made his way onto the highway, he needed to talk to someone that could help him make sense of the whole thing. He picked up his cell phone and started dialing Rita's number and then he remembered; it was Wednesday and after 7 o'clock her time. His mother was probably at Bible Study or prayer meeting. He wished that he could telepathically message her to say a couple of prayers for him; he was going to need them.

He dialed Desmond, the line was busy."He's online or has two conversations going at the same time," Zander thought to himself,"Get off the phone thing!" He hit redial, this time it rang."Thank God come on D, answer the phone!" Desmond's voicemail kicked in.

"Thank you for calling, currently I'm unavailable and can't take your call. Please know that each of you are equally important..."

"Give me a break!" Zander thought.

"Please leave a message at the tone..." The message continued instructing the caller to be sure and leave a number and name. Zander disconnected the call and said a couple of choice words under his breath. He then remembered Desmond's pager number, he dialed that leaving a numeric message and their emergency code, *9-4-1-1. Desmond came up with the code to translate,"I need to talk now, its important tea!", tea being good dirt or information.

A few minutes later the cell phone rang and Zander answered before the first ring was completed.

"Hello," Zander answered with panic in his voice.

"You rang Mistah Vice President or is that Mistah partner of The PRDesign Group?"

"Partner..." Zander said with no enthusiasm.

"Z you don't seem to happy for a man who just went from a low six figure salary to co-owning a multimillion dollar company"

"I am happy," he continued,"but that's not why I called."

"Chile what is wrong wit you?"

"You'll never guess who sent me flowers at work today!"

"No he didn't."

Zander relayed the events of the day to Desmond, concluding his story with the account of the flower delivery and the card.

"So what are you going to do, don't tell me you're actually thinking..."

"I don't know what I'm thinking..." Zander snapped.

"Do you want to talk with him?" Desmond asked,

"I honestly don't know," Zander said, his voice laced with exasperation.

"Do you?" Desmond asked again, not letting up.

"I don't know!" Zander yelled,"I'm sorry D!"

"It's aiiight, but you are pushing it Z baby..."

"I mean a part of me wants to but there is another part saying that I'm asking for trouble. You remember how it ended."

"Yes, I do, it wasn't pretty!"

"Nope and for that reason, I don't wanna go there!"

"Z baby there are some things that are better left alone."

"You better say that!"

"I just did!"

"Well say it again!"

"Z baby there are some things that are better left alone."

"Okay bitch, very funny, verrryy funny!"

"Why I got to be all that! You asked me to say it again so I did!" They both laughed. It worked, Desmond thought to himself, he got Zander to laugh and stop thinking about Gage for a minute or two.

"So tell me more about the presentation!"

"Well, you know I looked good!"

"No doubt!"

"I smelled good."

"I'm glad, bathing is important."

"Very funny! I guess you planning to replace Chris Rock now!?! You are just the little comedian tonight. In rare form aren't you?!?!"

"Anyway!"

"I wore the cologne that you gave me for my birthday."

"Which one, oh!!! You mean the one I give you every year for your birthday."

"If it ain't broke..."

"Yeah, yeah I know... don't fix it!"

"I wore the links Mom's gave me for graduation..."

"Please tell me something I don't already know! I know you like a book...and an old one at that!"

"That's 'cause I'm a classic... you know like Moby Dick!"

"Oh, really... I was thinking more like.... hmmm... let me see... Little Women."

"No, you ain't go there..."

"Back to the presentation please. Time is money."

"I think I called you and I'm on my cell phone."

"Hey, you a partner now, you can afford it..."

"You better say that!" Zander smiled.

"I just did..."

"But a long story short, I went in a VP and walked out a partner."

"That's it, no details..."

"It's boring stuff! I gave you the juicy stuff. I looked good, I smelled good and was good."

"I taught you well...sniff, sniff!" Desmond said, faking a cry,"you make me proud to call you my bristah!" They both laughed.

"Oh, I forgot the best part..."

"Thank you Jesus..some dirt!"

"No, not really, but I thought that you would want to know this. My first real decision as a partner..."

"Please tell me that you fired Julian, that queen in the mail room! You know I don't like him. He gives Black Gay men a bad name."

Desmond and Julian were like two dogs fighting over a bone on his last trip to visit Zander. They were in PRDG's break room when Julian tried to clock Desmond and he wasn't having it. Julian made some comment directed towards D and it was on. He declared war on Julian and to this day he was still plotting his demise. Desmond had a heart of gold, but cross him and he wasn't soon to forget or forgive the party who slighted him.

"No, I did not!" Zander said laughing so hard he almost dropped the phone." Leave that boy alone. He's young and you know how this younger crop of 'children' can be."

"Well you should, lil' punk ass..."

"D! Are you gonna let me finish or not"

"I'm sorry continue..."

"Thank you!" Zander said still laughing at Desmond,"I promoted Asia to Director of Special Projects!"

"You go boy! She deserves it, she is a diva in her own right! If I was straight, I would.."

"You would what?!?!"

"You're right, what was I thinking? If I want fish, I'll go to Red Lobster."

"You are a mess..."

"And you love me for it, don't you frat?"

"And you know this! I love you like a sis..."

"If you say it, I'm hanging up!"

"Okay D! Don't be mad!" Zander said in an effeminate tone mocking a skit from"Living Color."

"Anyway, back to your first executive order," Desmond interrupted. He hated those skits, he always thought that they set Black Gay Men back 2000 years. He always compared those skits to the stereotypical way Hollywood showcased Black people as idiots, ass kissers and jigaboos.

"Anyway! She was shocked, I wish you could have seen the look on her face when I told her." Zander didn't tell Desmond about the awkward moment between him and Asia. He knew that he would make more out of it than there actually was.

"You did a good thing!"

"I'm glad you approve!" He told Desmond about the impromptu party in the office after Elle made the announcement. He gave him a quick rundown of all of the gifts that he had received from clients and well wishers after the press release went out. He promised to send Desmond a couple of the cooler gadgets that he had gotten. Desmond was like a kid at the idea of getting some new expensive toys, especially if he didn't have to pay for them.

"I think I'm gonna like your new position!"

"Yeah, me too, me too!" He sighed.

"Z, what's wrong?"

"Nuttin!" Zander said frowning at the thought.

"Lies! What is it! You know I know you like a book..."

"I just wished that Pops and Gramps could see this!"

"They are Z baby! They are! Probably braggin to the 'Big Guy' right now!" Zander smiled at that thought. It had been quite a few years since his father and grandfather died but he never stopped missing them, he missed them even more at special moments like this.

"Thanks D! You my boy!"

"Thanks for what?"

"Just being you... just being you!"

"That's all I can be..."

"And I wouldn't have it any other way..."

"You ain't had this!" Desmond said flippantly. He hated it when Zander got too sentimental.

"Never wanted it!"

"Lies, you tell... every man wants this... but only a few can say they had it!"

"Now who's lying..."

"Moi?"

"Yeah you...."

"Hmmph! You think so do you?...don't hate me 'cause I'm beautiful."

"Anyway..."

"Whatever..."

"Back to you and your male suitors..."

"Why Mistah Eady whatever are you talking about?..." Desmond said, doing a rather bad Southern Belle.

"Don't even.... I guess I'll have to bring you back..."

"Wha..."

"One word... FlyBoyee... how soon they forget... remember, you're lil' heaven on earth, Mr. Green Eyes..." Zander was about to ask him if the eyes were real or contacts.

"Let's not even talk about that..."

"Why not, I thought he looked okay..."

"Looks can be deceiving...that's all I have to say on the matter!"

"Okay..." Zander figured that Desmond would tell him the rest of the story when he was ready. He promised that he would send Desmond a ticket to come and visit as soon as the renovations to PRDG were finished. Elle had left him an email saying that his office was no longer suitable for a partner and that she thought that they should acquire the remaining suites on their floor. He really hadn't thought about that, he liked his office, but who was he to argue with progress?

Eight

He continued his drive home thinking about the events of the day; it was one he wouldn't soon forget. He smiled as he remembered the look on Elle's face when she received her Sinjaro and Asia's reaction to her promotion. Zander liked making the people in his life happy, this brought him more joy than anything. Thinking about the two ladies in his professional life made him think about the lone woman in his personal life, his mother. He pondered what he could send Rita as a sort of celebratory gift. He thought about a new piece of jewelry or a fur coat, but he knew that his mother probably wouldn't accept it or fuss before finally doing so. He decided that maybe he would send a ticket for her to come for a visit when Desmond came. After all she thought of him as her other son too.

"What a difference a day makes" Zander thought outloud.

He thought back to their first encounter with Desmond and laughed at the thought. The first time Rita saw Desmond she warned Zander to stay as far away from him as he could. She informed her son that she suspected he might be 'funny,' Rita's term for gay or queer. Zander was moving into his Freshman dorm and Rita was there helping him get settled. As they took his belongings to his room, who should they be behind but Desmond. He was attempting to carry this steamer trunk up the steps and had this twist in his walk while doing so. The very thought of that sight still made Zander laugh even after all these years.

Rita and Desmond were his family, so he thought that this 'family' reunion on him would be a great gift for the both of them. He began planning the itinerary in his head. He would send limos for the both of them and make a big deal of their visit. They would get a kick out of that and seeing them was just what he needed. The thought of having them there with him put him in a good mood for the rest of the drive home.

As he pulled into the driveway his mood changed. Gage was standing on the steps with another white rose. That had become his signature with Zander; he always said that it signified the purity of their love.

There he stood, 'father fine' himself looking like one of the cover models for *Men's Health* and *Ebony Man*. The white linen shirt graced his body making it apparent that he was wearing it and not vice versa. The first three buttons were undone teasing you with glimpses of his chest. He had on a pair of black jeans that fit like no other, as usual he looked like they were made just for him. He had cut his hair all off so he was bald now. Of course he had the perfect head for it. You know how some people just look good no matter what. "Some things never change," thought Zander to himself, Gage just got better with age. Before he knew it, his body was beginning to respond to Gage's innate sensuality. That million dollar smile cinched his seduction. Zander thought to himself, "I have to be strong!"

As he got out of the car he gathered up his organizer and brief case, removed his coat from the hanger and locked the car with remote arming the alarm. He had to take things slow; because the closer he got to Gage the more his knees began to buckle.

"Surprise!" Gage said as if he actually thought Zander would be happy to see him.

"What are you doing here?" Zander asked coldly trying to regain his composure.

"Is that anyway to greet an old friend?"

"An old friend...no, you on the other hand..." Zander recanted.

"Z..."

"That's Zander or have you forgotten?" He said as he rushed past Gage. He couldn't help but be entranced by his cologne. He was weakening again.

"How could I forget you..."

"Easy, like I forgot about you..." He was lying through his teeth.

"Is that so, well I could never forget about you!"

"Sounds like a personal problem..."

"Hey Z! It's me Gage, why you trippin like this..."

"Like what?"

"Like this... I can remember a time when you couldn't wait to see me..."

"That was then...this is now." Zander was at the door by this time, hoping and praying that Gage didn't suffer from the delusion that he was even coming in his house."

"Did you get the flowers?"

"Yes, I did...."

"Did you like them?"

"You really shouldn't have!" Zander was trying to figure how he could open the door when he felt the organizer slipping from his grip, its contents spilling everywhere.

"Here let me help you..." Gage offered.

"I can manage, just fine..."

Embarrassed Zander knelt down to pick up the items. When Gage attempted to help he spotted the card from the flowers he had sent earlier among the spill. Zander tried to pretend not to notice. He could have kicked himself for bringing the card home. He thought to himself that he should have torn it up in a million pieces just like his heart had been when Gage had broken it years back.

"So you were going to call?" Gage asked holding the card and flashing that smile of his.

"I don't even have a clue as to what you're talking about..." Zander said not even acknowledging the card.

"...the card..."

"Oh, that....as you can see I had more than one..." Zander said pointing to the other casualties of his clumsiness."Good save," he thought to himself.

"Yeah right... you never could lie to me."

"Who are you calling a liar?"

"You..." Gage said laughing.

Zander could feel his face going flush.

"Whatever..."

Then there was this extremely awkward moment of what seemed to be never ending silence. Zander finally recovered all of the things that had spilled except for the card in Gage's hand.

"You want this?" Gage asked.

"What do you think?" Zander asked in a flustered tone.

"I think you wouldn't have kept it if you didn't..."

"You think huh?"

"Yes I do," Gage said smiling.

"Well that's what you get for thinking..."

"Tisk, tisk..."

By this time Zander had managed to get the door open and was standing in it's threshold. His body purposefully blocking the entrance, hoping that Gage would get the not so subtle hint.

"Well, I wish I could say it was good seeing you but..."

"Damn, you cold!" Gage said with an almost sincere hurt look on his face.

"What do you want?" Zander asked in a harsh tone trying to conceal his nervousness and his ever growing vulnerability.

"I wanted to talk....that's what this said...remember?" Gage said referencing the card he was still holding.

"And people in hell want ice water, what makes you think I want to hear anything you have to say less alone talk to you."

"Z! I mean Zander..." Gage said correcting himself in attempt not to upset Zander.

"How did you find me?"

"I have my sources!" Gage said.

"Those tell-all queens in Orlando, I knew I should have cut my ties with most of them. Some of them talk too damn much."

"Who says it was them?"

"Then who ?"

"Like I said..."

"Whatever. Well it's been real, gotta go... long day and all..." Zander said as he attempted to shut the door in Gage's face.

"Zander don't do this..." Gage said with the look of a wounded bird on his face.

"Give me one reason why I shouldn't.."

"Give me one reason you should..."

Having said that Gage moved in closer to Zander, he could feel the heat from Gage's body.

"Please let me in!

"I can't!"

"Can't or won't?"

"Both."

"Why?"

"Just because."

"Not good enough."

"Says you! Need I remind you that I live here, I pay the mortgage, me! Not you, not us, me! Remember there is no *us* anymore! So what I say goes!"

"And you said that to say..."

"This is a game with you isn't it?"

"No it's not..."

"Let's cut to the chase here, what do you want, why are you here?

"I told you..."

Zander didn't like being so mean to Gage, but this was his only defense. If he didn't he would cave in and Gage would have the upper hand.

"I have nothing to say to you Gage, so could you please leave...now"

"Okay, cool..."

"Finally!"

"No I mean cool, you don't have anything to say to me, but I have a lot to say to you..." With that he pushed past Zander and walked through the door."And you're going to listen. Come on in and close the door."

Zander took a deep breath, rolled his eyes up toward the sky, mouthing"why me?"

Nine

Zander stood at the door in disbelief. He watched Gage as he walked around the living room taking it all in as if he was on a museum tour or a thief casing the joint. Zander thought it to be the latter, after all he was good at stealing things, especially heart.

"Nice place..."

"Thank you, I like it."

"Nice car too.."

"Thanks, it was gift."

"Oh you got it like that?"

"And I worked hard to get it like that."

"I'm sure you did, you've never been afraid of hard work."

"That makes one of us..."

"What is that suppose to mean?"

"Did I stutter?"

"I work..." Gage said with a defensive tone

"You're a freaking artist and you own a gallery that your father-in-law and wife underwrite! How hard is that?"

"Excuse me! Mistah VP, everybody can't..."

"That's partner if you must know!" Zander interrupted.

"What?"

"I'm now a partner and co-owner of PRDG!"

"When did this happen?"

"Like you really care, but it happened today!"

"Z... I mean Zander, That's great, I'm so proud of you!"

Gage was genuinely sincere and seemed to forget that they were in the middle of a knock down drag out argument. He walked over towards Zander and attempted to hug him.

"What the hell are you doing?"

"I was trying to congratulate you!"

"Thats quite all right, I've had enough congratulations for one day!"

"Zander, why are you treating me like this. It's me Gage, you used to love me. We used to be each other's biggest support. We used to...."

"Aahhh, 'used' to be that is the operative phrase here, now you have a WIFE to support you and be your best friend...."

"So that's what this is all about? You're jealous!" Gage began laughing.

"You think it's funny?"

"No, you're funny!"

"Stop laughing at me, this is not funny! How dare you laugh at me! Get out!"

Gage stopped laughing when he realized that he was the only one that found his last comment humorous. He tried to regain his composure and get Zander to listen to him.

"I'm not leaving until I say what I came here to say!"

"Get out now or I'm calling the police!"

Zander pulled out his cell phone to dial the number, but was so frazzled that he couldn't even remember the number. He walked over to the door swinging it open and gesturing for him to leave.

"And what are you going to tell them, that I should be arrested for hurting your feelings or telling the truth. Yeah! Right!"

"Truth, truth, according to whom? GET OUT... NOW," Zander screamed.

Gage walked over to the door, but not to leave. He pushed Zander out of the way and closed the door.

"You need to calm down, this is me! Let's sit down and talk this out..."

"You've got a lot of nerve, you're in my house in case you have forgotten, you don't call any shots around here...."

"How can I forget ! You just reminded me?"

"First, you barge in uninvited and then you push me out of the way telling me that you're not leaving. I don't know who you think you are..."

"I know who I am, but I don't know this person before me!"

"I know who I am! And I also know that I want you out of my house. Now! Gage, I really am getting rather sick of this. I'll ask you again! Who do you think you are?..."

"I'm the person who loved you like no other and you loved me, remember. I'm the person you told that loving me was like breathing to you, remember?"

"What was I thinking? I have asked myself over and over again, how I could have allowed myself to love you in the first place."

"Simple.."

"Far from it! Maybe it was in the beginning, but in the end it was me loving you and you loving her."

"Aahhh! Back to Suzzette!"

"Yes, speaking of Suzzette, why don't you take your sorry..."

"Why are you trippin like this?"

"You honestly don't know..."

"Nooo, I don't!"

"Lies and more lies..."

Gage couldn't say anything. This was nothing like the reception he expected. He knew that he and Zander had departed on bad terms, but he thought that time had healed old wounds. Why was he was acting like this? He looked at Zander, he didn't even recognize him. This wasn't his Z, this was somebody else. Maybe showing up wasn't such a good idea. He was actually hurt that Zander would treat him worse than some stranger off the street. He thought surely he meant more to Zander than this. He didn't deserve this kind of treatment or at least he didn't think so!

"What? Cat got your tongue?"

"Zander, please tell me what I could have ever done to you that would warrant you treating me like this?"

Zander was floored. He asked himself how on God's green Earth could Gage stand there looking all innocent. He couldn't be that thick; or could he? No this was an act, it had to be. Zander didn't know whether to be mad at him or feel sorry for him.

"Get out!"

"No!"

"Get out!"

"Nope!"

"Get out!"

"Not a chance"

"Get out!"

"Sorry, I can't do that..."

"Okay, you stay, I'll leave! But I want you out of here when I get back!

"Zander..."

"Lock up when you leave," Zander said as he left, tossing him the key!

"Zan..."

The door slammed before he could finish calling his name. He ran to the door to try to stop him, only to see him pulling out of the driveway. Gage was dumbfounded. What was he going to do? Zander's last words rang in his ears. He made it clear that he didn't want him there! Suddenly, Gage started to laugh. It dawned on him; he didn't have a way home. He had taken a cab out to Zander's and the ride had drained him. Besides it was now dark out and no cab was coming to pick up a brotha this late anyway.

Ten

Zander sped off not really thinking about what he had done until it was too late. He couldn't go back now. How could he leave Gage standing in his living room?"Stupid, stupid, stupid!" he said out loud. He looked for his cellphone.

"Damn!" He said as he remembered that he left it at the house. What he wouldn't give to be able to talk to Desmond right about now. He thought about stopping and calling from a pay phone, but he had left his calling card in his organizer.

He thought about what had just transpired, he couldn't believe it. Gage Gregory was at his house acting as if nothing had happened and this was just a reunion of old friends."Old friend my ass!"

"I am not his friend!" Zander thought. "Why was he here? What was so damned important that he had to talk with me about it?"I ain't hearing it! How dare he come back into my life after all of this time? Just when my life is where I want it! He shows up!" Zander said holding a one man conversation.

"And what was this crap about me being jealous?"

"Of what and whom?"

"Yeah right!"

"The nerve of him to stand in my house and tell me that I was jealous of her! that..." Zander stopped mid-sentence.

"Why am I mad at Suzzette, she didn't do anything?" Zander questioned. She was an innocent party in this just like he was. If anything he should be pitying her. She was married to Gage, she had to put up with him. Better yet he thought may be he should be thanking her for taking him off his hands. After all, he wouldn't be where he was today if Gage was still in his life.

"I need to talk with you..." Zander mocked Gage,"About what ?!" he asked himself. He racked his brain trying to think what Gage could possibly have to say to him that was so damned important!

Zander continued to drive. He cranked up the volume on the car's stereo to drown out all of his thoughts. Janet Jackson's CD was pumping as"Throb" pounded out such a nasty beat that Zander was grooving right along with it. He loved this CD and played it more than any of her other stuff. He hoped that he had removed all of the other romantic music from the magazine of the player. He thought to himself that the last thing he wanted to hear was a damn love song."Love, who needs it?" Zander thought to himself."Love is never having to say you're sorry..." Zander laughed outloud, at his new thought,"Love is never having someone sorry in your life." He laughed even harder. But his laughter was defeated by the memory of what he and Gage had when they were a couple. Those were his good old days! Gage had always said that they were going to conquer the world together. He loved their life together, he never thought it would end. He thought that they would grow old together. They were so good together. He had always thought that their love was worth holding on to and worth fighting for, no matter what. He looked at their love as an investment and one with definitive purpose. Not to sound cliche, this wasn't an ordinary love, it was once in a lifetime love. He believed from the bottom of his heart that Gage was his soul mate. Zander thought that nothing and no one would or could ever separate them. He had always told himself that there was nothing that they couldn't work through. He was always proud of the fact that they didn't work at their relationship, it just was. He remembered the happy times and wondered how things could have ever gotten so bad. That was then, this is now! It had been three and a half years since their relationship ended and Zander had moved on. His dreams had come true only to be turned into a nightmare at the resurfacing of Gage."Damn him!" he thought to himself.

Zander just drove, he had no real destination; he just needed to drive. He thought about what had happened in the past twenty four hours. That was his future, Gage was his past, why was he trying to be a part of his present. His mere presence brought up painful memories of another time and place; with a sigh he found himself being transported back in time.

Zander stopped going out after the break-up, not because he was afraid of running in to"him", but because it was too painful. The first time he tried to go back to *Secrets* it was like somebody stabbed him in his heart. He was consumed by the memories. He thought about their meeting , the Friday nights sojourn; it was their place. Just being there hurt so much that he ended up leaving in tears. He was depressed for weeks after that. He lost so much weight behind the break up that people rumored that he was terminally ill. He found this out, when he ventured out to a party after finally feeling a little better and heard these queens whispering about how bad he looked and that he must have the 'sistahs,' a colloquial for AIDS. That night when he got home he took a long look in the mirror and could understand why people were saying that. His clothes didn't fit, his face was gaunt, his eyes were empty and his heart was still broken. That night's experience was the kick in the ass he needed to start him back on the road to recovery. He decided to take this time to get to know himself again.

In time he got used to being alone. He actually started liking and cherishing his time alone; he caught up on his reading and learning his computer. He saw movies he wanted to see, instead of having to settle for something that he really didn't want to see. No more action movies with bad dialogue or bad acting, not to mention audiences that talked back to the screen. He started working out again. Before long he was back in shape and looking good, even if he had to say so himself. He even threw himself into his work, spending longer hours at the office, which actually worked in his favor. Maybe being dumped was the best thing that could have happened to him after all.

"Hmmm, maybe I should be thanking him, instead of trying to kick him out. NOT!" he said outloud.

It was a long time before he started dating again. He was through with men he told himself. He didn't want to ever experience the hurt that this relationship had caused. He refused to ever let anyone in again. If and when he dated again, he would make it clear to his dates that he wasn't looking for a relationship and if they were; he couldn't be bothered. He met some really nice guys but they weren't what he wanted; how could they be when they weren't Gage. He admitted that he was jaded and that 'love' was only a word to him. He told himself that he would never allow the words"I love you" to be spoken to him, again. He would watch other couples and long to be in Gage's arms again. He remembered what it felt like to have those muscular arms around him, in them he felt safe. From time to time he wondered, if she felt as safe in them as he did. Did he hold her the same way he had held him? Did they make love with the passion that he and Gage possessed? Did she satisfy him the way he did? Did he love her more?

By this time he had been driving for hours, it was time to head home. He used to think of his house as his sanctuary, but now it had been violated by the unwelcome visitation of this ghost from relationships past. He hoped that Gage had locked up. He would have the locks changed first thing tomorrow; he didn't want to give him any excuses to come back. If only he could lock Gage out of his heart. Zander sighed again. He reviewed their meeting tonight hoping for some clue as to why Gage was there? Could he be there to ask him back or to finally explain why he did what he did? Why now? What did he want?

Eleven

Zander pulled into the driveway, he was beat. The drive had done him some good and now all he wanted to do was take a shower and get right into bed. He looked in the mailbox for the key, thats where they would leave the key in their old place. It was there. He unlocked the door and it dawned on him that he didn't set the alarm before he left that morning, that was unlike him but he was in a hurry to get to the office and his sensual thoughts in the shower regarding Gage had unsettled him. Needless to say, he wasn't quite himself this morning. He shut the door behind him looking to see if the coast was clear. All of a sudden he got mad at Gage all over again. Never in the three years that he had been living there did he ever feel unsafe in his home, until now. He put the keys on the hook where they always resided, went to the kitchen to see what he could find to eat. Nothing. He was too tired to eat anyway so he grabbed an apple and juice thinking that would keep him until breakfast. He shut off the lights, set the alarm and headed up to bed.

As he showered he thought about the happenings of the day and smiled. "Zander Eady, partner and co-owner," he said outloud. He had done what some thought to be impossible. He landed one of the biggest clients in the country. This was only the beginning he thought to himself; he and Elle were going to set the industry on its ear. They were destined for greatness. He was on top of the world. He just stood there as the water soothed his fatigued body. He thought back over the past few weeks and realized just how tired he really was. He was coming off of his adrenaline rush and he was heading for a crash landing. He picked up the soap and prepared to lather the loofah and opted not to use it. After all, look at how much trouble it had caused earlier! He let the water baptize him and seduce him into a peaceful state. He was going to sleep like a baby tonight and get some much needed rest.

He stood in the mirror debating whether he looked any different because he felt like a new person. He was little worse for wear, but refreshed and ready for bed. He found a pair of pajama bottoms and slipped into them. He was tired but keyed up and not as sleepy as he was prior to his shower. He decide that he would read for a bit and then call it a night. He arranged the pillows on the bed and settled in. As he read he thought he heard a noise down stairs. He listened again and heard nothing; it must have been his imagination. He continued to read when he thought that heard it again. "C'mon Z, now you're hearing things," he told himself as he turned the page. Just as he had convinced himself that his mind was playing tricks, he heard the noise again. "That's it, I am not going crazy nor am I hearing things," he said in a "see I told you so..." as a matter of fact manner. He pushed the silent alarm button by his bed notifying the police. He went to the closet and lifted a golf club from his bag. He looked at the nine iron palming it to see if it would do enough damage if necessary. He debated as to whether he should wait on the police or be a man and handle this himself. He cursed Gage again; he had him paranoid in his own house. Machismo took over and he decided to go downstairs to investigate. He tipped down the steps trying to be quiet, praying that the cops would get there before he discovered anything or anyone. As he neared the kitchen and den he heard the noise again. His heart began to race and little beads of sweat began to settle on his forehead. He thought about tip-toeing right back upstairs and waiting on the city's finest to show up. What if the noise was an intruder, an intruder with a gun. He decided that if he got a chance to get a good swing he was aiming below the waist. As he got closer to the noise, he gripped the club ready to swing; he could actually hear his heart beating. "Calm down, you can do this," he told himself. He moved in slowly, trying to breath quietly. He tip-toed in the direction of the noise passing through the kitchen and headed down the hall to the den because he had determined where the noise was, it was definitely in the den. He could see a glimmer of light coming from the room. He continued to move slowly and cautiously, the beads of sweat were now streams of sweat, he was even sweating underneath his arms. As he made his approach, he gripped the club even tighter trying to choke it for the swing. As he entered the room, he saw someone crouched over the CD player talking to himself. Zander was about to swing when the prowler yelled,"What the hell..." dropping the stack of CD's. "Yo! Z...I mean Zander, its me Gage!"

"What are you doing here?"

"Man, I didn't bring enough money to get back into town!"

"So you're hiding in my den?"

"I wasn't hiding, I fell asleep and didn't hear you when you came in."

"So you decided to make yourself comfortable..."

"I told you I fell asleep waiting...."

"Yeah right..."

"I'm telling you the truth, I..."

"The truth? What would you know about the truth?"

"I know that I'm telling you the truth!"

"Gage, put some clothes on!"

Gage realized that he was wearing nothing but the dumb grin on his face. Zander turned his back to give Gage some privacy.

"What are you doing?" Gage asked mid chuckle.

"Giving you a chance to put some clothes on..."

"Like you ain't nevah seen this before."

"That was then, this..."

"..is now, yeah, yeah I know."

"So if you know, get your clothes on so I can call...." Zander suddenly remembered, "...the police."

"The police!!!!" Gage yelled, "why you trippin like this?"

"No, I'm not calling them, I called before I discovered that I knew this intruder."

Like clockwork the bell ran. It was the Sheriffs deputy at the door.

"Sheriff's Department!" Zander and Gage heard him yell.

Zander ran to the door and opened it.

"Yes Officer, I mean deputy!"

"Someone sent a silent alarm, distress signal from this address."

"Yes sir, I did, but everything is okay. "

"Are you sure?" He said noticing Gage as he appeared from the shadows.

"Yes sir, like the man said, we're fine!"

"Who are you sir?" The officer asked.

"I'm a friend of Mister Eady! An old friend!" Gage said putting his hand on Zander's shoulder.

Zander stood there embarrassed by the entire situation and even more so by Gage's public display of affection.

"Sir, is this true?" The officer asked still looking at Gage with an eye of suspicion.

"Ah, yes, yes sir! He is an old friend. I didn't realize that he was still here when I arrived home." Zander said looking like a kid caught with his hand in the cookie jar.

"Mr. Eady is it?"

"Yes sir!"

"Could I see some identification?"

"What!" Zander asked shocked at the officer's request.

"ID, I need to make sure that this is you and that you are indeed the owner!"

"Officer, this is my house, look at the way I'm dressed, do I look like I'm a burglar. Does he?" Zander said pointing at Gage.

"Hey! Man I don't know what you're problem is..." Gage started.

"Gage, I'll handle this..." Zander interrupted. "Officer, I am Zander Evan Eady, I have lived here for three years. I am the vice president, I mean co-owner at PRDG, there must be some mistake. Everything is fine, so good night." Zander started to close the door when the officer pushed it open further.

"Sir, you're ID, now!" the officer said with an ugly tone and an edge in his voice; placing his hand on his gun.

"My ID is upstairs, I'll have to go get it, if that's okay!" Zander said as his voice began to tremble. He realized that the officer was serious and wanted to avoid a bad situation.

"Look man! You are way out of line. Do you realize who this is? Are you out of your f..."

"Sir stay where you are!" the officer said drawing his gun.

"Gage, he's not playing! Please..." Zander pleaded.

"Shut up, both of you!" the officer commanded entering the house and closing the door.

"Okay officer, I'm going to go get my ID, cool?"

"Zander, hurry up get your ID, please!"

"I gave you a chance, now get down on the floor, both of you. Hands where I can see them!"

They both dropped to the ground exchanging terrified glances. Zander couldn't believe this. The officer radioed for backup identifying Zander and Gage as possible burglary suspects.

"Officer, may I say something?"

"I told you once..."

"Let him get his ID officer and you'll see that this is all a big mistake." Gage pleaded with the officer.

"Shut up boy, I'm about sick of you and your mouth!"

"Man, you better be glad you got the gun or I'd kick your..."

"Gage, chill, right now!" Zander said through clinched teeth.

"No let him talk! The big bad black boy.... "

"Is that it? The color of our skin? What..."

"Shut up!"

"Sir, this is a really bad mistake. This is my house! I can prove it. Please let me get my ID and the mortgage papers..."

Zander tried to get up when the deputy aimed the gun right at him an cocked the trigger. Zander slid back on his knees. He looked at Gage. At that moment he looked to him for strength, something that he used to do when things were rough. The loss of his father, the disappointments at work when he didn't get a client or the promotion that he deserved, the loss of their friends to AIDS; he needed to see that look in his eyes at that moment. It was there. For a moment he was calm and rested in the feel good moments of the past, but he was jolted back to the present by the officer yelling at Gage.

"Boy, you sure talk a lot for a man in fancy designer draws."

"Don't hate me because I got a big..." Gage said sarcastically with that "I know, I'm the deal" look on his face.

"Gage! Not now!" Zander yelled. The moment was gone, "gee thanks you guys", he thought to himself.

"I've about had enough of you ni..."

"Deputy Anderson..." a female voice called out from the outside.

"Yeah, in here!"

The deputy approached the door with her gun drawn. She looked at Zander and Gage with a puzzled but curious look while putting her gun away.

"What's the deal?" She asked.

"I got a silent approach call and when I arrived at the door, I was greeted by these two. When I asked for ID, my request was questioned.

I grew suspicious and told them to hit the ground."

"Ma'am, may I..."Zander began.

"Shut up!" the officer scolded.

"Deputy with all due respect, I think that you are in the wrong here." the female deputy began. "How could you think that these men were...to use your term...'suspicious?' And I think you can put your gun away."

"Well, I...." the officer began stuttering.

"Well nothing, its obvious that these men reside here..." the female deputy said really looking somewhat ticked at this point.

"Gentlemen, you can get up!" She said looking at both Zander and Gage.

"Thank you" Zander said.

"Finally, someone with some sense.... this guy is an idiot!"

"No, just new on the job! And a lil' gun happy. On behalf of the department I do apologize, Deputy Anderson had just transferred from Biloxi and he isn't use to certain things..." she said with a severe frown, "don't you have something to say to these gentlemen, Deputy Anderson?"

"Yes em' I am indeed sorry for my misinformation and any anxiety that I may have caused you boys! My mistake."

"Mistake! Boys!!! First things, first! Do I look like a damn boy to you? You dumb asswipe! Take your mistake and shove..." Gage said as Zander interrupted.

"Deputy Anderson, I don't know how you do things in Biloxi, but as Mr. Gregory just so profanely demonstrated... African American men do not like to be called boys and as far as a mistake, I don't think so." Zander said as calmly as he possibly could while inwardly cheering for Gage's outburst.

"Once again, gentlemen, on behalf of this county's Sheriff Department for what its worth I do apologize and I will handle this matter from here." She bid the guys good night and could be heard telling the deputy what a big mistake he had made and that his job was now in jeopardy. Zander stood in the doorway looking as the cars left, he wanted to get angry but he was still too unsettled at the thought of what could have happened. He took a deep cleansing breath. What a day, what a day!

Twelve

Zander tried to close the door, but he couldn't. He just stood there staring out into space. He wanted to move, but he seemed bolted to the floor. He was angry, hurt, mad, pissed, relieved and glad to be alive, all at the same time. This was the 1990's, how could this still be happening? This was not L.A., law enforcement officers were supposed to protect and serve. That deputy couldn't do his job for seeing two Black men in a nice house with a great car parked in the drive way; why couldn't he believe that they belonged there? Zander could feel Gage looking at him so he looked back, smiled and then laughed. It was all he could do to keep from crying. Gage didn't see the humor, but what he did see was the pain in Zander's face.

"You aiight?"

"I don't know, I really don't know."

"Z...ahh. I mean Zander, were you scared?"

"More like terrified... did you see the look in that guy's eyes!"

"Yep, looked like those guys in the Klan movies, you see the hate in their eyes."

"You ain't never lied!"

"Nope..."

There was an eerie silence as Zander and Gage reflected on what had just happened moments ago. They both thought about what could have happened if the female deputy hadn't shown up. They just stared out into a nonexistent void pondering. Gage walked over to Zander put his arms around his shoulders and just held him. Zander turned looking into those same eyes that had given him comfort, and just stared. He laid is head on Gage's shoulder and whispered, "Thank you Gage."

"For what?"

"For being my rock when I needed you in the past and tonight..."

"No problem."

Zander couldn't help but feel at peace. He couldn't even find the strength to be mad right then. At that moment this felt right and that's all that mattered. He felt like he did the first night they were together. He felt safe and like the world was his when he was in Gage's arms. If there is such a thing as a one true love, then Gage Garrison Gregory was it for Zander.

"Z, I mean, Za..."

"Z is fine..." he said smiling at Gage.

"Z, I'm really sorry...."

"Sorry for..."

"You know..."

"For...."

"Come on, you playing me... you know what I mean."

"Gage, you don't have anything to be sorry for..."

"Yes I do..."

"Okay, then tell me what you're talking about!"

"You ain't kiddin' you really don't know what I'm talking about."

"Just tell me..." he whispered.

"About tonight..."

"What about tonight?" Zander asked quietly lost in the moment

"It's all my fault!"

"What's your fault?"

"This whole mess...."

"Ohhhkaay"

"If I hadn't fallen asleep..."

Zander began to laugh, he looked Gage in the eyes and put his finger up to his lips.

"It's cool, it's over and we're safe."

They walked back in the house and closed the door. They made their way into the living room and sat on the oversized chair by the fireplace, falling into the chair. They continued their conversation just above a whisper.

"Z, let me talk..."

"Ok, so talk..."

"None of this would have happened..."

"I know, but stuff happens and there's nothing we can do about it, right?" Zander said, putting his finger back to Gage's lips.

"Yeah but..." Gage managed to muster past Zander's finger.

"Shhhh, no buts...just hold me.... please."

Gage was shocked by Zander's request, but he gladly obliged.

"Man, I'm really sorry!"

"Yes, you are....but in a good way!"

They both laughed as Gage pulled Zander closer and rubbed his fingers through his hair. He had to admit that he hadn't felt like this in a long time.

"Z!"

"Yes?"

"Did you think that one of us was going to get hurt tonight or maybe even worse? I mean, I really didn't know how this would turn out? Barney Fife was trippin big time! I don't mind telling you that I was freakin' scared. There was a moment there that I saw my life flash before me."

"Really?"

"Yeah, I thought I was gonna use the bathroom on myself!"

Zander just started laughing and Gage took the throw pillow and hit him with it.

"Oh it's on now!" Zander said taking the pillow and hitting Gage back.

"Okay boy, come on make my day!" Gage said imitating the deputy and Clint Eastwood.

Zander pushed Gage on the floor and leaped on top of him. They wrestled, bumping into furniture and rolling all over the place. Much to Gage's surprise, Zander was actually getting the best of him.

"You give!" Zander said trying to be tough.

"Give what?"Gage said laughing at Zander's tough boy act.

"You think its funny?"

"No you're funny!"

"Oh, I am...." Zander said through staggered breaths

"Yep!" Gage said still laughing.

Zander started laughing as he tickled Gage knowing that this would render him helpless.

"No fair, Z, you know that I can't do anything when you do that!"

"I know..." Zander said with a devilish look on his face, "I know!"

Zander and Gage were like two kids on a sleep over. They had a pillow fight and a tickle challenge all within fifteen minutes. They were actually getting along. Zander felt alive again. He was happy. He was breathing. While Gage may have been right about this being his fault, Zander didn't care. He liked what he was feeling. A part of him wanted Gage to make love to him. The other half asked if he was out of his mind. His heart said just enjoy the moment.

Tomorrow was soon to come and things would be back to normal, but that didn't matter. Zander basked in the glow of the warmth that he felt when he was in Gage's arms, like now. It was the first time in ages that he felt like everything was right with the world. He felt whole again. No one made him feel like that, but Gage. He wanted to enjoy it while it lasted. It wasn't as much sexual as it was emotional. What they had in the here and now couldn't be disturbed by anything, not the past, not the future, nothing, because at this moment, it was like breathing again.

Thirteen

The brightness of the morning subtly danced around the room as if to wait for the reaction on Zander's face. He opened his eyes praying that he had been dreaming, but he soon realized that this was no dream. He thought of the roller coaster ride he had been on within the last 24 hours, the good, the bad and the ugly. He couldn't shake the thoughts of the officer, the look in his eyes, the hate in his voice. He asked himself how one person could harbor that much hate for people he didn't even know.

The thought saddened Zander all over again. This was one of those things that you don't ever forget, but you have to force yourself to get over or it will consume you. He sat on the side of the bed with his head in his hands massaging his temples. His head throbbed. His heart ached and was heavy from the thoughts of what had happened in a home that he had always considered to be his haven. He thought about the fact that this used to be his retreat from the world. It would never be the same again after last night if he didn't get rid of the pain and hurt of what had transpired. He took a deep cleansing breath trying to get rid of the tension that was struggling to possess his body. It wasn't working. He sat silent, the hurt permeated his body and tugged at his heart. He couldn't help wondering if he would ever get past this. He told himself that he had to or it would consume him. He knew that if that happened he would be just like the deputy. He had to get over it.

"But how?" He asked himself.

He slid to his knees and began to pray:

"Father God, I thank you for this day, one that I've seen and never shall again..." he prayed, "for safely being able to return to your arms and for being able to feel the warmth of your love, for life in and of itself." He said that as the thoughts of the deputy's gun cocking penetrated his mind, he continued, "and for sending your angels of protection and peace in the midst of my trials and tribulation. Thank you for guiding me through life's situations." He prayed referring to both the female deputy and Gage. That thought led him to the next. "I pause to remember those who have graced my life both present and past. Thank you for granting me the privilege to have known them. For those you have called home and those who still reside on the planet, I thank you for allowing me a place in their shadows to hide and for shelter." Zander's potential brush with death caused him to remember the people in his life that were so dear to him. He couldn't help but to think of "Gramps" and "Pops," he knew that they must have led the charge with his angels of protection through last night's ordeal. He continued, "And Lord, God, I pray for those in so much pain that all they can do is hate; please regenerate the love that has been chased away. Help me to find it in my heart to forgive those who are blinded by hate." Zander said as he thought of Deputy Anderson. "Lord, I pray for the people in my life and those I don't even know who are suffering from AIDS and HIV. Comfort them in their hours of pain and suffering, let them know that there are people who care about them..." he prayed remembering the friends and family that he had lost to the dreadful disease. He continued his prayer remembering another group, "Lord, please let those who feel alone know that you love them and that there are those who have walked in their shoes who share in their pain and wish them your joy and peace." He paused thinking of other gays who have been estranged from their family and friends because of their sexual orientation. "Thank you for your blessings, numerous and plenty. Thank you for being there when I asked you, needed you and even when I didn't know that I did. Thank you for seeing me through. I praise your name with a humble and grateful heart. God bless my family and friends, keep them and protect them letting them know that they are loved and held in high regard. May your will continue to be done in my life. Lord work through me as a vessel and bless the lives that I touch and the people that are placed in my way on the journey." Before he realized it tears had settled in his eyes. He stayed on his knees in silence. "Amen."

Fourteen

Zander sat back on the bed when Gage's voice startled him. Zander wiped the tear from his eye as it started to fall. Gage could see that Zander was still bothered by last evening's unfortunate event. He stood in the door watching Zander, wishing that he could take away his former partner's pain, but he felt somewhat helpless because he too was feeling that same pain. Once again they were a team. Unfortunately they both felt like it was a loosing team.

"You okay?"

"Yeah...you?"

"You ain't know?"

They laughed halfheartedly.

"You sleep okay?"

"Yeah, the couch in the den is the bomb, thanks for the hospitality!"

"No problem!"

"Z, about last night..."

"Gage..."

"Let me finish..."

"Okay."

"Thank you...geeze...what does a guy have to do around hear to get a word in edge wise?"

Gage frowned to make Z smile. His attempt was successful.

"As I was saying.."

"As you were saying..." Zander said mocking Gage.

"Smart ass..."

"At least it's a smart one."

"Zander Evan..."

"Yes sir!"

"Don't have me put you ovah my knee..."

"Ooo daddy! Beat me!" Zander said in his best Mae West voice.

"Are you finished?"

"Yes, I'm sorry..."

"I won't even go there... as I was saying...about last night! I am sorry for the trouble that I caused."

"Trouble, what trouble?"

"If I hadn't showed up on your door step and insisted on seeing and talking to you none of this would have happened."

Zander had actually forgotten the circumstances surrounding their visit from the county's finest. His thoughts were understandably directed to Deputy Anderson's racist and unreasonable behavior. Having Gage there was actually a blessing. So he couldn't be mad at him, even if he wanted to be.

"As Gramps would say, The Lord works in mysterious ways." Zander added. He could see that Gage was really blaming himself for this whole ordeal. He wanted to reassure him that he wasn't angry.

"Gage, listen to me, look into my eyes I am not angry with you or at least not about last night! I am just glad that you were here. I was scared."

"Me too."

"I still keep thinking that this is some bad dream and that I'll wake up..."

"It's not a dream, its a harsh reality...unfortunate as it may be."

"Do you think that we should report him?"

"The other officer said that she would handle it... I guess she will!"

"Maybe we should do it too!"

They looked at each other hoping that the other would have an answer. Neither did. They sat thinking and silently thanking God for the other being there. Thinking that probably they wouldn't be alive if the other had not been there.

"Gage, I said it before and I'll say it again, I couldn't have made it without you here last night. Thank you."

"Stop thanking me Z, this wouldn't have happened if I hadn't been here. If I had just stayed away."

"Why did you come, you said that we needed to talk on the card and then you showed up... so tell me what was so important that it couldn't wait?"

"It's nothing... I thought that I had to see you... that's all"

"Nothing huh?"

"No..." Gage said with a certain sadness in his tone and his eyes.

"You're lying Gage, what's wrong? Remember I know you like a book."

"Yeah you do, you're probably the only person that really knows me like that..."

"What about Suzzette?"

"Humph... no not even her?"

"Well..."

"I know you.... you told me so."

While he thought it, he didn't dare say it. Gage was obviously down and why would Zander kick him now. Zander could hear Desmond, "ready, aim, fire...Houston we've made contact! Man down."

"Nope, what good would it do."

"I know I deserve it..."

"Maybe..." He paused and thought about it and then added, "maybe not!"

"No maybe's about it I would if the shoe was on the other foot."

"No you wouldn't, vengeance ain't your style G!"

"True dat, but..."

"But nothing, getting back does nothing, but set you back!"

"Deep Z! When you right.."

"And we know that I'm nevah wrong." Zander said with a snap for emphasis.

"Miz Raj!" they both yelled as they started to laugh uncontrollably imitating a character in George C. Wolfe's *Color'd Museum*. He was the original self proclaimed "snap-queen." In the play his claim was that he could snap his enemies into oblivion. They had fallen in love with the character and occasionally they had paid homage with a salutary snap or two quoting lines from the play. They would spend evenings cracking each other up over a bottle of wine. Those were the good old days.

"I hadn't thought about Miz Raj in a long time." Gage said still laughing.

"Occasionally, when I'm here alone I do a line or two and keep his memory alive."

"Those were some great times, nobody but you, me and the misses..."Gage laughed. "I miss those days. Do you ever think about the good old days?"

Zander squirmed. He hated when Gage would do the 'eye' thing. He always felt that Gage was reading his mind or hypnotizing him to answer his question. He didn't want to answer, but he couldn't resist those eyes or Gage for that matter.

"Why do you ask that?" he said clearing his throat hoping to reverse the situation.

"Don't answer my question with a question, what part didn't you understand?"

"I am not sure... I do not understand the question..." Zander said imitating a deaf person using his version of sign language.

"Ha, ha! Very funny Mister man!"

"Gage, I would be lying if I said that I never thought about us because I'll hear a song or run across a photo that reminds me of us or I accidentally put in a unmarked video of a party or a trip."

"You still have all that stuff?" Gage asked surprised.

"Yeah, don't you?" Zander asked sarcastically.

"Yes I do, but of course given the circumstances, I have to keep them tucked away and only get to revisit them from time to time." Gage said with a sad look in his eyes.

"G, what's this stroll down memory lane about...I thought you were..."

"Happy? Yeah right..." Gage said sighing synonymously.

"What's wrong, talk to me..." Zander said with genuine concern.

Zander shocked himself with that question. Did he really care about Suzzette and Gage's life together? He didn't know her, but he felt sorry for her as well. She was living Gage's lie too! No matter what he said, Zander knew that Gage was gay and that was all there was to it. Zander didn't have a problem with bisexuality like Desmond did. Desmond was quick to say that self-proclaimed bisexual men are one of two things, confused or "ho's who want their steak and fish on the same platter." But Gage Garrison was gay, not bisexual, not confused...just a plain ole' "man in my life is all that it takes to make me happy"gay. Zander never understood exactly why he married Suzzette. The look on his face told the story; he wasn't happy and it was tormenting him. While he still looked like the old Gage - still fine, still sexy, still all that and the bag of chips with a chilled pitcher of grape Kool-Aid garnished with lemons on the side- something was missing...something different. Even in his eyes, still intense and overwhelming, but some of the intensity was missing; so was the happiness from his voice. His laugh used to fill the room, now it only made its presence known. Maybe he was just bummed about the ordeal from last night.

"Maybe, maybe not," Zander thought to himself.

"Z, *Z*!" Gage called snapping to bring Zander back, "Man where were you?"

"Wha..." Zander said in a daze.

"Where were you? You left me for a minute, I was about to answer your question, but you seemed to be preoccupied."

"Well I'm back now, you were about to say..."

"Never mind, it's not important."

"Gage! Talk to me. Something was important enough for you to send the roses and show up on my door step! So now spill it!"

"Z, baby, it ain't important anymore. Maybe I just needed to see you. It's been a long time... and maybe I needed just see you!" Gage said with a smile and wink combination.

"Gage Garrison Gregory! You lie like a rug! I know you and its more than a lil' reunion."

"Nope! Hate to disappoint you but that's it!" Gage said hoping that the he had convinced Zander.

He could kick himself for showing up at Zander's. He didn't care what Zander said, this was a really bad idea, he should have left well enough alone. He should have just lived off the occasional trip down memory lane, but no! He had to see him. He thought of him when he needed inspiration, when he was making love to Suzzette and he thought of him when he needed to "handle" his bizness. He was in his thoughts more than he wanted to admit. Sometimes thinking of him was the only thing that bought joy to him. He had to face facts. No matter what he told himself, there was only one person that he would ever love, really love and he was looking at him.

Fifteen

The phone rang at The PRDesign Group.

"Good morning and thank you for calling The PRDesign Group, the nation's information architects. How may I direct your call?"

"Good morning Mildred, is Elle in yet?"

"Good morning Mr. Eady, congratulations again sir! and sir she's not. I can patch you through to Joy if you would like."

"No, that won't be necessary, I'll try reaching her on her cell. Thank you again for your sentiments. You have a good rest of the week!"

"You too sir, we'll see you on Monday..."

"Thank you again Mildred, see you then."

Zander didn't want to take the time off, but Elle said that her last order as his boss was to give him the rest of the week off. She wanted her partner rested and ready to take on his new responsibilities with a clear head. He dialed her cell number and got her voicemail. He didn't leave a message. He dialed her private number and Elle's voicemail answered.

"Damn," Zander thought to himself waiting for the tone.

"Hello partner, this is Zander. When you get a moment please give me a call. I can be reached at home or by cell if I'm not in, you know the numbers, but just in case...." Zander left the numbers to make it convenient for Elle to reach him. "Please call soon, Elle, I need to talk with you as soon as possible," Zander thought as he hit the flash button on his cordless. He needed to talk; he couldn't talk with Gage given his mood.

He dialed Desmond's number.

"Good morning Zander and how are you?"

"You and that damn caller ID."

"Modern technology...you gotta love it!"

"Yeah, yeah! whatevah..."

"Are you busy?"

"Never to busy for you Z Baby"

"Thanks."

Zander told Desmond about Gage's surprise visit and the events of the evening. He told him how afraid and how he thought that the deputy might kill the two of them. Desmond hit the roof.

"So did you get Barney Fife's badge number?"

"Yes I did and so calm down, diva!"

"Calm down! Some racist Neonatzi Aryan sheriff's deputy nearly kills my bristah and his ex and you want me to calm down, I don't think so!"

Zander began to think that it was a mistake calling Desmond; he forgot that he had a doctorates in drama.

"Desmond, come on bring Butch out!"

"Wait one damn minute Mistah thang, I am always Butch. Don' you ever think otherwise. I am simply expressing my dismay at what happened to you. Forgive me for caring!"

"D!"

"That's Desmond to you..."

"As in Nora!"

"Ha, ha, ha! very funny. Go on with you lil' story!"

"N-knee-way, I think that I'm going to press charges or file a grievance against this deputy. What he did was inexcusable and he has to face up to his demons of hate and prejudice."

"You go boy!"

"I know that it's going to be his word against ours, but I think that the female deputy will testify on our behalf. She seemed to be equally as appalled..."

"That's good...speaking of ours"

"Oh, Gage?"

"Yes, Gage, who you think I'm talking about, Tyson or Shemar Moore, duh...dizzy diva!"

"No, you didn't!"

"Yes, I did...continue..."

"He's here. He stayed the night and..."

"He stayed the night!" Desmond interrupted.

"Yes...." Zander said coyly smiling in anticipation of Desmond's outburst.

"Ok, thing spill it! Did you do the do?"

"No! Hell, no!" however the idea did intrigue Zander.

"Okay, so tell me another one... when you two were a couple, you couldn't ever keep your hands off each other and you're telling me that you came that close to being taken out and you didn't do it! I mean..."

"One word...married!"

"And...you said that to say..."

"Rule one, I don't sleep with someone else's man. Even if he was mine first!"

"Neither do I...well not if I can help it..."

They both laughed at Desmond's true confession.

"But, no Desmond we didn't sleep together. He held me and that was it..."

"No kissing, no b&g?"

"B&G?!"

"...bump and grind, duh!"

"No!" Zander said blushing.

"Booooring, I mean come on, while G3 is not my favorite person, I know what he meant to you and you yourself told me that when you made love to him it was like breathing..."

"Yeah, well that was then and..."

"this is now! Yeah I know that but you were in the arms that, according to you, made you feel safe and you are telling me that you didn't even kiss!"

"Okay, he kissed me on the forehead and the cheek, but that was it."

"That's it, you are slowing down in your old age."

"Excuse me diva one, but we are the same age!"

"That's besides the point!"

"N-knee-way!"

"When you were in his arms, did it seem familiar?"

"Like, I never left!"

"You go boy!"

"But it wasn't like that. I think we needed each other at that moment..."

"And you didn't get a stiff one?"

"Now I didn't say all that..." Zander said laughing.

"Hmmm, you grew and didn't do the do? Oh no, that's a direct violation of the gay boy rules and regulations. I believe that its Section 10, Article 126A, wasting a perfectly good hard on when a fine man is present! The council may want to speak with you on this one!"

"You are sick!" Zander said trying not to laugh at Desmond's antics.

"Chile, what is this world coming to? I'm calling the gay boys council together and we may have to revoke your life membership."

"Whatever, it just didn't feel like we needed to do anything; sex would have clouded the issue. I just needed to be in his arms."

"How *sweet*, sniff, sniff, sniff" Desmond said pretending to cry.

"Bitch!"

"That's diva bitch to you!" Desmond retorted.

Zander just laughed.

"So, okay, you say that you didn't do the do.."

"No, we didn't. Now if I was going to tell anybody, wouldn't it be you!?!"

"And you know this!"

"But I must confess." Zander paused

"Yes..."

"It did feel good to be in his arms again"

"Allllllrighteeee then!"

"Support, not sex!"

"Tisk, tisk..."

"Whatever, you are such a pervert!"

"Not moi!"

"Vu!"

"Amore, ain't it grand!"

"So is he getting off the Titanic and coming back to the Ranch or what?"

"We didn't even talk about it, which is the second reason that I called!"

"Oh, okay! tell daddy all about it!"

"Something is definitely wrong with Gage, he isn't himself..."

"That's what fish will do for ya!"

"Desmond!"

"Well!" Desmond said doing his best Samantha impression.

"I can't put my finger on it, but something is wrong with him and he won't tell me what it is."

"Bad fish, it will do it every time. Oprah may have stopped eating beef, but baby give me her portion too!"

"Desmond, be nice!"

"Z, you don't even know miss thang, so why are you telling me to be nice to her. She has your man and it's known throughout Judea and Samaria that Zander Evan Eady, the fourth and Gage Garrison Gregory, the third belong together."

"Thanks D, but that was a long time ago and things change, people change...."

"And some things don't, like the two of you! If two people ever belong together it is you."

"Thanks but I think that Suzzette would beg to differ!"

"What does she know?"

"She knows that she's got the man and the 5 carat diamond to prove it!

"But her man is here with his man!"

"Former partner..."

"Don't get pc with me!"

"Whatever!

"Okay one last question?"

"If he stays tonight, will he be sleeping alone or with you."

"I don't know D, I don't know."

Sixteen

Zander showered and made his way down stairs to check on Gage. He couldn't help but think about Desmond's last question. He really hadn't thought about anything happening between Gage and him. If he had to be honest with himself, he would give anything to be in a relationship like the one he had prior to their breakup, but there was no sense in thinking about that because the circumstances wouldn't allow it. Nor would he as long as Gage was married. Besides, when he and Gage were consoling each other there were no physical signs that Gage was even remotely turned on by Zander's presence. Had there been, there would have been no concealing it even at the slightest signs of arousal on Gage's part. In fact he admitted that he was embarrassed when he started to get aroused. Since he was being honest, he was disappointed that he no longer had that effect on Gage.

He made his way to the kitchen to see if Gage had made breakfast for himself or if he was even hungry. If this was even a shadow of the former Gage, he would be hungry. To be as fine as he was, the boy could put away some food when it came to getting his grub on. It was their joke that Gage was a growing boy in all areas. Zander smiled at the memory of their moments together.

There was no evidence of Gage's culinary excursion, so Zander figured he must be in the den. He made his way down the hall passing the guest bath, when he heard water running and the familiar off key song stylings of a tone deaf Gage. The boy was hot, but singing was not his forte'. The door was cracked and Zander was ashamed at even the temptation to peak in. He tried to escape unnoticed when Gage opened the door wearing nothing but a smile. Zander felt his knees weaken at the sight, but managed to regain what resembled his composure.

"Hey you!"

"Sup?"

"Nothing yet!" Gage said with a wink and a smile, "but that could change..."

"That so?"

"Yep! "

"If you say so..."

"I see somebody is in a better mood!"

"What can I say, you bring out the best in me!"

"Do tell..."

"Being with you has been like a breath of fresh air, I think that's one of the reasons that I needed to see you Zan..ah..Z."

Zander didn't know what to say, so he just looked at Gage.

"What?!!!" Gage asked surprised by Zander's non reply.

"Nothing, nothing at all!"

"Are you sure? You've never been one to be quiet!"

"Some things change...now don't they. You haven't been around in quite a while, I've grown quiet in my old age!" Zander said laughing nervously.

"Things may change, but you haven't."

"Think so, do ya?"

"Know so!"

"Oh really?"

"Yes really, Mr. Man!"

"Hmmm..."

"Hmmm..." Gage mimicked Zander like he had done so many times before.

For a moment every thing felt like it always did and Zander basked in that feeling. He would give almost anything for it to be like it used to be. Life was simple. He loved Gage and Gage loved him. No gray areas, no hidden agendas just plain ole" love. The fact of the matter was that they never even had a cross word until last night with the exception of one other time. That thought brought Zander back to the here and now.

"So did you eat yet?" Zander managed to get the words out somehow.

"No sir! I was waiting on you..." Gage said as he started to dry himself off.

"Oh, okay so what do you want for breakfast?"

"Can I have anything I want..."

"Sure, what are you in the mood for?" Zander regretted the words before they could get out good.

"Okay cool. Then I'll have a hearty helping of you..."

"Ha, ha....very funny... I'm not on the menu!"

Gage almost looked disappointed.

"So what do you want to eat?" Zander said trying not to gawk at Gage as he continued to dry off.

"I don't know surprise me!"

"You hate surprises!"

"Depends on what or who the surprise is..." Gage said with this very devilish smirk.

"Food, Negro...what do you want for breakfast?"

"You gonna cook?"

"Yeah, you got a problem with that. You used to...." Zander caught himself mid sentence.

"Used to what? I wasn't talking about your cooking, because Rita taught you well. I was going to offer to take you to breakfast to try and make this up to you. I ruined your great day."

"Let's not go there again, I told you..."

"I know what you told me, but I can't help but feel the way I do about this whole situation."

"Gage!"

"Zander, look..."

"I'm looking, been there, done that..." Zander said trying to change the subject.

"And...you came back for more," Gage said grabbing his crotch.

"Anyway....."

"Truth hurts don't it! Huh, huh!" Gage said poking at Zander. He knew that Zander was ticklish so he grabbed him by the waist of the boxers attempting to tickle him. Zander didn't expect it so he was an easy target. He begged Gage to stop and let him go, but Gage wasn't paying him any attention.

"I said let me go! Ga..."

"Say please..." Gage said continuing to tickle the helpless Zander.

"Pleaaaaassssseeeeeeee," Zander yelled.

"Say pretty please!"

"Pretty please with hot chocolate syrup on top."

"Hmmm, when you put it that way...." Gage paused as if he was giving Zander's request credence. "Nope!" Gage said as he continued to tickle Zander.

"Please, Gage, please, I've had enough. Please stop!" Tears were beginning to settle in his eyes from laughing so hard, He actually felt like he was going to pee on himself. "I'm gonna pee on myself in a minute, please."

"Getting a lil' kinky huh?" Gage joked.

It was then that Zander felt something that he hadn't felt in a long time. Gage's rather erect self pressing against him. He managed to get free because if he didn't there was no telling what would happen.

"Finally! Don't you think you should be getting dressed!"

"Or maybe you should be getting undressed. Those look like their getting a little tight," Gage said smirking as he referenced the apparent bulge that was maturing in Zander's boxers.

Zander didn't know what to do. A part of him wanted to run back into Gage's arms and kiss him as passionately possible. On the other hand, he belonged to someone else and Zander wasn't about to share. It would have to be all or nothing.

"So...." Zander said thinking, "good answer fool," to himself as he tried to conceal his embarrassment.

"Look me straight in my eyes and tell me you don't want this as much as I do!" Gage said grabbing at Zander.

"Well then go home to Suzzette! I'm sure she would love for her husband to make love to her!"

"Zander you didn't have to go there!"

"Like you always said desperate times..."

"Yeah but that was a low blow! I need you..."

"What you need is a good lay?" Zander said going for the jugular." Is that why you were online the other night. Huh! Yeah I saw you online the other night! Tell me you aren't 'Phine9Bro.' Looking for a lil' romp in the hay, couldn't find anything you liked, so you decided to give your old partner a call. Thought I would be so easy, Huh! Is that it? Now I'm just a trick. A place to lay a lil' pipe...excuse me, I mean a place to service your nine!"

"What are you talking about?"

"You're telling me that you're not Phine9Bro on AOL!"

"No, I'm not!"

"Really..."

"No, I don't do chat rooms, I wouldn't risk it...but it's obvious you do or you wouldn't have thought that this was me, this Phine9Bro person." Gage informed Zander.

"Well, if you read the profile you might think that it was you too, I mean you are 6'2" and you are gifted in the endowment area. And there's nothing wrong with meeting people online." Zander said.

"I'm flattered that you would think I had it like that but it's not nine; close but definitely not nine..." Gage said smiling at his hurt friend, "...So is that why you're so angry with me, you thought that I was screwing around and just came here to get laid."

"Gage, I don't know what to say! I'm embarrassed as hell here."

"Well..."

"Z, of all people I thought that you knew me better than that."

"It's been a long time, people change. I mean look at me. I have no life and depend on my online friends for interaction."

"So, there is nobody in your life?"

"No, unfortunately not!" Zander said sighing at the sad, but true fact of his life.

"I find that hard to believe. You're handsome, successful, sexy, intelligent, sexy, articulate, sexy, giving, did I mention sexy?"

"Yeah, I think you did..." Zander said blushing. "Thanks, I'm glad somebody thinks so."

"Yeah, I do...and always will."

"I'm sorry about before G.."

"Hey at least I know you still care..."

"Yeah I do...like a friend of mine said, I always will."

"Smart ass..."

"Sticks and stones..."

"Yeah, yeah, yeah..."

"Whatever..."

"Z, I'm sorry about earlier, I don't know what came over me..." Gage said hoping to smooth over their earlier rift. "Well actually I do, but know that I'll always have it like that for you."

"It's cool..."

"No, its not!"

"To be honest, I'm flattered."

"Z, you were the best thing that ever happened to me. I thank God every day for having you in my life..."

"And I you!"

"That's what I wanted you to know; that's why I sent the flowers and showed up here."

"Just to tell me all of this."

"Yes, I think that you'll agree that we didn't end on the best terms..."

"No we didn't."

"For two years, six months and 7 days I loved you. We woke up to each other, we said good night in each others arms after saying our prayers together. We never argued or fought, but on the eighth day I messed up..."Gage said with a sadness in his voice.

Zander was touched that Gage would remember the exact amount of time that they were together. He thought that he was the only one that knew that. It meant something to hear Gage say that he messed up. All of the hurt and resentment began to melt away. His Gage was standing before him. The man that he loved was back. He needed to hear him say these things and for the first time in a long time he actually could feel his heart beating.

Gage continued, "I came home and told you that I needed space, moved back to my parent's place in Seattle and six months later I call you asking you to be my best man. I could still kick myself for doing that to you, but I needed your support. I needed you to understand and be there for me. When you hung up without saying anything I stopped breathing. I never explained to you what was going on in my life. I know now that if there was anyone that I should have been able to talk to, it was you. Instead I shut you out. It wasn't anything you did, it was me giving into the pressures of my family. My mother was whining about grandchildren and my dad was dying from colon cancer, so I thought that if I produced a girlfriend that would be enough. It all just got out of hand. The family was questioning our relationship and I caved. Instead of having faith that we could endure this, I did what they wanted me to do; instead of doing what was best for us. My father used to tell me all the time that it would kill him if he found out that he had a gay son. I never forgot that and when he was diagnosed I knew I had to do this. I had known Suzzette since first grade and we had always been in each others life. I took her to prom, that was our only date! Everybody said that we were the ideal couple after that and started predicting that we would get married one day. When I went home, I ran into her in the grocery store and we began to talk.

She came over for dinner and my father looked so proud. I wanted him to be happy now that I had someone in my life that the family could approve of."

Gage told Zander that he thought that he would grow to care about Suzzette and eventually love her.

"I always thought that our relationship was the type that together we could conquer anything together. But when it was time for me to marry Suzzette I needed your support. I really needed you and you weren't there."

"Well maybe if you had told me all of this I would have understood. I always told you that loving you was like breathing to me and so the day you walked out I began to suffocate." Zander said chocking back the tears. "I blamed myself for what happened and for months it was this slow painful death of a part of me and I resented you for that. I gave you my heart and you handed it back in a million pieces. G do you understand what I'm saying?" Zander asked with hurt and pleading in his voice.

"Z, I can't say anything that will justify what I did. Know these two things; one I am so sorry for the pain that I caused and secondly, I've never stopped loving you." Gage said sincerely.

Zander melted and began to cry. Gage pulled him into his arms and held him, rubbing his head and whispering how sorry he was and that he loved him. After all this time, Zander had the answers that he had given up acquiring and Gage was where he knew he truly belonged. The two just held each other, not saying a word, not moving, just breathing.

Seventeen

Gage held on to Zander for dear life, whispering how much he loved him and that he would never stop. Zander sighed at the thought. His body radiated from Gage's statement. He assured him that he felt the same way. No matter what happened they knew that they would always have each other. That one fact gave them both enormous comfort. Gage kissed Zander softly on the check, caressing the very same spot. He looked into his eyes; Zander could see that the warmth and intensity that had once vacated had now returned. This gave him great joy.

"Attention! All American Airline passengers..." the voice over the airport loud PA system began, disrupting Zander and Gage's farewell. They both frowned as the announcer continued to give boarding instructions reiterating that this was goodbye, for now anyway.

"You got everything?"

"Yep! Still some room in the garment bag if you wanna jump in!"

"As tempting as that sounds, I think I'll pass. Suzzette might not like that!"

"You didn't have to go there!"

"I know..."

"Let me know what happens with the Barney and all okay..."

"Will do, I talked with a friend in the Mayor's office and I have an appointment first thing Tuesday morning! I think that Mayberry's finest will be sorry that he messed with us."

"And you know this!"

Zander smiled as Gage winked reassuringly that everything would be okay. His face transitioned as he thought of what he wanted to say to Zander.

"Thank you."

"For?" Zander asked.

"Giving me my life back."

"How did I do that?"

"By being you..."

"All I know how to do...is be me!"

"Glad about it!"

Zander smiled trying to choke back the tears. He smiled at Gage.

"Thank you too!"

"For..."

"The past 48 hours..."

"Are you sure about that?"

"Don't start that again!"

"Z, let's recap..."

"No let's not, I don't care about Barney Fife. Like Gramps used to say, "Everythang happens for a reason, nothing in life is a mistake. You just have to find the good in any sit..i..ate..shun."

"What was good about nearly being shot in your own home? Please help me see that!"

"Baby, if Barney hadn't cut the monkey like he did, our walls never would have come down. His ignorance reminded us of what we once had and summoned it to the forefront. If none of this had happened, would we honestly be here today?"

"When you're right, you're right!"

"You better recognize!"

They both laughed watching the sparkles dance in each others eyes.

"So what are you going to do?"

"Truth..."

"And nothing but..."

"I don't know. When I found out that I was coming to town to meet with the art gallery, the first thing I thought of was seeing you. I wasn't certain that I should, could or would, but I wanted... no make that needed to see you. I knew that Suzzette wouldn't be coming since the doctor didn't want her flying in her last trimester. She's due any day now." Gage paused at the thought of being a father, "I had to clear the air and get things straight between us. I need you in my life. Your absence has been unbearable. You are the one constant. I needed to tell you how sorry I was and explain everything that I didn't get a chance to explain before. I needed you to know that I would always love you and only you. I really need you to know that...I have to see this thing through. But no matter what, you know that I'll always have you back..."

"What about the rest of me?" Zander said jokingly.

"You are such a lil' smart ass..."

"One of the many things you like about me, right?"

"No, one of the many things I love about you!" Gage winked.

Zander smiled trying to curtail the blush that was emerging. He was too late. Gage laughed at his friend as he continued.

"The mere thought of never having you in my life again; has haunted me. I'm glad to know that no matter what, this will never happen again. Right?"

"Hmmm, can I get back to you on that?"

"Z, I'm serious!"

"Well if you insist..."

"I do!"

"If I must, it is a far, far better thing that I do..."

"Hah, hah! I hear VIBE is looking for a new host!"

"No you didn't go there, leave Chris Spencer alone, just give him time."

"Negro please he is so... no you don't, trying to get off the subject!"

"Gage, I'll always be here for you. We may not be able to ever have what we had in Orlando, but we will always be the best of friends. I love you, that will never change. And I need to thank you too!"

"For what?"

"Helping me to breath again..."

"Huh?"

"These past 48 hours resuscitated my heart and now I can breathe again. When we ended, I felt like I was gasping for air, feeling that each breath might be the last. I couldn't breathe on my on. Moms, Desmond and PRDG were all like oxygen for me. Now I can breathe again, on my own. Thanks to you." Zander's voice began to tremble, "and that's a wonderful feeling!"

They both took a deep cleansing breath as a toast to life.

"Final boarding call for all American Airline passengers on flight number seven - seven-six -two flying non-stop to Seattle..."

"I guess this is it."

"Yep!"

"You sure you won't take me up on my offer and stow away in the garment bag..."

"I'm sure..."

"Can't blame a guy for trying..."

"I ain't mad at ya..."

"Not this time anyway!" he said managing a small smile.

"I guess I should go!"

"If you don't want to miss your plane!"

"Don't tempt me..."

"Git.."

Zander and Gage hugged one final time.

"Talk with you soon..."

"You better!"

Zander watched Gage board the plane; he waved as Gage turned to say good bye. He took a deep breath. He wondered if there was still time to get in the garment bag, the thought produced a wide grin. There may have been no room in Gage's luggage, but he knew that there was plenty of room in his heart.

Eighteen

"Ladies and Gentlemen...the Diva of Rock and Soul... Miss Patti LaBelle."

"Finally," Desmond thought as the overture began. He thought the comedian was funny, but it was time for the real show. Before Patti hit the first note, Desmond stood to his feet yelling the songtress' name at the top of his lungs. He was in heaven and never wanted to leave. He loved Patti more than life itself. To him she was an angel sent by God. He had been a fan since the summer before he went away to college and thought that she just got better with age. By the third or fourth song, Desmond was hoarse and by the time she got to "You Are My Friend," one of his favorites, he was a wreck. That song always reminded him of his favorite cousin and his first gay bar experience.

The summer before Desmond started his freshman year in college, his father had sent him to Tampa to spend the summer with his aunt, Leah and her only son Treyvon. She was his father's oldest sister and Desmond's favorite because she didn't take stuff off nobody. To Desmond, she was a second mother; he loved her like one since his own mother had died when he was two. She loved Desmond too, she always spoiled him and would take up for him when he got in trouble. But the real reason that he loved his aunt so much was because unlike the rest of his family, his being adopted wasn't an issue with her. His cousin Treyvon or "Trey" as he liked to be called, was born on the same day as Desmond and was three years older than him. He had been his hero for as long as he could remember. When they were younger, Trey would defend him from his bully cousins or the neighborhood kids, later teaching him to fight and defend himself. He also taught him to play basketball, run and swim. Desmond appreciated his teaching him those skills because he later would parlay his athletic ability into a college scholarship. He was smart, always wore the coolest clothes and like his mother, didn't take stuff off nobody. But what he admired most about his cousin was that his cousin never hid the fact that he was gay from anybody including his mother. But he didn't flaunt it either. To this day Desmond wished that he could be more like Trey in that aspect.

Desmond couldn't wait to get to Tampa because his cousin had promised him that he would take him to Busch Gardens since he worked there, and teach him to drive. Desmond's father worked three jobs so he never had time to do stuff like that with him. That was also the year that Desmond discovered a world that he never knew existed. One night Trey and Desmond were talking and he asked Trey how he knew that he liked guys. Trey told him that he just did, that it was like breathing. He never knew anything else except that he liked guys and guys liked him. Plain and simple. Desmond later confessed that he liked guys too to Trey. His cousin informed Desmond that he had known that for a long time and that was the reason that he was so protective of him. He went on to explain that he had been raped by an older kid in the neighborhood when he was ten because the older kid said that he could tell Trey was 'funny,' a colloquialism for gay. Trey said that he knew if Desmond didn't know how to take care of himself that the same thing might happen to him someday and he wasn't having it. Desmond asked Trey if the rape had made him gay and he informed his cousin that rape wasn't a sexual act, that it was about power and violence. And no that wasn't the reason that he was gay. Desmond learned a lot about being gay and life that night.

On his last night in town Trey told him that he was going to take him out. He set down several ground rules for Desmond to follow. First, no drinking, second, no dancing with men unless he cleared it with him and lastly, no car sex or making out with anyone; he was too good for that and if he didn't think so neither would anyone else. He also knew that Desmond's good looks would be a magnet for the club kids to come sniffing. Since Desmond already looked older than he was and turning eighteen in a month, Trey didn't see any harm in taking him to the club; afterall he was going to be legal soon. Trey knew the host, Fruity, so he was able to get him in without having to produce his ID. At the door, he was given the last rule, no staring. Trey knew that since this was a new experience for him, it would be difficult not to stare. He was right, Desmond couldn't stop looking at all of the attractive men who were coupled off or dancing and having the time of their lives. He felt like he had died and gone to heaven. Trey's intuitions were right, Desmond became the flavor of the night and boys were hitting on him left and right. Desmond felt like Cinderella, only with facial hair and pecs, no pumps. Trey couldn't concentrate on having a good time for having to play protector, a role that he had become used to over the years. At around 11:30, Desmond heard this page, "Five minutes to show time folks!" Desmond asked Trey what kind of show was it. "You'll see," Trey said winking at his club virgin cousin. That night he saw exactly what his cousin was talking about. The announcer bellowed, "It's show time folks!" and the show's cast took center stage doing a number from "Dreamgirls". The show's MC, Brenda Dee, a heavy set woman with a big red wig who reminded Desmond of his fourth grade teacher Ms. Pointer, only better looking, ascended the stage and welcomed the crowd. She told dirty jokes and chugged drinks with the crowd in between acts. When Desmond asked Trey why there were women performers in a gay club, Trey nearly fell of his chair laughing at his cousin's naivete.

"They're guys, men, chicks with dicks."

"No way!"

"Yes way!"

Desmond sat there amazed at his cousin's revelation. For the rest of the night he was in awe of the beautiful men in beautiful dresses lip syncing to the tunes of some of the businesses' best. There was this beautiful blonde named Dana Douglas who did some slow song by Olivia Newton John; then there was Lakesha Lucki, a stunning black performer with a long ponytail that did Stephanie Mills "Home" from the Broadway musical "The Wiz," and this guy who looked just like Prince did a medley of his hits. All throughout the night, people would walk up and give the entertainers tips and they would hug or kiss them. Desmond was in awe. This was the coolest, it was like being at a concert with the hottest stars. It was that night that the principal entertainer and special guest performer, Tiffani Middlesexx, came and performed "You Are my Friend." Trey tipped her about ten dollars throughout the song. Desmond even got in on that act and tipped her, too. It was a night he wouldn't soon forget. That was also the night that he fell in love with Patti LaBelle.

As Patti sang "You are My Friend" Desmond's mind drifted to Trey. He wished that he could be there with him. Trey had been the victim of a hate crime while vacationing in DC during the spring of Desmond's freshman year in college. The service had to be closed coffin because he was beaten beyond recognition. As Patti worked the song, he knew that Trey was in heaven listening to Patti croon his favorite tune. A smile graced his face at the thought.

Nineteen

Rita really hadn't given much thought to dating since the death of her husband. It had been ten years since he had died. She had joined the widow's support group at the church about two months after her husband passed. Thinking that being with other women who had gone through the same thing would help ease the pain and help her work through the grieving process. It wasn't until recently that she had given thought to having someone in her life again because as far she was concerned there was only one man for her and he was gone.

Zander Evan Eady, III or Eady as she called him, was the love of her life. She could be heard bragging to her girlfriends that she had loved Eady from day one. They were childhood sweethearts. They graduated high school and college together and were the proud parents of one son. He was the only man she had ever known and they were married for forty-five years when he died. Their marriage was one that most people dreamed of having. They took their vows seriously and fulfilled them. They were together in sickness and in health, for richer and poor, and only in death did they part. When Eady died, Rita said a part of her died with him. She had spent all of her life making sure that the house was filled with love and a place that they could proudly call home.

Rita and Eady, wanted a house full of children, but she was unable to carry to term and had three stillborns. The doctors predicted that if she conceived again she would never carry to term. So when they discovered that she was pregnant with Zander, she took great care and made sure that she did everything that the doctor said to insure that Zander would make it. His birth was unanimously the greatest day of their lives. When he was born his father beamed with pride. He had a son and Rita had the baby she was told she would never have. She knew that their prayers had been answered.

She loved the two men in her life and made sure that they wanted for nothing. She loved spoiling her boys. This was her way of showing God that she was grateful for being blessed with a loving husband and beautiful son. They were the "Three Musketeers." While most families were going in separate directions, the Eadys could be found having dinner together, worshiping together, going to the movies together and enjoying each other's company. Zander knew that his parents "had his back" no matter what. While most of his friend's parents were divorced, Zander was proud of the fact that he had both parents living at home.

Eady was a handsome man. Rita always said that Billy Dee and Harry Belafonte had nothing on her man. They made a stunning couple. His wavy hair was like silk and his brick brown skin was equally as smooth. He had a cleft chin, like Cary Grant and teeth as white as snow. His smile lit up the room and his laugh was infectious. Rita made sure that he was always as clean as the board of health. She was the envy of all of her girlfriends. She always said that there was nothing worse than a good looking man that didn't look good, Rita made sure that both of her men always represented her well. She always made sure that they smelled and looked good. Cologne was always one of the presents that she gave on birthdays, anniversaries and Christmas. She believed that their appearance was a reflection of her. She made sure that their shirts were always starched and that their pants were creased so sharp that you could cut yourself if you weren't careful. Their shoes had to have a shine to them or her boys would have to answer to her. Eady cherished "His Rita" too. He loved lavishing his wife with jewelry and other tokens of his affection. He was one of the few men in Rita's circle who actually remembered important dates like their anniversary and his wife's birth date. He said that it was easy to remember their anniversary because that was the day his heart began to beat and her birthday was the day an angel was born. Rita could be heard saying at any given time, that she was the luckiest woman in the world. Zander even thought that he had the best looking parents in the world, well maybe not the world, yeah the world.

Their life together was not without it share of problems, but the difference was that they didn't see them in that way, they saw them as challenges for growth. Challenges that they endured. Their endurance was something that Zander admired and wanted for himself. They endured two miscarriages, three stillborn and a high risk pregnancy. They survived the racism and hostility as the first Black family to move into an all-white neighborhood and some how beat all the odds. With every challenge Rita and Eady grew closer. No matter what happened in their lives, there wasn't anything that they couldn't handle as long as they were together. They planned to grow old together, but not before they would travel the world and move to Florida to spend their golden years. Funny how plans change sometimes.

Shortly after he had retired, the doctor had suggested that he come in for a routine physical. He obliged knowing that everything would be all right and that they would give him a clean bill of health. Eady got up and showered and put on his brand new wind suit and tennis shoes that Zander had given him as a retirement gift. He saw that he had a little time and thought that he would get a cup of coffee, watch a little TV and then leave for the doctor's office. He sat down in his favorite chair, a Lazy Boy recliner that Rita had given him for a retirement gift. Zander speculated that this was to ease her conscience since she had taken a hacksaw to the other one when he was away on business years back because, to quote her, it was "broke down." It was ten til ten and his favorite show, "Knight Rider" was about to come on. No matter what he was doing he would stop to watch that show. People knew not to call during this time because he didn't want to be disturbed. While watching television Eady suffered a stroke and died.

Rita was the one to find him. She had just returned from having her hair done. As she passed through the den her initial thought was that he was asleep. This wasn't uncommon because Eady always said that the chair put him to sleep. He kidded her about having put a spell on it. At first she didn't disturb him until she realized that he was going to be late for his doctor's appointment, if he didn't leave soon. That set off an internal alarm because Eady was probably the most punctual person you would ever meet. He would always say, "Time waits for no man, so be a man and don't be late." We're talking about a man that had never been late or taken a sick day in 40 years of employment. In fact when he retired, his boss said that they would have to get a clock because their living clock wasn't going to be there any more. Rita gently touched his forehead like she always did to ease him out of his sleep. He felt cold and this alarmed Rita. She gently shook him, but he didn't respond. She called his name and he didn't respond, she called him again, no response. Rita called 9-1-1 and like lightning they arrived, only to confirm Rita's greatest fear. She told Zander that it felt like the world had been snatched from under her. What would she do with out her Eady? She even blamed herself for leaving the house and going to get her hair done, she should have been there. The only consolation that Rita found was in the fact that the paramedic said Eady didn't suffer. In fact he had probably fallen asleep and just didn't wake up.

She called Zander at college and told him the news. He hopped on the first thing moving and was there before the day's end. He remembered sitting on the plane numb; his hero was gone. He thought back on the life that he and his parents had shared. Not one important moment was void of them being there; why did this have to happen now? He had always envisioned his father being in the audience when he graduated, giving him the thumbs up beaming with pride. He had been there for everything else, why did he have to miss this one. Rita had sent one of the neighbors to the airport to pick him up. When he arrived Rita told him that she was going to need him to be the man of the house and take over the arrangements because it was too painful for her. His father knew that this would be to difficult for his family so he had made arrangements with the funeral home to ease the burden at the time of his death. Every detail was covered. That was Eady, always looking out for his family. The one request that he had of his family was that they be strong and for Zander to deliver his eulogy because he wanted the last words said about him to come from the man who knew him best, his namesake and pride and joy.

Zander was amazed at the number of people who showed up for the service. Their church, Calvary Temple, was packed to capacity. Black people, white people, people from the community and his old job all had come to pay their respects to Eady. Zander knew that his father would have been proud of the turnout. Zander Evan Eady, III, met no strangers. From a child his grandmother had told him that "she would rather see a sermon any day than hear one." He lived his life trying to exemplify Christ. That example had paid off.

At the funeral, Rita sat stolid and lifeless. It was almost as if she wasn't really there. The fact of the matter was that she wasn't. She just sat there quietly remembering the good times and the not so good times when Eady would prove to be her rock over and over again. She stared at the mahogany casket, draped in white roses. She didn't want to believe that her husband was actually in that box. "How could a man as big as life itself be contained in such a small place?" she remembered asking herself. The thought of him not being there was what really hurt the most. What would she do without him? A steady stream of tears cascaded down her left cheek. She didn't carry on like some Blacks do at funerals, hollering and screaming, falling into the casket asking why. She knew why, it was God's time and as much as she didn't like it, He knew what he was doing. She managed to listen long enough as Zander delivered his father's eulogy. His words were about the only thing she remembered about the entire service. She told him that his father would have been so proud of him, she sure was.

Twenty

"Hello, this is Rita."
"Good evening lovely lady!"
"Well, hello stranger!"
"You haven't returned my email, you bad boy you!"
"I haven't gone near the computer in days."
"Well the phone still works too."
"Point well taken, I'm sorry! You forgive me?"
"We'll see, what are you going to do to make it up to me."
"What do you want?"
"How about a great big hug? And a kiss would cinch the deal."
"You drive a hard bargain!"
"Hey they don't call me Big Mama for nothing!"
"This is true!"
"Were you busy?"
"Just getting ready for my group meeting..."
"That's right it is tonight! Well let me let you go."
"But first I need to know, you doing okay?"
"Yes ma'am, I doing good."
"That's good, anything new I should know about?"
Zander then began to tell his mother about the incident from the

nights before. She could sense a source of confusion in his voice and Rita told Zander that she would be on the next plane out and that she would stay as long as he needed her. The offer meant a lot to Zander, but he really needed to be alone and access the previous 48 hours.

"Ma! I know that God sent angels of protection to watch over us, I don't mind telling you I was scared."

"God always protects his children, you know that."

"Yes Ma'am, I do!"

"What's this world coming to when the people hired to protect you are the ones you have to be afraid of?"

"Don't worry Ma, Deputy Anderson will regret ever treating Gage and me like that. We didn't deserve that, he treated us like thugs..."

"He better be glad I wasn't there!"

"Ma, what would you have done, beat him with your purse."

"You better believe it, Big Mama packs a mean wallop!" Rita said letting out a hearty laugh.

They shared a laugh off Rita's last statement. Zander loved hearing his mother laugh. It was one that brought you joy just hearing it.

"Son are you sure you're okay?" Rita said taking on a serious tone.

"Yes, ma I'm fine."

"So are my ears playing tricks or did you say that Gage was there when all of this happened?'

"You heard right..."

"If I'm being to nosy, please let me know."

"No Ma, you're not being nosy... So are you ready for your big date?"

"The question is...is he ready for me?"

"You go girl! I'm scared of you"

Rita knew exactly what Zander was doing, but she wasn't having it.

"Now, back to you and Gage..."

"Ma!"

"Don't Ma me. Now that boy broke your heart and now he just sachets back into your life. Why? Did he come back with his tail between his legs wanting you to take him back?"

"No Ma! We needed to talk and get some things out in the open!"

"So are you gong to get back together? What happens now?"

"Ma! I wish, but I don't know what's going to happen? Suzzette is expecting, the baby is due any day now. Gage certainly has an obligation to his unborn child and I can respect him for honoring that!"

"Sounds like Gage is caught between a rock and hard place..."

"Yep!"

"Well things have a way of working themselves out, so all we can do is pray, wait and watch."

"True, Ma, true!"

"So when am I going to see you?"

"Ma! Didn't we just talk about this the other day?"

"Just checking"

"Ma! We will see each other soon and I promise that we'll spend time together."

"And a promise..."

"is a promise."

"Love you son!"

"Love you ma!"

Rita hung up the phone, Given the conversation with Zander she felt compelled to pray. So she did:

"Lord keep my chile safe, you made him and know all about him. Keep your angels of protection around him. Take him safely from place to place. Ease his burdens, touch his heart and remind him that you're there. Strengthen him when he's weak, prop him up when he's weary and encourage him when he's doubting himself. Thank you for hearing my prayers concerning my child, thank you for honoring the prayers of those who came before him for him. Lord, thank you for blessing him and taking him further than we all imagined, but then God we all know you're able. Thank you for just being you all by yourself. Lord, let your will be done in all of our lives. Let us always hear you when you whisper and when you have to speak a lil' louder. Thank you for loving us when we didn't love us ourselves. And least of all, remember me your humble servant. These things we ask in your darling son Jesus name. Amen." A tear rolled down Rita's face as she sighed reflecting on the goodness of the Lord. She sat there for a moment longer humming a stanza of her favorite hymn. She thought to herself, God is good.

Twenty-One

"It's a girl!"

The next sound Gage and Suzzette heard was their baby's first cry. The nurse placed their new daughter in Suzzette's waiting arms.

"Oh Gage look at her, she's beautiful."

"Yep! She looks just like her mother."

"She has your eyes." Suzzettes said adoringly.

"What are you going to name her?" the nurse asked.

"Zandrea Evan Gregory." Suzzette said with pride.

"What a beautiful name for a beautiful little girl." the nurse commented.

"Her father thought it up."

"Great name Mr. Gregory."

"Thank you!"

"I love you Gage."

"I love you too, Suzzette!"

"I'm so tired, but I don't want to stop looking at this angel that we created in love."

"Get some rest, you'll have a lifetime together."

"We'll have a life time together..." Suzzette corrected.

Gage didn't say anything, he just smiled.

"Sweet dreams," Gage said as his kissed Suzzette on the forehead and left her to rest.

Ever since he got back from his visit with Zander he couldn't help, but think about how good it felt to be back in his arms. He knew that he had to stay with Suzzette, especially now that Zandrea had arrived, but no less it was good to have Zander back in his life. He stopped in the hall way to call his mother.

"Hello."

"Hey Grandma."

"The baby is here, Gage why didn't you call me. I would have been on the first plane out."

"There wasn't time mother, Zette went into labor unexpectedly and so we had to get here as quickly as possible."

"How is Suzzette doing? And how is my first grandchild doing?"

"Mother and daughter are both doing fine... both resting and beautiful as ever!"

"It's a girl! Oh how marvelous and what is my granddaughter's name....and don't feel obligated to name her after me..."

"I'm glad you feel that way, her name is Zandrea Evan..."

"Where on Earth did you and Suzzette get that name from..."

"Why, don't you like it?"

"To be honest, no I don't...it sounds so...so ethnic...so... so common."

"Well, I'm sorry you feel that way, like it matters to you, I chose her name and Suzzette loves it so I guess that's all that matters...isn't it mother?"

"I guess, I'll get used to it in time. Are you sure you can't..."

"Change it? Mother, don't start this. I call you with what I thought would be good news and all you can do is complain about my daughter's name! You are a real piece of work mother!"

"How dare you speak..."

"No mother, how dare you!"

"Gage Garrison Gregory, I have had enough!"

"So have I mother, good bye!"

"Gage..."

"Good-bye mother, I love you. I'll talk with you soon!"

Gage didn't even give his mother a chance to say good-bye before he disconnected the call.

"Somethings never change," he thought. It seemed that he couldn't do anything right as far as his mother was concern. When he announced that he was going to art school instead of some Ivy league school, his mother threatened to disown him. If it hadn't been for his father she would have had her way that time too.

To Drucilla Douglas Gregory, image was everything. You had to go to the right schools, be seen at the right social events, associate with the right people and yes, even choose the right name for your children. It wasn't all her fault, her mother and her mother before her all ascribed to the same values and philosophy. Her family spent their summers at Martha's Vineyard on The Oval, a section of the vineyard where affluent light-skinned blacks spent their summers. She was a member of a sorority that was associated with accepting only beautiful black women who could pass the brown paper bag test, from, you guessed, it "the right families." For as long as he could remember his mother drilled into him and his other siblings that status was everything. She would screen their friends and if they didn't meet their criteria she would tell them to never bring that friend back to their home. And when they started dating, they would be instructed to invite their potential date to the house for dinner and if they didn't say the right things, wear the right clothes or come from, you guessed it "the right family," they were not allowed to go out with them. "Dru" as a self admitted snob, made no excuses for who she was. When Gage confronted her about her elitist ways, she simply said that she was doing what she thought was best for her family. He vowed that she would not poison his daughter with her racist viewpoints and behavior. As much as Gage loved his mother, he resented her as well.

He took a few minutes to regroup from his latest encounter with his mother. He then made calls to his sisters, other family members, Suzzette's family and their friends announcing the arrival of an angel. He was about to leave the hospital when he decided to make one last call.

"Hello..."

"Congratulate me!'

"Congratulations, who is this?"

"My how soon we forget!"

"Oh, Gage, how are you? You didn't sound like yourself"

"Gee thanks Z!"

"Why am I congratulating you?"

"Suzzette had the baby..."

"Already? I didn't think that it was due for at least a couple of more weeks!"

"She came early!"

"She! Congrats, what's her name?

"Zandrea Evan Garrison."

"Ha, ha, very funny, now tell me her real name!"

"I'm not kidding that's her name! You like...."

"Yeah, I guess, I'm just a little surprised."

"Hey I named her after someone very special, someone that means the world to me!"

"I'm very flattered!"

"No problem..."

"So how is Suzzette...and the baby?"

"Both doing great!"

"...And you?"

"I'm actually on top of the world, I guess fatherhood will do it for you!"

"Okay Pop!"

"Be happy for me, okay..."

"I am happy for you, I just want you to be happy!"

"I am...."

"Then that's all that matters..."

"Z..."

"Yes....

"I love you, always know that!"

"Ditto, and congratulations again, give my namesake a kiss from her uncle Z!"

"That reminds me, one other thing..."

"What's that?"

"Will you be Zandrea's godfather?"

"Whoa! I don't know about that!"

"Why not! It would mean a lot to me if you would."

"Gage, I'm honored that you would want me to be your daughter's godfather, but how are you going to explain that to Suzzette? Especially with the similarities between the two names? I think you're asking for trouble!"

"C'mon Z, it would mean the world to me..."

"I'll have to think about that one...."

"What's to think about?"

"Gage, I don't think that you've really thought this through..."

"Yes, I have...."

"I don't think you have...not thoroughly!"

"Z..."

"Look, think it over and I'll do the same, but my first inclination is to graciously decline because it's going to send up a red flag to Suzzette and anyone else..."

"Maybe you're right, I guess I just want you to share in this happy time with me..."

"I do, but I just think that this is the best thing for everyone, especially Zandrea and her daddy."

"I guess I wasn't thinking..."

"Yes, you were, but it was with your heart and not your head."

"I guess I'll head on home; I need to get the nursery finished. I'm painting a mural and I had to wait until the baby was born. Now I'm inspired; I want this to be my best work yet. Nothing but the best for my little angel."

"I'm sure that it will be beautiful. Take pics of it and the baby, I'd love to have one and I'm sure Ma would too!

"How is Rita doing?"

"She's doing great! I told her about our ordeal and needless to say she was concerned, wanted to get on a plane right then to come out here. You know Ma!"

"Give her my love and tell her to keep me in her prayers!"

"Will do."

"Take care..."

"You too and take care of your family. I take it that you've decided to make a go of this."

"I'm going to try..."

"It'll take more than trying, but if it helps, know that I support your decision and that I have your back. Okay!"

"Just knowing that you care helps more than you'll know!"

"See you Pops!"

"Very funny!"

"I thought so!"

Gage hung up and sighed. He hoped that he was making the right decision. There was no turning back now.

Twenty-Two

"Good Morning and thank you for calling The PRDesign Group, how may I direct your call"

"Zander Eady please"

"May I say whose calling please"

"Desmond Lowe."

"And you're with?"

"I'm an associate of Mr. Eady"

"Hold please, I'll check and see if he's in!"

"Thanks."

Desmond listened to the on hold message and found himself beaming with pride as it announced the changes at PRDG.

"Mr. Lowe?!"

"Yes!"

"It's my pleasure to connect you, have a good day..."

"Thank you."

"This is Zander..."

"It bettah be, wassup?"

"You, baby love, you."

"You got a minute?"

"For you, I've got two!"

"I'm flattered, how white of you!"

"I was just thinking about you, great minds..."

"Yeah, good thoughts I hope."

"But of course, what else could they be!"

"Depends on who you ask."

"I'm sure you're right and what do I owe the pleasure of this call!"

"You were on my mind and I had a few minutes before my next appointment..."

"Everything is cool."

"Okay so now tell me the truth!"

"I'm fine..."

"No you're not, you're not even supposed to be in the office today. Elle gave you the rest of the week off."

"And you said that to say...."

"Okay be a bitch..."

"I learned everything I know from you!"

"Well then I guess you're one helluva bitch then."

"But seriously, Des, I'm fine, just a little preoccupied..."

"With..."

"Gage's wife had the baby..."

"O....k...a.....y..."

"And you'll never guess what they named the baby..."

"I couldn't even begin to..."

"Zandrea Evan Garrison."

"You lie like a rug..!"

"Could I make this up!"

"And that's not all."

"There's more..."

"What?"

"He wanted me to be the Godfather..."

"Tell me you didn't..."

"As tempted as I was, I declined. He seemed to actually be disappointed."

"I'm sure he was..."

"D, stop...he's in a bad place and I feel kind of sorry for him..."

"Nobody told him to get married. He had a wonderful relationship with a good man and he decided to go fishing..."

"Stop, boy you are crazy!"

"You know I'm only speaking the truth..."

"N---knee-wayeee..."

"Why you still taking up for him..."

"I don't take up for him..."

"And I quote, 'he's in a bad place and'..."

"Maybe I do take up for him but old habits die hard..."

"Yeah, like loving him..."

"Yes that too..."

"So are you telling me that you're still in love with him?"

"I don't know what I am. During our visit you would have thought that we were back together..."

"So you did do it!"

"No we didn't..."

"Yeah tell me anything, I don't believe you..."

"When have I ever lied to you?"

"Well there was that time..."

"Go on..."

"And then there was the time..."

"Yes, bristah horny one..."

"Why a bristah gots to be all that...."

"As you were saying?!"

"Okay so you've never lied to me..."

"I didn't think so..."

"But I still believe that you did something..."

"We didn't even sleep in the same bed..."

"Why not, afraid that it would be to hard to resist..."

"Damn straight, he's gotten better with age. Tyson has nothing on him."

"Now lets not go that far. How dare you blaspheme against my baby?"

"You don't even know Ty..."

"And you do..."

"Well he is one of our clients..."

"You've been holding out on me..."

"Psyche!"

"You know I only have one name for you bi..."

"Don't go there..."

"Don't play with me like that, you know how I feel about his Phiness!"

"Whatever..."

"Anyway, back to you and the baby's Daddy."

"No you didn't go there..."

"Payback is a bitch, ain't it sweetness."

"And you call yourself my friend."

"I am your friend, but you need to face the truth Z Baby, you still love him and he's back in your life and wants to be there in a big way!"

"But he knows and more importantly, I know that what we have is over and as long as he's married we can't even think about being together not even for one last stroll down memory lane as badly as I wanted to. I never thought that I would be saying this, but I would give anything to have him in my life, but I know that this can't happen. So I have to resign myself to being a friend and believe me, he needs a friend right now."

"No what he needs is a man. Instead he has a wife and a baby named Zandrea, go figure."

"I mean Des, it would have been so easy to pick up where we left off, but I couldn't. I wouldn't want anyone to do that to me..."

"And you know what the good book says about reaping and sowing..."

"Yep! That's one needle that I don't want be stuck by..."

"You ain't never lied!"

"So how are things with you?"

"As he said changing the subject..."

"Well what's going on in the life of Desmond Thomas Lowe?"

"Nothing much I met someone new and I think I may actually want to settle down if he acts right."

"Excuse me, I didn't really hear correctly?"

"Yeah you did," Desmond said blushing.

"Operator, I think we have a bad connection..."

"Zander, stop it.."

"Minerva, get me my pills, the yella ones! I think I'm gonna have a heart attack..."

"Okay, see how you are, that's okay forget it..."

"No c'mon D tell me".

"Nope"!

Zander realized that his friend must be serious about him if he was acting like this, because Desmond hadn't talked about a man in this manner in years. He knew that this guy must be something if Desmond wasn't spilling the beans about a sexual escapade and how he turned the guy out.

"Why haven't I heard of him before now..."

"I didn't want to throw him up in your face when you were going on about the G-man."

"Desmond, I want you to be happy no matter what's going in in my life, you know that right?"

"Yeah, but..."

"No buts!"

"No buts! Oh my, perish the thought!"

"Fool... you know what I mean."

"So tell me about this new man in you life..."

"Well...."

"C'mon D! Don't hold out on me!"

"Remember the last man I wrote you about online...."

"FlyBoyee?!"

"Yep! I thought you said he wasn't about nothing!"

"He wasn't!"

"So...."

"When I got to the room he seemed to be nice, but as the evening went on he started to get on my nerves..."

"How?"

"He just didn't, it didn't feel right and I wanted to get out..."

"What did you do?"

"I left just as he was telling me that he wanted to rape me and make me feel like the bitch he knew I was..."

"What did you do?"

"I told him that if he wanted to see tomorrow, he would let me walk out that door and forget that I ever knew him!"

"See, D that's why I worry about you...what if he wasn't going to take no for an answer... "

"Go ahead, say it.."

"Say what?"

"I told you so!"

"No, I'm not going to do that, I'm just glad that you're all right!"

"Of course, I am...nobody does the diva!"

"Work it out boy!"

"And you know this..."

"Okay so if it's not him,..."

"I got off the elevator, went to the bar to get a drink to calm down and there was a guy sitting at the bar. We started talking..."

"Tell me you didn't"

"What? Ohhhh, no babe doing the do was the last thing on my mind....especially after what had just happened..."

"Okay, just checking, no don't even try at getting all new, you know how you can be when it comes to men..."

"No he didn't just say that, paging Dr. Click!"

"Des, I'm just playing. Lighten up and finish your story!"

"So anyway!" Desmond said as if to dismiss Zander.

"No you didn't!"

"As I was saying before I was so rudely interrupted..."

"Okay, I'm sorry, continue..."

"Never mind!"

"C'mon D, I'm just giving you a hard time..."

"I won't even touch that, but back to Eli..."

"Eli, huh Hmmm..."

"He was sitting in the bar and we started talking and we talked until 5:00 in the morning. We closed the bar down and them we went and sat in my car. I didn't want to leave and neither did he but he had an early meeting and was flying back to Dallas later that afternoon."

"So did you kiss him good night," Zander said in a school boy tone kidding with Desmond.

"No, I was a gentleman..."

"That's a new one for you..."

"What are you trying to say..."

"Nothing..."

Zander started laughing and Desmond couldn't help, but laugh himself because he knew that he was notorious for going in for the kill and leaving his conquest in the dust.

"Anyway, he asked if he could kiss me good night and I said..."

"I knew it! "

"I said that I would rather not..."

"You lie like a politician at a debate..."

"You're right..." Desmond said laughing, "I obliged thinking that he was going to lay it on me and he leaned over and kissed me on the forehead and the cheek."

"Get out! All right Mr. Eli, you get major cool points for style."

"Z, I floated all the way home."

"So where is he now?"

"Right here, you wanna speak to him?"

"You lying..."

"Hello?"

"Ah, hello and how are you?"

"Fine and you? Zander it's a pleasure meeting you via telephone..."

"Same here."

"I don't want you to worry about Desi, he's in good hands.."

"Desi," Zander thought to himself, "Desi?" He said again.

"He better be! Cuz if he isn't you'll have to answer to me..."

"He said that you would say that..." Eli said laughing.

"He was right!"

"I look forward to meeting you soon..."

"Same here..."

"Peace, here's Desi!"

Eli handed the phone back to Desmond caressing his hand as he took it. Desmond leaned down to kiss his forehead. As he put the receiver back up to his mouth, he just sighed.

"Oh Lucy, I'm home...."

"Shut up! You sick man!"

"No your the one sick! Love sick. Desi and Eli sitting in a tree..."

"No you didn't."

"Be happy, babe, I've never heard you this happy before...and I have to tell you I like it on you. You wear it well."

Twenty-Three

Zander had settled in for a long afternoon planning the media campaign for their newest clients promoting their existing and new projects. While he could have turned this project over to someone else, he still wanted to handle this client personally. After all, it was their signing that helped him achieve his partnership. He felt that he owed it to them. His train of thought was interrupted by Mildred's page.

"Mr. Eady..."

"Yes Mildred?"

"Ms. Page on three..."

"Thank you, Mildred."

"Hey partner wassup?"

"Hey stranger and how are you? Listen could you do me a huge favor?"

"Depends..."

"On what..."

"What the favor is..."

"I'll tell ya, give a Negro half your company and they get all new on you!" They both laughed knowing that Zander was just giving Elle a hard time.

"No, you didn't take me there. What can I do for you?"

"Something has come up and I need to take care of it, but I need to be away from the office for a couple of days."

"Anything I can help with?"

"Just being there is enough."

"Are you sure, you're okay? You don't sound like your usual self..."

"Well, like I said there is something I need to take care of and I'll be fine."

"Well if you say so, know that I'm here if you need me.."

"I know that! And knowing you're near helps...Hey don't forget you have to speak with the Sheriffs' Office and the Mayor's Office regarding that idiot!"

"Yeah, thanks for making some calls, we appreciate it!"

"What are friends for..."

"Thanks again! Take care of yourself partner, need you back in tip top shape..."

"I will be..."

"Peace sistah friend."

"Bye..." Elle whispered as she hung up.

Zander couldn't help but worry. Elle was more than a business associate. She was like a sister and a friend to Zander. His mother always said that she was the daughter that she never had and joked with Zander about her being the daughter-in-law that she never would. Zander smiled at his last thought as he reflected on the call. He then became concerned because he knew that it wasn't like Elle to take time off without good reason. She was an even bigger workaholic than he was. His concern led him to whisper a quick prayer for Elle. He was just finishing as Mildred paged him again.

"Mr. Eady, I hate to disturb you but a young man is here to see you. He says that you're his big brother..." Mildred said with a tone of doubt in her voice.

"Yes, Mildred, send Hakiem in."

"You can go in now..." Mildred said as she disconnected the call.

Zander stood up from his desk and went to the mini fridge pulling out two IBC Root Beers and looking to see if he had any snacks in one of the gift baskets that Asia had left for him in the office. Hakiem was his little brother from the mentoring project that Zander helped start a couple of year's ago. The whole idea of the project was to show young gay men that they didn't have to fall into any stereotypical group as a young black or gay male. One of the counselors for the youth group that had been started in the high school for openly gay teens thought that the men's group would be an ideal partnership to help guide these boys into manhood in a positive light. Hakiem was a handsome teenager who wore the typical baggy jeans and big shirts which always looked odd on him because he was rail thin. He has big brown eyes, and thick eyebrows. When he and Zander met, he was bald and had a faint goatee. Since that time he had let his hair grow back. His honey golden skin accentuated his blondish brown color which was now styled into a Caesar cut that showcased his wavy hair.

Zander had been paired up with Hakiem shortly after his fifteenth birthday. His parents kicked him out when he came out. Zander helped find him a place to stay and made sure that he stayed in school and that he was okay. He had been so busy lately that he hadn't had a chance to devote any time to Hakiem. He had beeped him earlier to see if he could meet him for lunch or to catch a movie so that they could spend some quality time. He needed to be brought up to date about the happening in his ward's life.

"Hey lil" bro wassup? Long time no see!"

"Nuttin man! Yep its been too long. Thought you ain't love me no more!"

"Never doubt that! We're cool! right!"

"Yep! This office is phat!"

"I take it you approve...."

"Man you must be large and in charge up in here..."

"Well I do own half the company now."

"For real, can you hook a brother up with a job, I need to be gettin paid!"

"I think I can arrange that. You'll need some money for school in the fall. So what do you want to do?"

"Anything, as long as it's got a check connected to it!"

"Okay! then consider it done, but know that I expect you to make me proud..."

"Z, how you sound? You know I ain't gonna let you down!"

"You won't let me down.." Zander said correcting Hakiem's grammar.

"I meant I won't let you down, sorry"

Zander was always on Hakiem about his use of grammar. He was always stressing the importance of speaking correctly when he was in a professional or social setting outside of his crew.

"So what would you like to do here at PRDG?"

"Can I be your assistant? I can answer the phone or run errands."

"Yes you could do that, but what interest you? What do you want to do when you finish high school?"

"I ain't... I mean I haven't given it much thought"

"Why not, you graduate this year. What about college?"

"Not going!"

"What do you mean you're not going? Your grades are 200% better than they were in your sophomore year, you're great at basketball, you're intelligent. Hakiem you owe this to yourself!"

"Don't think that college is my thang!"

"We'll talk about this over lunch!"

"Nuttin to talk about! I ain't going so squash it!"

"Who do you think you're talking to like that?"

"Look dawg, you ain't my Daddy!"

"Hakiem, chill!"

"Look Z! Maybe this wasn't such a good idea. I'll check you later. Let me know about the job," Hakiem said as he prepared to make his exit.

"Hakiem, sit your narrow butt down; you are not leaving until we talk about this!"

"Man..."

"That's right, I'm a man and so are you and we're going to discuss this like men."

"What is there to discuss?"

"What is there to discuss! Your future boy!"

"Boy! I got your boy"

"You don't want to go there!"

"Man..."

"Don't start that man crap. If I didn't' give a damn, I wouldn't be in you life"

"Whatever..."

"Hakiem, let's stop or squash this here and now.."

"Cool, I ain't...I mean I am not going to college. I can't afford it, I'm not smart enough..."

"Okay, thats it! If you are saying this because your parents aren't going to help, there are scholarships and if that doesn't work out, I've got you covered, I'll pay it and as for you not being smart enough, that's a lie and you know it."

"You would pay for me to go to school..."

"That's what I said!"

"But..."

"No buts, when I agreed to mentor you I made a pledge to myself to be there for the long haul and to always have your back..."

Hakiem didn't know what to say. It had been so long since an adult genuinely cared about him. He really was untrusting of men because some of them were always trying to get up on him because he was young.

"Thanks man, nobody has ever done anything for me without wanting something in return.You cool that way g."

"You're welcome and the only thing that I want is for you to realize your fullest potential and live your dream..."

"My dreams... it been a long time since I had any of those, seems like I have more nightmares than dreams lately."

"Why is that?"

"I just do."

"Hmmm, you wanna talk about it?"

"Naw! But man back to college and stuff... I really wanna thank you, but I don't think you should waste your green. I'm probably not smart enough!"

"Stop that madness right now! As far as school, not a problem, but I know that this not smart enough reasoning you're screaming is a front. So fess up!"

"That's really it. My grades are up, but school is boring and I don't like it."

"Why is that? You get good grades and you're active in drama and speech..."

"I just don't want to!"

"Not good enough!"

"Man.....Oops, I'm sorry, but Zander school ain't my thing!"

"Okay, tell me this then. What is your thing..."

"I like fashion, art, dance, drama... I like acting a lot, but I like costume design the most..."

"That's it!"

"What man!!!"

"There you go! If you really like costume design then maybe thats your calling."

"You really think so..."

"When we come back from lunch we're gonna research some schools on the web and start charting your future, time is of the essence."

"Sounds good to me...I really don't think about the future kinda live day to day, especially lately."

"Why lately?"

"Just cuz..."

"Cuz what?" Zander said smiling at Hakiem. He knew that the boy had something on his mind because he had never seen him this negative and down before.

"Nuttin, I don't want to talk about it?"

"Obviously something is bothering you so lets hear it. Maybe I can help."

"Nah, can't nobody help me wit dis, except the man upstairs."

"Is it that bad?"

"Yeah...but like I said..I don't wanna..."

"But we are talking about it so you might as well tell me..."

Suddenly Hakiem started coughing uncontrollably, so much so that he couldn't stop. Zander handed him the soda and he took a swig.

"You okay?"

"Yeah, just a lil' cough...I'll be aiight?"

"You sound awful, you taking something for that cough..."

"Just some cough syrup?"

"Is it helping?"

"No, not really!"

"Have you been to the doctor?"

"Yeah, he gave some medicine and ran some tests."

"Did he tell you what was wrong?" Zander said growing concerned.

"Yeah, but I don't want to talk about it, I'm not trying to be all like that, but I just don't wanna talk to you or anybody else about this. So can we change the subject? I'm starving! We gonna go eat or are you busy?

"No, I'm never too busy when it comes to you!. But don't think for a minute that you are fooling anybody you know. When it comes to you, I know you like a book so start talking."

"Look. I said I don't want to talk about it!"

"And I said were are going to talk about it..."

"I ain't hearing it!"

"Hakiem, what could be that bad? You're only 17!"

"Man a lot of shi... I mean stuff!"

"Like what?"

"Stuff!"

"Stuff like..."

"Man leave me alone... please..." Hakiem started to cry, turning his back to Zander trying to conceal the tears.

"Hakiem, it can't be that bad, talk to me..."

"I got..." Hakiem said mumbling so low that Zander didn't hear what he said.

"What did you say?"

"I'm H.I.V. positive!"

Of all the things that Zander expected to hear he never thought that it would be that. He got up out his chair and embraced him. Hakiem collapsed in his arms sobbing.

"H.I.V. positive, are you sure? I mean..."

"I'm sure, so that's why I don't think that I'll be going to school. I probably won't be around."

"Hakiem, I'm sorry...I'm so sorry... but you do know that people are living longer and healthier lives, this isn't the death sentence that it used to be."

"Thats what the doctor said, but I'm full blown. I have 11 T-cells. I'm dying!"

"Is that what the doctor said?"

"No, but if I only have eleven cells then how am I gonna do this?"

"lil' bro, they have medicine that will build you immune system and your T-cell count, didn't they tell you that!?!"

"Yeah but I can't afford the medication and I don't want to go to the health clinic. Somebody may see me there and it might get out and then nobody will want me or even be my friend."

"That's not true, your friends will be friends no matter what and you will always have me!"

"Thank you..."

"And as far as medication and your doctor's care, there are programs to assist with that and you know I'll do whatever you need me to do! Okay lets take a deep breath!"

They both took deep breaths and Zander looked into the eyes of this boy who now was faced with man sized problems. Zander reminded him that he wasn't alone. He told Hakiem that they were going to fight for his young life and do whatever it took to make the best of this bad situation. Zander was numb, but he couldn't let Hakiem see how his news had affected him. They went to lunch but neither of them really felt like eating.

After lunch he dropped Hakiem off, but not before hugging him and telling him that he loved him. He knew that he needed to know that right about now because he was really down on himself and blaming himself saying that his father was right; this was God's punishment on fags and queers. The fact that he might believe this saddened Zander even more. He reminded him that God was about love and not hate or punishing people for being who they were.

When he got back to the office he asked Mildred to hold his calls. He turned off the lights and just sat there. Out of all the times that someone has told him that they were H.I.V. positive or that they had AIDS, never had it knocked the wind out of him like Hakiem's revelation. As he reflected on the past two hours, tears trickled down his cheek. He took a deep breath and cried some more. He was angry, sad and frustrated. Hakiem was only 17 and wanted to give up on life. He told himself that he wasn't going to let that happen. He was determined to help him live with AIDS and not lay down and die from it.

Twenty-Four

"We're home..."

"Finally."

"Look into the camera..."

"Gage, please I look awful..."

"You look beautiful sweetheart..." Suzzette's mother Marlena chimed in.

"Your mother's right, you're positively glowing; motherhood agrees with you."

"You're all too kind, but I caught my reflection in the mirror in the hall, Gage put down the camcorder please." Suzzette said fussing with her hair.

"I want to record your arrival for our video library. Come on Suzzette, give me that million dollar smile of yours..."

"There, are you happy?" Suzzette said through clinched teeth forcing a smile for Gage.

"Hold Zandrea up so we can see that beautiful face."

"Say, 'hi daddy, I'm ready for my close up.'"

"Hey angel! Let me see that beautiful smile..."

"Son, that wasn't a smile that was gas." Marlena said laughing at Gage.

"I knew that..." Gage said trying to cover his embarassment.

Suzzette made her way to put the baby down hoping to escape Zander's camera lens but it was no use. The "daddycam" was on her trail. Suzzette opened the door to the nursery and was met by the faint aroma of new paint, but the smell seemed insignificant as she looked at the mural that Gage had painted.

"Gage, it's beautiful!" Suzzette cooed.

"Thank you, nothing's too good for daddy's angel!"

The room was painted in a cloud motif with African American cherubs playing on the clouds with mother nature and a bald guardian angel watching over them. Gage got the inspiration for the mural after reading an article on acclaimed sculptor, Thomas Blackshear, and his Ebony Vision's collection. Gage new how much Suzzette loved angels and since Zandrea was an angel, it only seemed natural.

"I wanted to get it finished before you got home with angel girl... but don't worry about the fumes, I used non-toxic paints so they won't harm the baby."

"You read my mind."

"I figured that you would be worried."

"Yoohoo! Where is everybody?"

The voice changed Gage's entire mood.

"We're back here!"

"Oh there she is," Drucilla said reaching for Zandrea.

"Hello to you too mother!"

"Oh forgive me everyone, I was just awestruck by the baby! She is absolutely beautiful"

"Thank you..." Gage and Suzzette said in unison.

"So to what do we owe this unexpected pleasure?"

"You didn't think that I was going to let this precious bundle come home and not be here to greet her?"

"And we're glad you did," Suzzette interjected sensing the tension mounting between Gage and Drucilla.

"If I had known that you were coming, Dru, I would have postponed my visit until a little later in the month."

"I was sitting at home bored out of my mine and so I said to myself. "Self, there's a new baby in the world and her Nana Dru needs to be there to welcome her home."

"We're glad you're here, Mother Gregory."

"I'm sure you are dear, but my son may not agree..."

"Mother, I am glad you're here..." Gage said rolling his eyes when his mother wasn't looking. He would give anything for his mother to turn around and walk out of the door just as quickly as she entered."

"So what do you think of the nursery Dru, isn't it absolutely the most charming?"

"It's nice if you like angels. We don't want the baby to grow up and be some religious zealot, now do we..."

"Well, I think it's wonderful; Gage is so talented. He worked very hard on it trying to get it ready for the baby's arrival. It was a present from her father."

"Oh! you did this..."

"Yes mother I did, remember I'm an artist, it was a labor of love..."

"Quaint, really quaint..."

"I'll take that as a compliment..."

"Look at your new home, Zandrea! You love it don't you my darling?"

"Well mother, where are you going to be staying?"

"I thought that I would stay here and help out, but Marlena beat me to the punch...."

"Well, we can both help since we're both here..."

"I feel honored to have both of my mother's here to help," Suzzette said attempting to make Drucilla feel more welcomed since Gage wasn't doing such a good job.

"Let me take you bags mother."

"Thank you dear..."

"Suzzette now that it's just us girls, may I ask you a question?"

"Sure..."

"Why on earth did you let Gage name the baby Zandrea..."

"Mother Gregory with all due respect...."

"My dear, I don't mean any harm, but where did he come up with that name?"

"He says that the baby's name was inspired by an old and dear friend and so I really didn't have a problem with it."

"An old friend, who?"

"Zander, his old roommate from Orlando."

"You let him name your daughter after some friend of his..."

"Mother, drop it!"

"I was just..."

"You were just sticking your turned up nose into places it doesn't belong..."

"How dare you..."

"No, how dare you come here uninvited stirring up trouble?"

"C'mon you two not in front of the baby..." Suzzette interjected trying to keep the peace.

"Suzzette is right! I won't let even you mother spoil my daughter's homecoming..."

"I didn't mean any harm..."

"You never do.."

"That's enough you two..."

"Suzzette is right, this is not the time nor is it the place. Dru we're glad you're here. We're going to help our baby girl take care of her baby girl and give Gage a hand too!" Marlena interjected trying to assist her daughter in breaking the mounting tension in the room.

"Okay, so let's get some pictures for the baby's album and then I'll put some steaks on the grill and fix you girls a dinner you won't soon forget."

Gage took pictures and video of the baby, the nursery, the women in his life and his mother. He looked at Suzzette and the baby through the viewfinder and sighed. He thought to himself, "I'm a lucky man; how come I don't feel like one?"

Twenty-Five

The sun was setting as Desmond pulled into his parking spot. He was glad to be home. He had been looking forward to getting home since he left. He removed his briefcase from the backseat and made his way into the house. He was greeted at the door by the sweet smell of dinner being prepared by Eli. He tiptoed into the kitchen as Eli was busily preparing dinner. The table was set with fresh flowers and candles. Desmond quietly tip-toed behind him and placed his hands over his eyes.

"Guess who?"

"Denzel?"

"No guess again..."

"Damon!"

"No guess again..."

"I give up!"

"Ha, Ha, you're so funny!"

"Hey babe, how was your day?"

"Couldn't wait to get home!"

"And why is that?"

"Take a guess..."

"Because I was here..."

"No, I thought I left the stove on...."

They both laughed and kissed each other gently on the lips. Desmond closed his eyes and embraced the sweetness of what he was feeling at that very moment. He now understood what Stephanie Mills meant when she said that she never knew love like this. While he and Eli had not been together long, he knew that this was the genesis of love, because he never wanted a relationship before. All he ever wanted was sex and they hadn't even done the do yet, so it had to be more than just lust.

"What you thinking about?"

"You, us..."

"What about us?"

"Just how good it is to have someone in my life, someone that I want to stay around for as long as forever."

"Forever? That's a long time boo!"

"I know that, that's exactly what I want."

"You sure about this?"

"Never been this sure about anything in all the days of my life."

"Okay, then forever it is!"

"You mean it?"

"Desi, I wouldn't say it if I didn't!"

"Okay, cool!"

"Cool," Eli said taking Desmond into his arms and kissing him passionately. He had never had his breath taken away, but he liked it.

"So whats for dinner?"

"Me!"

"I'll definitely want seconds..."

"If you're for dessert, so will I!"

They just stared at each other letting their eyes finish the conversation. Over dinner they talked about their lives before each other and why this felt so right. Desmond told him about his days on AOL and why he never wanted commitment before. Eli said that neither of them were perfect but as long as they were honest about their pasts and didn't keep secrets that they could make this happen. Desmond agreed. After dinner, they listened to Luther, Barry White, Mikki Howard, Anita Baker and of course, Patti LaBelle while sipping wine and gazing into each other's eyes. As Eli laid in Desmond's arms, they both felt safe and secure emotionally. They whispered sweet nothings to each other watching the candlelight and basking in its glow. Desmond liked what he was feeling and so did Eli. No pressure, no promises, but a whole lot of potential. This was the beginning of something special.

Twenty - Six

The room was still filled with the aroma of the lavender roses that Gage had sent. Zander smiled and sighed all in the same moment. He took a deep breath and hoped that he was happy. He shut off the lights and made his way to the elevator.

As he drove his mind drifted back to lunch and Hakiem. He wished that he could take the pain away and make everything okay for him, but he couldn't; that frustrated Zander more than anything else. So he did the only thing he knew to do, he prayed. He wanted him to begin healing and accept this place in life and go from here. No, AIDS wasn't going away, but he didn't have to lay down and die from it either. Zander racked his brain on how he could get him to understand that simple fact. He told himself that come hell or high water, he was not going to let Hakiem give up without a fight.

He pulled out his organizer and looked up the number of Miles Robertson, one of the guys that he had met through his men's group, Brother's United, to see if he would agree to counsel Hakiem if he wanted it. "God know's he needs it," Zander thought to himself.

"The Umoja Project, this is Miles..."

"Wassup my brotha?"

"You and only you!"

"And you too my friend..."

"And to what do I owe this pleasant surprise and honor.."

"I need a favor..."

"Hmmm..."

"Don't even go there..."

"What?" Miles asked trying to sound innocent.

They both laughed at his feeble attempt at playing the innocent and caught up on what was going on since they last saw each other. Miles told Zander that he had been meaning to call him because he had an idea for a campaign targeting youth of color regarding AIDS education and prevention. This was the perfect lead in for Zander to talk about his young friend. He explained to Miles what he needed; he wanted someone in place if and when Hakiem agreed to join the youth support group or at least have one on one counseling.

"He's like a lil' brother to me, I love this boy and don't want him to give up living. I thought that if anybody could get him to see that this isn't the death sentence it used to be it would be you."

"Boy, I've been fighting this fight for nearly fifteen years and I can't give up now. These youngsters that get this sh... mess don't have a clue of what the early survivors went through. Compared to the meds from as little as four years ago, living with AIDS is a stroll in the park now." Miles said reflecting on his own battle with H.I.V.

"Well I don't know what you're doing, but you looked like new money the last time I saw you..."

"You flatterer. What you want name it, its yours big daddy..."

"You need to quit!"

"Nevah, as long as there is breath in this body..."

"Okay Scarlet..."

"No Suzanne Sugarbaker..."

Zander laughed and thanked Miles for all of his help. He told him that they would meet for lunch to finalize PRDG's commitment to the project by the end of next week. He also asked Miles to say a couple of prayers for him as he pitched Hakiem with the idea about attending group or individual counseling. They exchanged goodbyes and Zander felt a little better. If anyone could help Hakiem it would be Miles.

"Mr. Eady..."

"Yes, Mildred..."

"You have a call holding on line three..."

"Thanks Mildred, and you can go, I'll be heading out, too, after I take this call..."

"Thank you sir, and have a good weekend."

"Good night and have a good weekend Mildred. Drive safely."

With that said Zander picked up line three and answered in his usual business tone.

"Zander Eady here..."

"Hello stranger..."

"Wassup?"

"Not much, I thought I would have heard from you by now..."

"I've been swamped..."

"How did I know that you would say that?"

"You got me, so what's been going on?"

"Nothing much, working hard and waiting by the phone for you to call..."

"I'm sure you have plenty of people waiting for you to give them the nod..."

"Yeah right, the line forms in the rear, no pun intended..."

They both laughed at the latter part of the statement realizing the inside humor of the joke.

"So Zander when are you going to take me up on my invitation?"

"When the time is right..."

"The time is never right with you, especially now that you're the CEO of PRDG..."

"Don't even try it..."

"How many times have I asked you out and at the last minute something always comes up, some emergency at the office, you have to fly out to meet a client..."

"Okay, I can see how it would seem like I'm doing these things on purpose, but I swear I'm not..."

"Okay then, prove it..."

"How?" Zander said almost holding his breath.

"Go out with me tonight..."

"Tonight?"

"Yes tonight!"

"Tonight..."

"What part of tonight didn't you understand?"

"See now, you're getting smart with me...."

"Don't even try changing the focus here..."

"I wouldn't do that!"

"Yeah right, tonight!"

"Hmmm..."

"So what's it going to be Mister Executive..."

"I don't know Mistah TV Man...."

"Tonight..."

"How about Saturday night?"

"Tonight..."

"It's been such a long day..."

"Tonight..."

"I would need to go home and change and by the time..."

"Tonight..."

"C'mon give a brotha a break..."

"Tonight..."

"Okay..."

"See I knew you would....wait a minute...what did you say?"

"I said okay..."

"Okay as in..."

"As in okay, I'll go out with you tonight....what part of that didn't you understand? And you call yourself a journalist..."

"Now you didn't even have to go there..."

"But I did..."

"So what time should I pick you up..."

"I have my car, why don't I just meet you?"

"I'm not taking any chances..."

"No, I need to meet you, I promise nothing will keep me away from meeting you..."

"Okay..."

"You have my word..."

"What are you in the mood for? I mean for dinner that is..."

Zander smiled at his date's sense of humor. "You tell me..."

"How about Prima Donna's?"

"Italian, hmmm..."

"Or how about Allie Mae's?"

"Soul food with elegance...sounds good!"

"Okay so Allie Mae's it is..."

"In about an hour?"

"Cool, how are you dressing?"

"Casual chic..."

"All right then casual chic it is. You bettah work it out.."

"Just finished, so I know I'm looking good..."

"You are crazy!"

"Yeah about you!"

Zander blushed at his date's last flirtation.

"See you in an hour newsman..."

"Not if I see you first..."

"And for the record, I'm looking forward to it..."

"So am I, Mistah President, so am I!"

"Peace..."

Zander hung up the phone and decided to change into something less business. As luck would have it, some of his dry cleaning had been delivered to the office while he was out so he had something that he could slip into after taking a quick shower. As he looked through his choices he couldn't help but notice the butterflies that were beginning to stir in his stomach. It had been a long time since he had been on a date and Jordan Jacobs was nothing to sneeze at. He could do worse. He selected a black linen suit and a gray, short sleeved silk polo shirt that Desmond had given him for Christmas. He smiled approvingly at his selection and made his way to the shower.

As Zander removed his shirt and tie he looked at himself in the mirror. He removed his trousers and boxers to see if he was maintaining. He hadn't worked out in weeks and his little tension buster from the other night had hardly made up for the weeks of neglect. Luckily he was still eating right and not letting the PRDG vending machines seduce him to sample their fattening contents. He flexed to see if he at least had maintained his arms and some tone especially since he was wearing a short sleeved shirt that would cling to his body. He wanted to look like he was in shape, even if he wasn't in tip top shape. He gave himself a B but made a promise to himself that he would hit the gym first thing tomorrow morning. He turned on the shower adjusting the water's temperature giving it a few minutes to work up a steam. As he stepped in he was greeted by the mist and warmth of the steam. The water embraced his body as he lathered the looffah. He lost himself in the peace and serenity that the shower brought.

He shut off the water in the shower and toweled off. He looked to see if he needed to shave; he did. As he lathered he thought about Jordan and why he had never taken him up on his offer before now. It was nothing that Jordan had done or said, it was all his fault. "Well we're about to change all that..." he thought to himself. He finished shaving without cutting himself and finished his regime, got dressed and prepared to leave the office. He checked his voicemail one last time and made his way to the elevator. He checked himself via his reflection in the mirrored doors. He looked okay, but he wanted to look more than just okay, he wanted to look great. As he made his way, he began to question his choice of attire, maybe he should have worn something else. He was actually nervous, maybe this was a good sign. While he knew Jordan and they had been in social settings before, he wasn't taking him for granted.

"Oh well, ready or not, here I come."

Twenty-Seven

Jordan stepped out of his ebony Lexus handing the valet his key. The valet recognized him from television and greeted him with excitement.

"Good evening Mr. Jacobs, I watch you every night. You make me proud to be a brother..."

"So do you my brothah, so do you. Keep up the good work."

"Good evening Mr. Jacobs, welcome to Allie Mae's."

"Thank you!" Jordan said as he greeted and thanked the doorman as he held the door for him.

The hostess recognized him also and was more than happy to be the one escorting him to the table. Zander spotted him as he approached the table. Jordan was dressed in a gray mandarin linen shirt and charcoal linen slacks and a navy blazer. "He was truly a sight to behold," Zander said to himself.

Jordan Jacobs, was an anchor and talk show host of the station's morning show at the CBS affiliate and the most eligible bachelor in town. His drop dead looks and velvet voice made him a joy to watch and listen to. His skin was as smooth as ebony and richer than black gold itself. His eyes danced when he talked and his smile was equally as infectious. You could tell that he worked out and that he took pride in how he looked. As he approached the table, Zander smiled and stood extending his hand.

"Good evening sir!"

"Good evening to you too, you're looking awfully handsome tonight."

"So are you!"

"I was inspired by the company I would be keeping this evening..."

They both blushed while smiling at each other in mutual admiration.

The hostess rolled her eyes at the exchange between these two extremely handsome men of color. She was heard saying "such a waste" as she walked away shaking her head at the obvious flirtation between the two men.

"Bitterness, its such an ugly color" Jordan said as he observed the sistah's disdain.

They both laughed and settled in to enjoy each other's company.

"I took the liberty of ordering some wine, I hope you don't mind..."

"Not at all, I'm sure you made a wonderful choice..."

"Thank you, I'm sure you'll like it. It's one of my favorites..."

"Ouch!" Jordan said as he pinched himself.

"What are you doing?" Zander asked in amazement.

"Pinching myself to see if I am really here or dreaming..."

"Okay newsboy!"

Jordan laughed and his whole body joined in.

"But seriously, I'm glad that you're here tonight Zander. I've been looking forward to this for quite sometime..."

"Oh you just want to jump my bones and you know it..." Zander said jokingly.

"Hold up, is that what you really think that my persistance has been about?..."

"Jordan, I was just kidding, even though my sources did report that you were overheard saying, and I quote; 'I would love to have a piece of that'...that being me..."

"Mistah President, but your sources are mistaken. For the record, what I said is that I would love to wake up to that...that being you every morning, so tell these "sources" to get it right the next time. And these sources, as unreliable as they are, could only be Mason Gardner or Beau Reynolds or both...two gossiping queens who embellish anything in order to make their story more interesting..."

"Oh, so now you know my sources..."

"Everybody knows the Heda Harper and Rona Barrett of the gay world..."

They both laughed and gave each other dap over Jordan's last comment.

"While they are to be commended for a fifteen year monogamous relationship, those two have nothing better do..."

"True, but guess what, it was only after I was informed of your comments, as misquoted as they were, that I knew you were even remotely interested. So I guess you have them to thank for this evening..."

"I'm making a note now, 'send flowers and champagne tomorrow'.."

"You do that..."

"And, you know what..."

"What..." Zander answered as he took a sip of his wine.

"I would like a piece of that..."

Zander gulped as he nearly choked on his wine at Jordan's confession.

"That," Jordan continued, "being your heart!"

"You can have it if you want it!"

"Really now..."

"Sure, but you have to earn it..."

"No sweat, never been afraid to step up to a challenge..."

"We'll see, Mr. Jacobs, we'll see!"

"Yes we will," Jordan said raising his goblet to Zander.

"Cheers, to beginnings..."

"And happy endings..."

The waiter approached the table, and before asking for their order, he asked Jordan for his autograph. Jordan obliged and asked for a few more minutes before they ordered.

"I'm about to get jealous," Zander said jokingly.

"Part of the job, but tonight belongs to you!"

"Just giving you a hard time; I work in PR remember.."

"True dat!"

"So tell me more about you Jordan. I mean I know you, but I don't really know you..."

"Well I was born on the son of a poor sharecropper and..."

"Okay George Jefferson... be serious..."

"Okay, okay. Well you know what I do for a living... and you know my parents."

"Yep. Your pops is cool; he's the reason that I joined Mount Moriah..."

"I'm glad you think he's cool..."

"Spoken like a true preacher's kid..."

"No, I'm serious Z... my father talks a good game, but if you looked up homophobe in the dictionary, his picture would be prominently displayed..."

"Stop it, Rev. Jacobs is cool as all get out... if he wasn't he wouldn't have a choir full of family or a church orchestra that is happy as Robin Hood's band of Merry Men..."

"Zander, I wish I was lying, but my father knows that gay people in choir will give him the sound that he's looking for. But mark my word he doesn't like gay people. As he puts it; he has no room for nonessential queers in his church."

"Talking about embellishing and you call yourself a journalist.. God if you gonna strike please aim over there."

"Zander I love my father and wished I was lying, but I'm not!"

"Jordan..."

"Zander, trust me when I tell you this, he is one of the biggest supporters of the anti-Gay movement here in town. My father went as far as to say that if the Klan was marching against Gays he would join them..."

"Jordan, okay you've gone too far!" Zander said laughing at what he thought was Jordan's sense of humor. But Jordan was not kidding, he was dead serious..

"Okay fine, let's change the subject because I see that you don't believe me!"

"Jordan, I mean maybe your dad has issues with gay people but, the Klan..."

"If I'm lying, may God strike me dead right now!"

Zander looked to see if any lighting bolts were about to be thrown.

Jordan gave him the hand and had to laugh at the expression on Zander's face.

"Man, I am shocked!"

"What about your mom?! She's the minister of music! She has to know that there is family all in her music department!"

"My mother says that it's known that most church musicians have a little sugar in their tank. They are creative and thus her choir is the best in town. She tolerates other gay people, but not her own son."

"You are lying. Look at the way that she always talks about Harrison DeLeon, the musical director. She calls him her other son from the pulpit. The way she makes it sound, he was over at the house for

Sunday dinner every time the oven door opened. And I know for a fact that she is your biggest fan."

"My mother would make a great politician. The sad thing is that Harry thinks the world of my mother, too bad it's not mutual. He's never set foot in my parents home, nor will he ever. And as for me, while she knows that I'm gay, we never discuss it and she wants nothing to do with my life outside of being a local celebrity who happens to be her son. My mother still thinks that it's a phase and that I will eventually grow out of it. You know she has the same address as Cleopatra."

"Denial," they said in unison laughing even though they both knew it wasn't funny.

"I am shocked, but as my mother would say, 'it's known throughout Judea and Samaria that these are folks that make you stay on your knees just a little longer.' But your parents...that's deep" Zander said amazed at Jordan's confession.

"I pray for them everyday Zander. My love is the only thing that keeps them even in my heart. I have cried many nights after hearing them discount the gays in their congregation or even more the members that have died from AIDS. Notice how he's never available to do the services of the members that have died from the disease?"

"I never gave it any thought, but now that I think of it, you're right."

"Even though most of those who have left us held key positions in the ministry, my father didn't think that they deserved his care. He never goes to visit them in the hospital, he never consoles the family, he does nothing once they are useless to the ministry."

"My God..."

"I don't want to belittle my father; I believe that he was ordained by God and that he is one's of God's preachers." The gleam in his eye was being replaced by tears,"But if we're going to embark upon any type of relationship beyond just friendship then I thought you should know what you're getting yourself into."

"Hmmm, well I'm game if you are," Zander said touching Jordan's hand.

"Remember, you said that." He winked as he held onto Zander's hand.

Twenty-Eight

Zander pulled into the driveway still thinking about his evening. He was pleasingly surprised that he had enjoyed his date with Jordan. He always thought that he was attractive but really couldn't get a reading from him. His gaydar must have been in the shop when they initially met. He had to confess that prior to tonight he thought that Jordan was a stuff-shirt television personality who thought that the sun rose and set around his schedule. His thoughts of Jordan led to unhappy thoughts of the revelation regarding Jordan's father, his pastor.

He made his way to the steps and gathered his mail from the box. He noticed an envelope with Gage's return address. He stopped and opened it. He smiled at the photo of Zandrea dressed in white organza with angel wings. It read:

Mr. & Mrs. Gage Garrison Gregory, III

cordially invite you to share

in the christening and dedication of

their precious angel

Zandrea Evan

Zander stopped reading and smiled at the thought of Zandrea being christened. He only wished that he could be there, but he thought it best not to. He finished reading the invitation and thought of what he could do to make his God daughter's christening special. Without much thought he knew exactly what he would do. He decided to commission one of the artists that he knew and have him render a portrait of the entire family and one of Zandrea as a gift to Gage and Suzzette. He also thought that he would have his clients from the baby boutique make a christening gown as a gift as well. He was proud of his ideas and thought that the Garrison family would all know how special they were to him.

Zander couldn't get in through the door before the phone started ringing. He dropped everything on the foyer console and ran to get the wireless phone closest to him.

"Hello, this is Zander..."

"You made it home safely, I see..."

"Yes sir, I did..."

"Did you have a good time?"

"It was aiight.." Zander said giving Jordan a hard time, "just kidding!"

"See how you are!"

"No really, I had a great time..."

"So did I, I don't mean to be pushy, but when can I see you again?"

"When would you like to see me?"

"How about now?"

"What..."

With that, the door bell rang. Zander opened the door and there was Jordan standing with three dozen roses. Zander hung up the phone as he stood there in utter and total shock.

"I forgot one thing before we departed..."

"And pray tell, what was that?"

"This..." Jordan leaned over and kissed Zander lightly on the cheek. "There..."

Zander could do nothing but blush; he was speechless.

"Thank you...for the roses and for being so nice..."

Zander leaned over and gently kissed Jordan on the lips.

"Thank you too!"

"Well I just wanted to see you one more time before I turned in."

"Truth?"

"And nothing but..."

"I wanted to see you too!"

"Good night!"

"Pleasant dreams....Jordan..."

"Yes..." he answered hoping that Zander was going ask him to stay. He didn't want sex, he just didn't want the night to end.

"Call me when you get home..."

"Okay! I will..."

"Jordan..."

"Yes, Zander..."

"I had a great time and thanks for the flowers..."

"I aim to please..."

"Good night..."

"Night..." Jordan said as he turned returning to his car.

Zander stood in the door watching as Jordan drove down the street. As he watched, the phone rang.

"Hello..."

"So you really gonna let me leave..." It was Jordan calling on his cell phone.

"Yes, I am," Zander said laughing at how pitiful Jordan was sounding.

"Zander, I don't want to have sex with you, I just want to be with you."

"We'll have plenty of time for that and anything else you want, I just don't want to rush this..."

"I can appreciate that, but I would love to wake up to you in the morning...tomorrow morning!"

"Pushy little newsboy aren't you!"

"Only when I see something that I want..."

"Something?"

"You know what I mean..."

"Yes I do...just giving you a hard time, no pun intended..."

They both laughed,

"Zander?..."

"Jordan..."

"Zander, please?...."

"Don't beg! It isn't pretty on you..."

"I hate you..."

"Aahhh, so the truth comes out..."

"Nothing could be further from the truth..."

"So you wanna come back?"

"If its aiight with you!"

"I'll see you when you get here..."

"I'm turning around as we speak..."

"Jordan, I want to make one thing perfectly clear..."

"And that is..."

"I'm not easy, I'm no one's one night stand and I won't be taken for granted, clear?!?"

"As a crystal... Now can I make one thing perfectly clear..."

"Shoot..."

"I never thought of you as easy. I'm not looking for a one night stand, those are too easy to come by and I wouldn't take you for granted..."

"As long as we're on the same page..."

"Hey!"

"Wha..."

"Could you let a brother in?"

"You're back already?" Zander said as he open the door amazed at how quick Jordan had returned.

"Gee, maybe I should leave..."

"Okay..." Zander said as he closed the door in Jordan's face.

The phone rang again, but Zander didn't answer it. Instead he went out through the garage and out the side door sneaking up on Jordan.

"Nobody's home."

"You..."

They both laughed as Jordan shook his finger at Zander.

"So you wanna come in?"

"If you want me in..."

"Hmmm, let me sleep on it..."

"You do that..."

Twenty-Nine

Zander woke up in Jordan's arms. He tried to get up without waking him up. He wanted to stay in his arms, but he knew that if he didn't get up now, he never would. He reminded himself that he had committed to start working out again today. He looked over at Jordan sleeping so peacefully, how could he leave this Nubian god?

He could hear Desmond, "and if you want to keep him you have to be the finest thing he sees every morning before he leaves." That was enough to make him get up. As his foot touched the floor, Jordan stirred, grabbing Zander and bringing him back to his chest. He looked at him with those remarkable eyes and gently kissed his forehead.

"Where do you think you're going?"

"I was going, to fix you breakfast in bed..."

"Aahhh, thats so nice of you, but I would rather just have you for breakfast..."

"I'm sure you would, but I'm not on the menu..."

"Doesn't this joint take special orders?"

"Nope..."

"What happened to the customer always being right?"

Zander had no come back for that one and gave in as Jordan pulled him back into the bed lavishing him with quick kisses.

"So what do you want for breakfast..."

"Just coffee and you..."

"You have a one track mind don't you?..."

"You complaining?"

"No just an observation!"

"Oh..."

"So, how do you take your coffee?..."

"Why don't you let me fix breakfast for you?...."

"Because you're a guest in my home.."

"And you said that to say.....?"

"That in my house a guest is treated as...such..."

"So that means that you do whatever it takes to accommodate your guest?"

"Ahh..."

"Ahh...right?"

"Ahh wrong! Tell me what you want?"

"You, I want to take those boxers off you and make love to you..."

"Hmmm" at the very thought Zander could feel his boxers growing and pulsating.

"Hmmm what do we have here..." Jordan said pointing at the obvious bulge in the silk boxers that were doing such a poor job of concealing Zander's growing manhood.

"We don't have anything," Zander said embarrassed that he was reacting at the thought of being with Jordan. He had restrained all night long; it was important to both of them that they not rush into any sexual situation. But the thought of a morning filled with sensual passion and intimacy was more than he could take. He wanted Jordan in the worst way, but didn't want to give him the wrong impression. After all they didn't know where the relationship was headed.

"No need to be embarrassed..."

"I'm not embarrassed.."

"So is that a brush in your boxers or are you just glad to see me..."

"Ha, ha!"

"Come here..."

"Why?"

"Because I said so..."

"And..."

"And I want you here..."

"Here?"

"Now"

"Now"

"Right now..."

"Right now..."

"Yes..."

With that Jordan pulled Zander into his arms and on top of him kissing him with such passion and tenderness. Zander melted into his arms struggling to catch his breath. He had never felt like this. It was a reminiscent combination of all the firsts.... first kiss, first orgasm, first love and the first time you make love. The innocence of the moment was fused with sensuality and a pinch of erotica thrown in for good measure. This moment was like none that had ever surfaced before, not even with Gage. Zander returned the kiss with a passion he didn't even know that he possessed. He craved Jordan's kiss and found an insatiable place that was more emotional than it was sexual. He never wanted this moment to end. This place was where he wanted to spend the rest of his days. The moment almost eluded description. There was a rhythm, a pace. This wasn't sex this was synch. It was like breathing.

So much for working out.

Thirty

The phone rang as Zander showered.

"You want me to get that?" Jordan asked

"Please... "

"Hello??.."

"May I speak with Zander please?"

"May I say who is calling?..."

"Who is this?"

"This is Jordan, who is this?"

"This is Gage Garrison, is Zander there?"

"Hey! Gage wassup?...he's in the shower, can I take a message?"

"Just tell him that I called.."

"Sure thing, nice talking to you... peace"

"Peace, uhh...excuse me?..."

"Yes..."

"Never mind..."

Gage hung up the phone somewhat perplexed. "Who was that and why was he answering Z's phone?" he asked himself.

"Who was it?" Zander asked from the shower.

"Gage," Jordan said sticking his head in the door. "I think I should warn you..."

"About?"

"I think I really took him by surprise and he didn't seem too pleased..."

"He'll get over it.."

"If you say so.."

"And you know this..."

"So what did he want?"

"Nothing, except for you to call him..."

"Okay cool..."

Zander ascended from the shower, the water beading up on his toned frame glistening in the fluorescent lights that lit his dressing room. As he toweled off Jordan watched with lust in his eyes. Zander could feel his piercing eyes capturing his every move; he knew that if they started anything now they wouldn't get anything accomplished.

"So what do you want to do for lunch?..." Zander asked trying to get Jordan's mind off of an afternoon filled with more passion.

"You!"

"You already had me..."

"I want more, I'm greedy..."

"Tell me something I don't already know..."

"I can fix something for lunch and we could stay in..." Jordan said raising his eyebrow in a mischievous manner.

"And if we stay in lunch is the last thing we'll be doing..."

"And you said that to say...."

"I was thinking that we could have lunch in town and maybe catch a movie?"

"Sounds like a plan." Jordan said somewhat disappointed at Zander's unwillingness to stay in and see what they could get into.

"Why don't you hop in the shower and I'll make reservations at this lil' outdoor cafe I know..."

"Cool..."

"I won't be long.."

"Take your time... make sure you get rid of that funk of yours..."

"Who you calling funky.."

"Hmmm, let's see I've gone for a run, did my workout and taken a shower, I wonder who it could be?" Zander said doing his best "church lady" impersonation.

Jordan flipped Zander the finger as he grabbed a towel and made his way to the shower. He sniffed under each of his arms to see if he really was smelling. He did!

While Jordan showered Zander went downstairs to the office and checked his email. He deleted the junk mail and printed out mail from his mother and Desmond along with an article on homophobia and hate crimes that he had received from one of his online buddies who belonged to a gay men's support group in Dallas. He checked his voicemail to see if there was any word from Elle; there wasn't. He called the restaurant, made reservations for two and asked that his favorite table be reserved. With that done he made his way back upstairs.

Zander opened the closet and scanned his wardrobe for something to put on as Jordan sneaked up behind him grabbing him from the back. Zander jumped from the shock of the surprise attack.

"See, a brotha can get hurt like that, sneaking up on somebody..."

"Oh, I'll remember that the next time..."

"You bettah, cuz I'd hate to hurt such a cute brotha," Zander said as he assumed a lame Ninja pose.

"Ahhhh, okay..." Jordan said bursting into consuming laughter at Zander's feeble attempt.

"What's so funny, 'news nerd'.."

"Oh, no you didn't...It's on now..." he said grabbing Zander's towel and swatting him with it.

"C'mon give me your best shot..."Zander said pulling Jordan's towel from his waist to defend himself.

"I think that I should warn you I was the undefeated towel swatting champion at Camp Whatchamacallit...."

"Oh really, and how old were you?" Zander said getting a pop in on Jordan's leg.

"Don't even try it.."

"What was the name of that camp..."

"Camp Whatchamacallit!"

"You made that up..."

"Oh you think so..."

"Yep! And you ain't nobody's champion anything, you made that up to..."

"Famous last words...." Jordan said smiling as he delivered the final snap causing Zander's hands to loose his towel.

"Still champion of the towel snapping competition, Jordan 'King Snap' Jacobs."

"I wanna rematch, I was suckered..."

Jordan laughed at Zander's protest and snapped him once more for good measure.

"Its all technique my brotha and you ain't got none."

"Maybe not in snapping, but..." with that said, Zander pulled Jordan closer kissing him with every ounce of passion possible. Jordan surrendered kissing back. He was determined to take his breath away and wouldn't give up without a fight.

"You give..."

"Never!" Jordan said with the last ounce of breath he possessed.

Zander began massaging Jordan's lower back knowing that this was a trigger point for his opponent.

"No fair.." Jordan said protesting the sneaky move, "I want a rematch..."

"It's called technique..." Zander said winking at a defeated Jordan.

"And you have plenty, Mistah President..."

"Thank you sir"

Zander started kissing Jordan's neck, working his way down to his chest and gently kissing his pecs as he began slowly and methodically licking his nipples. Zander noticed that with every stroke of his tongue he could feel the nipple stiffening. Jordan's groans assured him that he was in the right spot. Hearing this caused an eruption of passion that was sure to last for quite sometime. Zander traced the crevices of Jordan's well defined chest with his tongue. Every moan encouraged him to search for a new place to tantalize.

"Stop!"

"Why?"

"I can't take any more?"

"Hmmm."

"Seriously, I can't..."

"Mmmmm...chocolate..."Zander said as he continued his erotic expedition.

Jordan groaned in ecstasy with Zander's next discovery of what was an obvious erogenous zone.

"Please not there!...

"Why not?"

"I can't be held responsible for what happens next,..." Jordan said barely able to speak. "Just remember I warned you!...." he said as he moaned even louder.

"Bring it on newsboy, cuz I'm just beginning," Zander said in a very sensuous tone.

Jordan and Zander made their way out of the closet on to the bedroom floor. Jordan laid on the floor as his boxers were removed by his passionate partner using only his teeth. He could feel his breath teasing his skin. His body trembled with each breath and tingled from every touch. He closed his eyes in anticipation of what was yet to come. He was now lost in a Utopia that made him desire permanent residence. No one had ever made him feel like this, nor did he think anyone else could.

Zander glanced over at Jordan as they drove into the city for lunch. He returned the glance, smiled and placed his hand on Zander's.

"Thank you for coming into my life..."

"I should be the one thanking you?"

"Why?"

"Because I never thought that I would ever have another chance at love..."

"Love, huh..."

"Yep!"

"We'll see..."

"Yes we will!"

Both of them knew that their encounter was like nothing that they had ever experienced before. Zander couldn't believe that he was allowing himself to feel again. He vowed after Gage that he would never allow himself to feel this way, but with Jordan he wanted to experience the joy and excitement of a new relationship. As he thought about the future, Jordan had questions about the past.

"Zander..."

"Yes..."

"Who is Gage?"

Zander had forgotten about Gage's call until Jordan brought his name up.

"He is an old lover and current friend, why?"

"He seemed very protective of you!"

"That's Gage!"

"If I didn't know better, I would think that he's still in love with you..."

Zander didn't say anything; he wondered if now was the right time to get into the delicate nature of his relationship with Gage.

"Zander are you listening?"

"I'm here..."

"Barely. What's wrong? I didn't mean to pry it's just an observation."

"One day I'll tell you the whole story, but for now let's just concentrate on us!"

"Us, huh..."

"Yes, us...you got a prob..."

"Not a one...just checking..." Jordan said as he settled back in his seat taking Zander's free hand.

"Cool..." Zander replied as he settled in for the drive.

Thirty-One

"Thank you for calling, The PRDesign Group, how may I direct your call?"

"Hello Miss Mildred and how are you?"

"Hello Mr. Lowe, it's so nice to hear your voice."

"Yours too..."

"Hold on, I'll get Mr. Eady....

"Thank you..."

"Hold please..."

"Mr. Eady, Mr. Lowe on line one."

"Thank you Mildred..."

"Mr. Lowe!..."

"My aren't we formal today? You busy?"

"Never too busy for my bestest friend in the whole wide world..."

"Yeah right, then why haven't I heard from you in weeks?..."

"And I could say the the same about you..."

"Touche' diva, touche'"

"How is Eli doing?"

"Fine as ever..."

"Spoken like a true man in love..."

"That I am.."

"And what's been going on in Zanderland?"

"Not much. Work, I've been seeing somebody and...."

"Hold up, wait a minute, put a pin in it...what did you say?"

"Not much..."

"No after that..."

"Been working, did I tell you..."

"No after that..."

"Oh that I've been seeing somebody..."

"Thank you Jesus, miracles never cease..."

"Shut up, you ain't even funny!"

Desmond stopped his praise when it hit him that Zander had not called to tell him about this latest occurrence in his life.

"Wait one cotton picking minute! How come I haven't heard about this before now?"

"Well, I've been really busy, Elle has extended her leave of absence from a couple of days to six months..."

"What's going on with diva one?"

"We don't know. She's not returning any of our calls. She leaves voicemail messages in the middle of the night and email."

"Sounds like Miss E has issues..."

"Desmond! That's not nice, after all if it wasn't for her I wouldn't be here today..."

"I know but you got to admit.... wait a minute, we were talking about you and this new beau before we got on Miss E... you thought I forgot, didn't you."

"No D, but there's not much to tell..."

"Oh hell yes there is..."

"Okay what do you want to know?"

"First of all, who is he, where did you meet him, is he good in bed, is he packin?...oops I guess that was a wee bit personal... anyway..."

Zander could do nothing but laugh at his rather inquisitive best friend.

"Okay spill it, give me all the dirt..."

"Well if you must know, his name is Jordan Ja..."

"Jacobs, the media hunk! Okay you're lying...who is he really? Now why you wanna play a brotha.You know I was lusting after him that last time I came to visit..."

"I'm not kidding, we've been seeing each other for about a a couple of weeks and it's wonderful..."

"A couple of weeks, where have I been?"

"Well you've been rather busy yourself!"

"Yep, we just celebrated our two month anniversary and I don't mind telling you that Eli rocked you mama's world on more than one occasion."

"Sounds personal..."

"So are you happy Z?"

"I am on top of the world.."

"If there's a cure for this...."

"We don't want it! Sho you right!"

"Let me give you a fiber optic high five on that one" Desmond said as he pushed the number 5 on the key pad!"

"That was my ear. Desi..."

"I'm sorry baby, but I couldn't resist!"

"Yield not to temptation next time okay!"

"Look at him, he's gettin some now and he's all that!"

"You ain't know?"

"Least' you're honest.."

"You know what they say about the truth!"

"It'll set you free..."

"How's Mom's doing?"

"She's fine..."

"She still seeing Daddy Warbucks?"

"Miss Thang is never home. I call and all I get is voicemail and her emails consist of hi and bye."

"You girl Miss Rita ghurl!"

"My mother the teenager, I don't know what I'm going to do with her..."

"Love her and let her enjoy her life!"

"Oh, I agree... Every since my mother met Oscar Lee Thomas, she's been on cloud nine..."

"Ain't that nothing we all got boyfriends..."

"Hey when you guys coming to see us?"

"Us," Desmond said faking a sniff. "My bristah is involved, will miracles never cease..."

"Hold on, mistah "I don't want a relationship,' what do you call the fact that you and Eli have been together for 2 months? That in itself is a major miracle, mistah f'em and forget them."

"No, you didn't!..."

"Yes, I did and there ain't nothing you can do about it..."

"Paging Doctor Click, paging Doc..."

"Desmond Arnez Lowe, if you hang up on me..."

"No you didn't use my middle name... see you can't tell niggahs nuttin..."

"N-knee-way! When are you coming to see us?... I want to plan it around the time that we open the new offices if not sooner, It's been ages since I seen your lite brite ass..."

"Oh no you didn't!"

"And you know this my bristah."

"I'll let the lite brite comment pass, but one more wise crack and Doctor Click will be making a house call..."

"Whatever, so when?..."

"How about in two weeks?"

"Let me check, hmmm that might work... no wait that's the weekend Zandrea is being christened..."

"And...."

"And nothing..."

"I know you're not thinking about going thing..."

"And what if I am?"

"Then you are one mo silly qu..."

"Watch yourself..."

"I stand corrected, you couldn't be a queen..."

"You bettah recognize..."

"Of course you couldn't..."

"That's bettah..."

"Don't be silly. Your mother is very much alive, so that would make you a princess..."

"No you didn't go there....."

"Yes I did. Wrote a song about it, wanna hear it..."

"You get a lil' peter in your life and you're out of control..."

"Whatever Diva..."

"No that's a title I'll leave to the professionals..."

"That's right and don't you forget it... speaking of which, forgetting that is... I haven't forgotten that the Gman sent you an invitation to your step daughter's christening..."

"Let me make this one thing perfectly clear, I have no children, steps or other wise, and as far as the christening, its a mute point. I'm not going... end of story!"

"If you say so! What if Gage himself asked you to come, I bet you would be on the first plane out of here..."

"Gage called the other day. I was in the shower and Jordan answered the phone..."

"And...?!"

"And nothing!... They spoke, Jordan took the message and that was the end of that!"

"Yeah right, I bet you Gage was fit to be tied."

"I wouldn't know, I didn't call him back yet!"

"Afraid of what might happen if you did..."

"Not in the least, I've just been so busy and besides I have everything and more in Jordan."

"Okay if you say so..."

"And I do, but you're still incorrect..."

"Whatever chile... whatever... but if you want my opinion..."

"And I don't..."

"Since when did that stop me?! I really think that you should go..."

"I couldn't have heard you correctly. This must be a real bad connection, because it sounded like you said that you think..."

"That you should go.. I don't stutter..."

"Why and for what?"

"Number one, the chile has your name. Two, it must have been awfully important to him for you to be there and thirdly...."

"Okay you've made your point! But I'm still not going..."

"That's what your mouth says, but your heart and certain other parts are saying, go, go, go!"

"Are they still giving two bags of sugar for the crazed?"

"Whatever, somebody is gonna be on a plane to Seattle...."

"Why would I want to go?"

"Because Zandrea is your goddaughter, Gage is her father and you will never ever get that man completely out of your system. He was your first love!"

"Was being the operative word... we settled all of that when he was here, we will always be friends and granted he will hold a special place in my heart, but I've moved on and so has he! I am happier than I ever was. Jordan's sexual orientation is a non-issue with him, thus his baggage is not even a carry on!"

"Okay....don't get your boxers in a bunch!"

"I'm not wearing any!!!"

"Thats's too much information..."

"Well you started it!"

"And I'm gonna finish it, I gotta run sweetness!"

"Sweetness? Yuk!"

"Z, I'm happy for you... but, I still say that Gage..."

"Bye! Love you Desi..."

"Okay, so it's gonna be like that..."

"Like what... bye..."

"See you Bristah..."

"Bye." With that Zander hung up the phone and went back to the review of the project he was working on, chuckling at Desmond and his warped sense of reality. Gage was the past and his future was looking brighter everyday with Jordan. He took a deep breath and smiled. Life as he knew it had never been better; he was breathing again.

Thirty-Two

"In our last session, Hakiem, we talked about your being outed by your guidance counselor..."

"Yeah, ain't that some shi..."

"Yeah major..."

"I don't really blame her. She thought that my moms knew I guess..."

"How so?"

"Well, I guess she thought that if she knew moms knew too...it never really came up..."

"I'm having a hard time with understanding that..."

"I was out at school. I was in the chorus and drama and I had a boyfriend.. it wasn't no secret.."

"It wasn't a secret," Miles corrected with Hakiem correcting himself.

"But how did it come up? A counselor doesn't call your home and in the course of conversation say 'oh by the way your son is gay, you must be so proud!'"

Hakiem couldn't help but laugh. "Man..."

"What happened when your mom found out?"

"Man, she ain't..."

"She didn't..." Miles corrected.

"She didn't," Hakiem said correcting himself, "...say anything for the longest time..."

"So how did you find out that she knew?..."

"Well, one weekend I asked her if I could stay at a friends house and she just blurted out,...'you going to stay with your boyfriend?'"

"And what did you say?"

"I was like; 'why you trippin?' and she went off.."

"And then what happened.."

"I just told you, she went off..."

"And..."

"She started calling me faggot and queer. She told me that she wished that she had aborted me..."

"And she said this? I mean, how did you feel, what did you say?" Miles asked trying to maintain a professional tone concealing his anger and hurt for his patient.

"I was blowed, man this was my moms telling me that she wished I hadn't even been born and then calling me names that even the kids at school didn't call me. I wanted to die right then." The later part of the statement really caught Miles off guard.

"Do you still feel that way, I mean about wanting to die?"

"Yes and no... I mean now that I got this shi...AIDS, what difference does it make? I'm gonna die anyway!"

"You really don't believe that do you?"

"Sometimes, I mean I miss my family and I even miss my step dad! At least we were a family! As screwed up we were, I had a place I could call home. I mean, don't get me wrong! I like where I'm living, The Kendricks are cool people but it ain't, I mean it isn't home."

"So do I hear you saying that you would go home if that were possible?..."

"In a heartbeat!"

"Why?"

"Haven't you been listening! I want to be a real family again!"

"Yes I was listening, but living in the same house doesn't mean that you're a family! Think about this, could you be really happy there? What's to say that you won't be thrown out again?"

"That's a chance I'm willing to take!"

"It means that much to you?"

"And you know this..."

Miles laughed. Hakiem had spent so much time around Zander, he was speaking Zanderese.

"As Zander would say, you really look up to Zander don't you?"

"Yep, the Z'man is my mentor!"

"Speaking of, have you talked with him lately?"

"Yeah we still get together for lunch and hangout every now and then! But he's busy with that guy Jordan these days so its not like it used to be..."

"But you know that he still cares and you are a priority, right?"

"I know, don't get me wrong, I'm happy for him and everything. I guess I'm a lil' bit jealous even though Jordan has been cool. I got to go to the TV station and I even taped a segment..."

"I'd like to see that tape sometime. Maybe you have a future in TV."

"Thats what Z and Jordan was saying... I mean were saying," Hakiem said trying to avoid Miles correcting his grammar again.

Miles smiled at the self correction and asked, "Have you given any thought to what you want to do when you graduate from school?..."

"Live..."

"And you can do that, if you stay on you meds and keep a healthy attitude."

"I hate taking that medicine, it gives me the runs and I keep forgetting to take it..."

"You have to take the medicine to stay well!"

"I know, you sound like Zander and Jordan..."

"Well they're right!"

"Whatever..."

"What is that about..."

"What?"

"The sudden change in attitude..."

"I just want to be a kid, hang out and have fun..."

"And you can have that... but you have to be healthy both physically and mentally!"

"If you say so..."

"And I do, but until you believe it...it can't happen!"

"I do..."

"Who are you trying to convince, me or you?"

"Man!..."

"Yep, that's what I am and so are you! You're a kid with adult problems, but you can still have a quality of life if you want it. However, the only person that can make it happen is you...Hakiem..."

"Yeah, how, you tell me how... my own mother doesn't want me around. She wishes that I was dead and now she may just get her wish..."

"Hakiem, pity parties are deadly and you sound like you're getting ready to throw one helluva bash and I don't want an invitation."

"You trippin..."

"No you're the one that's trippin! It's time to stop the pity party and live son! It's time to LIVE!"

"I'm trying, but what am I suppose to do?"

"Lets start with the thing that brings you the most pain, your family... now if you want them back, maybe you're going to have to make the first move..."

"How do I do that?"

"Do you think that your mother would meet you for lunch or come here for a counseling session?" "Would you ask her? I haven't talked with her in two and a half years..."

"I think that it would be better if the invitation came from you..."

"But she won't talk to me...."

"True, but why don't you call her from here and if you get stuck I got your back..."

"Okay you wanna me to call her now?"

"Is she home?"

"I think so... you wanna make the call now?"

"I want you to make the call and if you get in trouble, I'll pick up the slack. Cool?"

"Yeah, okay..."

Miles handed Hakiem the phone and nervously dialed the number. With every ring, his heart beat a little faster. Finally someone answered.

"Hello,.." a little voice on the other end said.

"Pookie, it's me Hakiem."

"Hey Hakiem, where you?"

"I'm here in town, how have you been?"

"Fi...Fine."

"Is Mama around?"

"Yes, you wanna... you wanna talk to her?"

"Yes please, and Pooh..."

"Yeah..."

"You be a good boy, okay..."

"Okay...I love you Hakiem!"

"I love you, too! Pooh..."

"Maaaaa, Hakiem's on the phone..."

There was a silence and then the little voice came back on.

"She says to tell you she's not home."

"Okay, tell her I called, okay..."

"Okay, bye...Ha, Hakiem you still there..."

"Yes, Pooh.. I'm here..."

"Question?"

"What?"

"You still funny?'"

"Huh?"

"Mommy told Grandma Jenny that you was funny and that's why you don't live wit us no more..."

"Oh, well I'm still funny...so I guess I won't be able to come see you anytime soon, okay...but know that I got much love for you..."

"Come see us sometime and take us to the Mc Donald's, okay?"

"Okay, I'm promise"

"And, Hakiem..."

"Yeah, Pooh!

"I don't care how funny you is, I like to laugh!..."

Hakiem had to laugh at the naivete of his young sibling. "Me too Pooh...bye"

"Bye, I looooove youuuu!" the child said as he hung up.

A tear coasted down Hakiem's cheek as he held onto the phone. Moments passed as he just sat staring into space, and then he spoke. "See what did I tell you, I'd be better off dead."

"Hakiem, you knew when you called that there might be a possibility that you mother wouldn't talk to you, but it doesn't mean that she won't talk to you..."

"You don't know my mom..."

"True, but I'm not giving up hope and neither should you."

"If you say so..."

"And you know this..." Miles said winking at Hakiem.

Thirty-Three

Zander laid stretched across the king-size bed letting the breeze from the ceiling fan cool his body as he listened to Trina Broussard belt out "Inside My Love" from the "Love Jones" soundtrack. He took the remote and adjusted the volume to enhance his mood. He bobbed his head to the beat mouthing the words. Before he knew it he was lost in the words and caught up in the song's seductive groove. His mind drifted to the last night he and Jordan spent together and he felt his entire body surge with heat as he reminisced. He could feel his manhood stiffening as he drifted further back into the newfound abyss he visited when he was with Jordan. He sighed at the thought of having to spend the night alone. He clutched the pillow next to him wishing that it was Jordan. The cool fabric only frustrated him more, he longed for the warmth of Jordan's body. As he clutched the pillow the faint aroma of Cartier teased his nostrils. He grabbed the pillow and tossed it across the room, it was of no comfort. After doing so he rolled over grasping the wine glass that rested on the night stand. As he took a sip he drifted back to recent memories of moments that he and Jordan had shared. By this time Cassandra Wilson had taken over the mike and was crooning "You Move Me," This wasn't helping...this was one of the first song's that they made love too. It only frustrated him more.

He took another sip; letting it slowly trickle down his throat, another sip and this time holding it in his mouth letting in warm before he swallowed. He ran his glass across his forehead, letting the water settle. The cool only provided temporary comfort. He sighed again, he was lonely. Just as he prepared to take another sip, the phone rang. Zander sat straight up in the bed. It was Jordan.

"Hey babe, wassup?"

"Nothing just chillin..."

"Do I hear "Sentimental Mood' playing in the background?"

"Yeah..."

"You must be lonely, I wish that I didn't have to work tonight..."

"I'm okay and you know that I understand," Zander said trying not to sound too disappointed.

"It's just that since the show is being expanded to an hour and renamed after me, I feel obligated to be here and help out until the new executive producer gets here. Thank God, I'm not anchoring too or I would never leave this place."

"Okay Oprah, Jr."

"And you know this..."

"We've been hanging around each other too much, you're stealing my lines now..."

They both laughed, knowing that they wouldn't trade a moment of the last six weeks that they had spent together.

"Hey who knows! You may be national before you know it..."

"Only if we can do the show from here..."

"You would pass up your big break for lil' ole me?"

"In a heartbeat! Being with the man I love means more than fame or fortune any day!"

"Remember you said that...."

"Like you would let me forget it..."

"And you know this!"

They both laughed.

"Well they're calling me..."

"Go, I'll be fine. Call me when you get home..."

"I'll do you one better, I'll wake you up when I get home..."

"Sounds like a plan..."

"Love you..."

"Wha..."

"You heard me, I love you!"

"Just wanted to make sure I wasn't hearing things..."

"Clean your ears, I'll see you soon..."

"Jordan..."

"Yes?"

"I love you too!"

"You better, I gotta go...bye!"

"Bye," he said as he hung up the phone. "He loves me!" Zander said repeatedly, With that Zander sprung out of the bed and began to dance around the room. As he settled down, he said it again,"He loves me," just one more time for good measure.

He thought about calling Desmond but he was fairly certain that Desmond and Eli were other wise engaged.

"The bastards" he thought to himself.

He could hear Desmond's response to his last comment, "Jealousy is such an ugly color on you."

Zander laughed and took another sip of the wine. He was in love.

Zander had almost drifted off to sleep when the phone rang startling him. He thought that it was Jordan.

"Hey handsome, wassup?"

"Well what a reception, so I still got it like that huh?"

"Gage?"

"Yeah who did you think that it was?"

"Not you..."

"My what a difference a day makes..."

"Hello Gage, wassup?"

"Why you acting like that with me, you trying to hurt a brotha's feeling?"

"I'm sorry, I just didn't expect your call..."

"Who were you expecting, the guy who answered your phone..."

"To be quite honest, Yes..."

"I bet you he didn't even tell you that I called..."

"Yes he did and you owe him an apology.."

"For what?

"You were rude..."

"Is that what he said?"

"No that's what I know. And another thang don't ever call here asking who is on the other end of the phone, the very nerve..."

"What's your problem?"

"I don't have a problem..."

"In case you've forgotten, you don't run anything here Gage. Why are you calling anyway.."

"I see I caught you in a bad mood..."

"I'm not in a bad mood..."

"You could have fooled me!"

"Whatever..."

"Look, maybe I should hang up and call again..."

"No, that's okay. Just remember what I said okay..."

"Cool, I apologize, if it helps, to both you and your friend..."

"Apology accepted, so what's up..."

"As you know we're getting ready for your goddaughter's christening..."

"Yes, I got the invitation..."

"So are you coming?"

"I don't think I'm going to be able to..."

"Zander, you're her godfather you have to be here..."

"Gage..."

"Zander, you're a crucial part of the service..."

"Gage, I agreed to be Zandrea's godfather and I will be the best one I know how to be, but I really don't think that it's a good idea to be there..."

"Look if it's a bad time for your schedule, we'll change it. But we both want you here..."

"Suzzette is looking forward to meeting you and you know that I want to see you!"

"Gage, things have changed since you were here..."

"You mean "the voice?"

Zander had to laugh at Gage's reference to Jordan."Yes, the voice...his name is Jordan and he's the new man in my life..."

"Oh, moving a little fast aren't you?"

"Gage, worry about your home, I can handle this one just fine...."

"I guess I had that coming...."

"And there's more where that came from if you don't watch yourself."

"I stand corrected... So are you coming?"

"No, I told you that I didn't think that it was a good idea..."

"Please Zander, I need you here."

"Gage, if I come, I'm bringing Jordan with me... you do understand that..."

"Okay, what, you don't trust yourself with me?..."

"You wish. No I don't trust you!"

"Moi?"

"You, your ego will get in the way and you'll be trying to prove that you're still the man..."

"You know me too well... I will always love you... you know that..."

"One more word and I won't be there..."

"So you're coming?"

"I'll talk with Jordan and we'll see if it fits into his schedule..."

"Do that, I look forward to seeing you." Gage said and then added "Jordie too."

"His name is Jordan and I'll give you a call....take care and give my regards to Suzzette and Zandrea also..."

"I'll give you a call within the next week..."

"Okay, take care and tell Jordi... I mean Jordan that I said hello."

"I will, take care."

Zander hung up the phone, hoping that Jordan wouldn't want him to go. He had already commissioned the paintings and the christening gown so he didn't really see the need to be there.

Thirty-Four

Jordan stood in the doorway watching Zander sleep, he looked so peaceful. On several occasions he found himself watching his partner sleep; he loved just watching him breath. He tried to quietly prepare for bed as Zander stirred.

"Hey babe, what time is it?"

"Almost two... sorry if I woke you?"

"No problem, I needed to talk to you anyway..."

"Okay...what's on your mind?"

"Remember when we first started dating and my friend Gage called?..."

"You mean Mr. Personality?"

"One and the same. By the way he apologized for being so rude..."

"Did he now? And I suppose you didn't have anything to do with that now, did you?"

"You're damn straight. I chewed him a new one; nobody talks to my baby like that..."

"While I'm honored that you felt it necessary to call him on the carpet, but it wasn't necessary...he is a non-issue with me."

"Cool.."

"Why are we talking about him anyway? I thought he was a closed chapter as far as we're concerned."

"Well he called tonight..."

"I gathered that..."

"Well you know that I'm his daughter's godfather..."

"Yes and..."

"Well the christening is two weeks away..."

"And now you're having second thoughts about going and you want to know if I think you should go..."

"Yeah that and I want to know if you would please go with me?"

"Baby, I would love to go with you..."

"But..."

"The new show premieres the Monday after the christening and we're got rehearsals, promos, voice overs, you know the routine and..."

"and you can't go. Well that settles it, we won't go..."

"Wait, nothing is settled. I can't go but that doesn't mean you shouldn't go..."

"So you think I should go..."

"I didn't say that!"

"So you don't think..."

"I can't make that call..."

"Help me..."

"Your goddaughter deserves to meet her goddfather and with Gage as her father, she's gonna need you sooner or later..."

"Be nice..."

"Look, from what you've told me Gage is on self destruct... hey see if we can have him on the show, "HONEY! I'VE GOT A SECRET."

Zander and Jordan laughed at the thought of Gage appearing on a show like that.

"C'mon be serious..."

"Okay... okay," Jordan said as he tried to stop laughing.

"What should I do?"

"What does your heart say?"

"It says go."

"End of discussion. I'll call my travel agent in the morning." he said smiling at Zander.

Thirty-Five

Donnie McClurkin's, "Just a Little Talk with Jesus" could be heard blaring from the boom box in Rita's kitchen as she prepared Sunday morning breakfast. She sang along patting her foot to the beat as she praised God. She thought that good gospel and good food were the the only ways to get ready for Sunday service. She always said, "the soul and your stomach are two things that you need to feed everyday."

The aroma of fresh baked biscuits welcomed Oscar Lee as he rang the bell.

"Good morning Mr. Thomas, I hope you're hungry!"

"Good morning Rita Mae, I sure am. I was hoping that you had made breakfast."

"Sunday morning wouldn't be the same if I didn't."

"I brought some fresh squeezed juice from the store; I know it's your favorite.."

"Why Oscar Lee Thomas, you sure know how to make a girl feel special..."

"That's cause you are special..."

Rita blushed as she looked at her suitor. They had been seeing each other for almost two months now and she welcomed his company. He was a honorable and decent man. Oscar Lee was about 5'11" with a slim build. He had caramel colored skin and the prettiest white hair she had ever seen. He was a retired school teacher and had been widowed for about seven years. He was a cross between the man who played Bill Cosby's father on his old "Cosby" show and Ed Bradley, without the earring. Since he had started courting Rita, Oscar had rejoined the church, not to mention the Male Chorus and was serving on Usher Board No.1. He was even reading his Bible again. Rita informed him that any man in her life had to have God in his life, if not they had nothing to talk about. He was the first to tell you that having Rita in his life was truly a gift from God.

"Something sho smells good in here?"

"You probably smelling my homemade biscuits..."

"No, that's not it?"

"Then maybe its the sweet potato pie that I'm baking?"

"Nope..."

"Then I don't know what it could be..."

"I do. It's you... Rita Mae..."

"Oscar Lee Thomas, you better behave yourself," Rita said blushing.

"It's true, I love that perfume you wear."

"You like it?"

"Yes ma'am I do!"

"Well now that you mention it, you're smelling awful nice yourself."

"This is my new Sunday-go-to-meeting cologne... I had hoped you would like it. I bought it with you in mind."

"Well I do, it smells clean and crisp, like those white shirts you wear..."

"Thank you! I'm glad you approve. I even bought the soap to match."

"Fancy that... you are sir debonair himself."

"I have to make my girl proud!"

"Well sit yourself down and we'll have our breakfast before we go to Sunday school."

"Don't want to be late for my favorite Sunday School teacher's class," Oscar Lee said winking at Rita. She blushed again.

"Stop it! Get serious and say the blessing."

They bowed their heads and he said the blessing:

"Lord we thank you for this bounty and for your blessings. Thank you for the sweet hands that prepared this meal..." he said squeezing Rita's hand, "bless them and keep them ever in your care. Amen."

"Amen,"Rita said opening her eyes as she smiled. "Let's eat, don't be shame, I made plenty."

"Never been ashamed to enjoy a good meal..."

They sat talking about the Sunday School lesson and current events over breakfast. Rita enjoyed Oscar's company. Not since Eady had she felt like cooking and pampering a man. Oscar was a kind man. He appreciated her company as much as she did his, it was a true mutual admiration society. "That was a mighty fine breakfast Ms. Eady..."

"Thank you Mr. Thomas,.."

"I'll just put these dishes in the sink and go get ready for church."

"I'll do these dishes, go on an get ready..."

"Oscar, we have plenty of time, I'll just take care of these and get ready."

"Missy, please let me do this. You cooked and you shouldn't have to do dishes too.."

"Well thank you sir..."

"My pleasure..."

Rita untied her apron and retired it to the hook where it always rested. Oscar hummed along to the music that was playing in the background as he washed the dishes. He quickly straighten up the kitchen and put his dish towel on the drain. He checked on the pie as Rita had instructed, it was fine and the aroma was divine. He loved anything Rita fixed because it was always prepared with plenty of love.

Rita hurried to get dress, she didn't want to keep Oscar waiting. She looked in the mirror fidgeting with her hair and then putting on translucent powder. She didn't wear much makeup; lipstick was a staple and she always put on powder to keep down the shine. She rummaged through her jewelry box looking for her pearl earrings and necklace. She picked up the diamond and pearl pendant necklace that Zander had given her three Christmas' ago; Oscar woud have to help her with that because she could never get the clasp. She took one final look and thought that the new pale yellow suit that Oscar had helped her pick out was a good choice. She sprayed on a bit more cologne just for him.

"Well now, don't you look pretty..."

"Thank you sir, I had a great fashion consultant..."

"I'll send you my bill..."

"Put it on my account..."

"Could you please help me with this necklace?..."

"With pleasure..."

"Thank you kind sir..."

"You're more than welcome beautiful lady..."

"You are such a flatterer..."

"The truth shall set you free..."

"Fly my brother, fly..."

"You look radiant, but something's missing..."

"What?"

"This..." he said as he pulled out a little black velvet box."

"What on earth?" she asked gazing at the box.

"Open it!"

Rita slowly opened the box; her hands were actually trembling. "Oh, it's beautiful..."

"You really like it?"

"Yes."

"I was really worried!"

"I love it!" Rita said as she removed the ring from the box.

"Ms. Rita Eady, will you make me the happiest man in the world and be my wife..."

"Oscar, are you sure about this?"

"I wouldn't be asking if I wasn't sure..."

"If you're sure..."

"Never been more sure of anything..."

"Then the only thing I can do is..."

"Yes?"

"Pray on it!"

"Okay. That wasn't the answer I was hoping for, but I can respect that..."

"Thank you Oscar, maybe you better take this back until I give you an answer..."

"No, I want you to keep it...look at it from time to time and maybe it will help you make up your mind..."

"We'll see, we'll see..."

Thirty-Six

As the plane landed the pilot welcomed the passengers to Seattle and gave them the weather forecast, overcast as usual. Zander took a deep breath and prepared to make his way off the plane. He stood and stretched opening the overhead compartment and removed his garment bag. He was glad that this flight was over. He had been the only passenger in first class so the attendant was constantly asking if he could be of service. Every time he looked up, there was Chandler. As he closed the compartment the flight attendant approached him and thanked him for flying with their airline. Zander knew that he was flirting and tried to be cordial, but he wasn't in the mood since he had gotten on his nerves the whole flight through.

He made his way down the concourse and on to baggage claim. He needed to pick up the portraits from shipping and then he would see if Gage had learned how to tell time. He made his way to shipping and reclaimed the portraits of the Gregory family and his new goddaughter. He couldn't wait to see the look on their faces when they unwrapped their presents. He had been able to get the portraits done from pictures that Gage had sent him previously. Sinjaro had done a beautiful job as usual.

"Zander..."

"Hello Gage and how are you?" he said hugging Gage.

"Fine as ever or can't you tell?" he whispered as he returned the hug.

"Same old Gage!"

"Where is Jordi..Jordan?"

"He couldn't make it; he sends his regrets and best wishes..."

"Tell him thanks, so he trusts you with me..."

"Yep! He knows where my heart is..."

"It ain't your heart that I'm after..."

"Well don't waste your time..."

"You've never been a waste of time..."

"Thanks," Zander said smiling a half hearted smile.

"So what's in the wrapper..."

"You'll see when we get to the house..."

"I hope it fits, I drove the Volvo..."

"Let's hope..."

Zander and Gage made their way to the car and Gage popped the rear entrance to see if they could slide the portraits in. It was tight, but they did fit.

"It was tight but it fit..."

"Whew, I'm glad. I didn't know what I would have done if they hadn't."

"You know me I know how to work even the tightest of holes...."

"N-knee-way!"

"In all seriousness, I'm glad you're here and I know that Suzzette and Zandrea are going to fall in love with you almost as quickly as I did..."

"We'll see..."

"You'll have nothing to worry about!"

"Oh, I'm not worried..." He was lying; there was a lot to worry about.

"So how long have you guys been together?"

"Two months, four days and..."

"Okay I get the picture.."

"So how are Zandrea and Suzzette?"

"They're fine...Suzzette is running around like a chicken with her head cut off. You noticed that she sent out the invitations two months in advance. She said she wanted to make sure that everyone had plenty of time to prepare and plan to be here."

"You won't read her for being inefficient..."

"Nope, she is efficient...."

"So whats on the agenda, for Zandrea's extravaganza?"

"Well there's a dinner tonight, a barbecue tomorrow and of course the christening and a reception immediately following..."

"Suzzette is quite the social planner isn't she?"

"That's my Zette..."

"So how are you really doing?"

"Better than I was when I came to visit you..."

"I'm glad to hear it, so you're going to try to lead a straight life..."

"Yep! I made my bed so now I have to lie in it.."

"Well you know I'm praying for you and we support you 100% no matter what the outcome..."

"Thank you so very much..."

"So is your family in for the christening?"

"Yes, mother arrived yesterday and I'm ready for her to get on her broom and go home..."

"Some things never change..."

Zander checked into the hotel and called Jordan at the station, his new home.

"The Jordan Jacobs Show..."

"Yes may I speak with Mr. Jacobs please?"

"May I say who is calling?"

"Zander Eady..."

"Hold please..."

"Hey handsome, how was your flight?"

"Interesting to say the least..."

Zander told Jordan all about his trip, Chandler the overzealous flight attendant and his ride in with Gage.

"How is Mr. Personality?..."

"He's fine..."

"Did you see the second Mrs. Gregory..."

"Funny, very funny! And for the record she's the first. I was never anybody's Miss or Mrs..."

"I stand corrected.."

"And don't let it happen again."

"Yes sir!"

"So how are things coming? You ready for premiere week?"

"As ready as I can be!"

"I should be back on Sunday night. I left my car at the airport so you won't have to worry about coming to get me, I don't want to add to your stress...."

"Babe, it's no trouble, I would have gladly picked you up..."

"Don't worry about it..."

"What time do you get in?"

"7:42PM..."

"Oh, okay..."

"Well a car will be here to pick me up for the dinner in an hour or so I'm going to take a shower and try and get some rest..."

"You do that, and Zander..."

"Yeah baby?"

"I miss you..."

"I've only been gone for three hours..."

"I know, but that doesn't stop me from missing you..."

"Truth?"

"and nothing but..."

"I miss you too..."

"Love you..."

"Love you more..."

"Bye..."

Thirty-Seven

Zander was waiting in the lobby for the driver when he arrived. He was carrying a sign that read "Zander Eady." He alerted the driver to his presence and the driver greeted him, took the packages that he had with him and escorted him to the car. Zander thanked the driver as he held the door. He got in and settled in the back of the limo and prepared to meet the woman that Gage married.

When he arrived at the Gregory estate, he swelled with pride. Gage had done well for himself. There were cars everywhere. The driver removed the packages and carried them to the door. A butler, greeted them and relieved the driver of the packages, ushered Zander into the living room. Gage caught a glimpse of Zander and excused himself to go and greet his friend.

"Hello, and welcome to our home..."

"Thank you, bro, you are living large...I'm so proud of you!"

"Thanks! I worked hard to get here thinking that it would make me happy and while I'm grateful, its just a big house with a lot of bills that come along with it..." As they talked, Zander noticed an absolutely gorgeous woman making her way over. Suzzette Katherine was tall and slender, very fair skinned and gorgeous; She could have been a model, her eyes were wide and very telling, Zander recognized her from the picture he had of them.

"Gage darling, who is this handsome man you're talking with, I don't believe we've met..."

"Suzzette this is Zander..."

"Oh, my Zandrea's goddaddy, its so wonderful to meet you..."

"Same here..." he said as he hugged Suzzette.

"I am so glad that you could make it; we would have all been crushed if you hadn't..."

"I couldn't miss this, I know that you guys are busy, but could I have a few minutes of your time..."

"Sure..." Gage and Suzzette said almost in unison.

Zander made his way to the foyer were he had instructed the butler to leave the packages.

"I wanted to do something special for you all to commemerate this occasion, so I commissioned my client and friend Sinjaro to paint these," Zander said as he unveiled the family portrait.

"Oh my God, it's absolutely gorgeous...Zander you shouldn't have" Suzzette squealed.

"Zander this is gorgeous!" Gage said stunned at the portrait. He admired Sinjaro's work a great deal.

"I also had him do a portrait of Zandrea for the nursery or where ever you guys want to put it..."

"It's just like the picture on the invitation..." Suzzette began to cry as she hugged Zander.

"No wonder Gage loves you..." Suzzette continued, "and so do I..."

"Zette is right Z... you the man!"

"And I took the liberty of having one of my other clients create a christening gown for my goddaughter..."

Zander pulled the silk and organza gown from it's protective covering.

"Oh my, won't our angel look absolutely beautiful in this...Zander you are too much..."

"Nothing is too good for my goddaughter and her family..."

"Thank you!" Gage and Suzzette said trying not to cry.

You're very welcome. Okay, now get back to the party before the rest of your guests start feeling neglected."

As the evening progressed Zander met the infamous Drucilla and Suzzette's mother, Marlena. He could see where Suzzette got her looks; they looked more like sisters. And he too wanted to hand Dru her broom as the evening progressed.

"You must be mighty special to my son..." Drucilla said with an evil tone in her voice.

"Good evening to you too, Mrs. Gregory," Zander said trying to maintain his cool.

"Let's dispense with formalities..."

"Okay.... so what are you asking, Mrs. Gregory?"

"I think you know what I mean, Mr. Eady! Please don't play me for a fool..."

"With all due respect, Mrs. Gregory, I stopped playing games along time ago, Please get to the point."

"Well, I never..."

"Whatever you say. Look, I didn't ask Gage and Suzzette to name the baby after me so if you have issues...and I'm sure you do, I suggest you talk to the parents and leave me the....leave me alone." he said in a whispering and polite tone as he tried to move away from Drucilla

"Don't you dare walk away from me, I'm not through with you Zander..." Drucilla said grabbing Zander's arm.

"Mrs. Gregory, I suggest that if you want to keep your hand that you remove it from my arm right now or I will be taking it with me. And I don't think that you want to ruin that beautiful hostess gown, now do you?" Zander said through clinched teeth.

Drucilla released Zander's arm and walked away but not before Gage had witnessed their confrontation..

"Mother, what did you say to Zander?"

"I simply asked why he was so special to you?"

"He was my best friend when I lived in Orlando and he helped me through a rough time."

"Then why wasn't he in the wedding?"

"He couldn't make it..."

"Some friend..."

"Mother drop it..."

"My, my...you both are awfully protective of each other, aren't you?"

"One more time, drop it or you'll be leaving on the next plane..."

"What are you trying to hide?"

"Mother, I'm warning you...I will have Thorton bring your broom if you don't stop your interrogation right this instant..."

"You may find this hard to believe, but I only have the best interest of my granddaughter at heart. And for the record, I didn't come by broom..."

"Mother do not make trouble and do not ruin this happy time for my family or my friends..."

"I wouldn't dream of doing that, why do you think the worst of me son, why?"

"I only go by what I know mother, now if you'll excuse me..." Gage said as he walked away.

"Gage...son," Drucilla said as she tried to grab her son to apologize for her behavior, But Gage was gone and she could tell he wasn't pleased. Maybe she had gone too far, she told herself.

"Are you having a good time Zander?" Suzzette asked.

"Yes, I am..." he said lying through his teeth and smiling. He kept telling himself that this was a mistake.

"Well, well Suzzette you already have a gorgeous husband so why are you trying to keep all of the hunks to yourself?"

"Oh you are so silly..." Suzzette said giggling at her friend. Zander blushed at the obvious flirting of Suzzette's friend.

"Zander Eady, IV meet Austin Fitzgerald Shaw, Esquire...Austin, Zander!"

Austin Fitzgerald Shaw was about 5'9", had a short cropped cut that was crowned by just a touch of gray. You could tell that she worked out and was very proud of her body, evidenced by the dress that she was wearing. It was cut low in the back and the front. Zander thought to himself, "even Toni Braxton would have to think twice about that one." She had pretty white teeth and a charming smile. She was very attractive and you could tell that she thought so, too by the way she moved and talked.

"Charmed," the bronze beauty said taking his hand with a firm grip, something that shocked Zander as they shook hands.

"Same here..."

"Austin is Zandrea's godmother..."

"Wait a minute, Zander...Zandrea! Oh you're Gage's friend. You're my angel's goddaddy!"

"Yes, that's me...speaking of which, where is Zandrea?... I'm dying to see her," Zander said hoping that this would be his excuse to be released from the snare of an obvious woman on the prowl.

"She's asleep, but I'm sure she'll be making an appearance before the night is out, after all this is her party," Suzzette said, "Well Zander you're in capable hands so I'll let you two get acquainted." she said as she made her exit winking at her friend and soror.

"So... Zander, are you staying here at the house?"

"No, I'm staying at the Four Seasons..."

"Oh, isn't that a coincidence, thats where I'm staying, I do like a man with taste..."

"That's...great..." Zander said as he made a mental note to change hotels if at all possible.

"So maybe we can meet for a lil' night cap later.."

"We'll see... "

"What are you afraid of? I don't bite."

"It's what you will do that I'm worried about..." Zander said under his breath.

"Huh, what was that?"

"Just thinking out loud..."

"Hmmm, I bet I know what you're thinking..."

"You think so, do you? Can you excuse me for a moment?" Zander said escaping the clutches of the amorous female.

"I'll be right here."

"Thanks for the warning..." Zander said as he escaped to the foyer followed by Gage.

"So I see you met Austin... "Gage said to Zander.

"Yeah I did and I think she was hitting on me..."

"You think?!?" Gage said laughing at the flustered look on Zander's face.

"I'm glad that you think that its funny, mind you, she is staying at the same hotel that I am..."

"Why are you surprised, all of the out of town guest are staying there...Suzzette arranged it that way..."

"Oh, did she? Well I'll be checking out and staying at an undisclosed location. I do not want to have to fend off the unwanted advances of the amorous attorney."

"Hey, I thought you liked seafood?" Gage said laughing.

Zander failed to see the humor. "to eat yes, to have sex with...no!"

"I'm sure Austin would love for you to..."

"Don't even go there..."

"Come on lighten up..."

"You're into fish, you do her..."

"Now you know I can't, I'se married now.." Gage said imitating Oprah in *The Color Purple.*

"Ha, ha,...ha very funny!"

"Austin is harmless..."

"Yeah right, and RuPaul is really a cute man!"

"Oooo, that was cold..."

"Where is the baby? I really want to see her and go..."

"Speak of the angel, here she is now..." Gage said beaming with pride as Suzzette brought the babe down the staircase.

"Zandrea, meet your godfather and name sake..." Suzzette said.

Zandrea just cooed and smiled at her godfather as Suzzette placed her in his arms.

"Hello angel, how are you?" Zander said as he smiled adoringly at his goddaughter and she smiled back at him. The feeling was mutual.

Thirty-Eight

Zander had just settled back in his room when the phone rang. He thought about not answering it. It might be Austin and he wasn't in the mood. He thought about having the front desk hold all of his calls, but decided against that. He finally answered the phone.

"Hello?"

"Zander?"

"Hey babe, wassup?"

"You didn't sound like yourself..."

"I probably don't."

"What happened, how was the dinner party?"

"Well, it had its moments..."

He told Jordan about the run-in with Drucilla and Suzzette's attorney soror.

"Well Seattle is known for its seafood..."

"Ha, Ha, Ha..."

"I guess you fail to see the humor..."

"That's cause there was none..."

"Well you're safe and sound now..."

"You think so, she's staying in the same hotel. I won't be safe until I'm back in your arms.."

"and you know this..."

Zander and Jordan talked for about another hour. They said their good byes and Zander decided to try finishing *One More River to Cross*; he was really enjoying it but hadn't been able to dedicate the time to completing it. Tonight was perfect, especially since he was alone and planned to keep it that way. About an hour into his reading he heard a knock at the door. He marked his place and put on his robe.

"Who is it?"

"Room Service..."

"I didn't order room service, you must have the wrong room..." he answered through the door

"It's the hotel's complimentary night cap." the voice replied

"No thank-you,..."

"Zander it's me...Austin."

Zander took a deep breath and looked to the heavens begging for help before he opened the door. On the way home from the dinner party, he had prayed that Austin would meet another guy that was equally as horny as she was and give her what she obviously needed. He cracked the door with the chain on.

"Hello, Austin and how are you?"

"I'll be better when you let me in!"

"I was already in bed, so maybe we can hookup tomorrow at the barbecue."

"I'm here now...c'mon let me in..."

Against his better judgment he opened the door. He didn't want to be rude to Suzzette's friend. He should have listened to his first mind, because Austin had changed into a black lace teddy and a satin robe.

"You like..."

"It's very... nice." 'Revealing is more like it.' he thought to himself.

"Is that all you can say?"

"It's really... you!?!"

"I'm glad you noticed."

"Austin, I think I know where this is going and while I'm flattered, I think I need to tell you that I'm in a committed relationship and my significant other lives with me..."

"And you said that to say...."

"This can't happen!" Zander said surprised at Austin's nonchalant demeanor.

"Can't isn't in my vocabulary..." Austin said grabbing at Zander's robe.

"Well it's in mine and I'm exercising it's use..."

"Zander don't play hard to get, we could have a good time and it would be our *little* secret."

"Austin, I think you should leave..." Zander said heading to the door to let his unwelcomed visitor out. As he turned to say good night, what he saw left him speechless.

"You mean you're going to turn down all this...' There was Austin, wearing nothing but a cunning smile.

"Please get dressed..." Zander said turning his back.

"No, I'm so sleepy. I can't move a muscle." With that she laid across Zander's bed.

"Austin, I want you out now!" Zander said in a no nonsense tone looking Austin straight in the eye.

"Zander..." she said in a seductive tone, "I want you... and I know you want me..." She said sitting up in the bed and spreading her legs open exposing herself to Zander.

He had had enough. Zander marched over to the bed and grabbed Austin's clothing and placed it on the side of the bed. "Get dressed and get out!"

"You don't mean it! Zander I can make this a night you won't soon forget."

"Believe me I won't... now get dressed."

"Zander..."

"Okay have it your way..."

"I knew that you'd come around!"

"I'm going to go for a walk, when I return you had better be gone. If you're not, I'll call security and have you removed... is that clear?"

"Be that way, I'm leaving...you don't know what you're missing..."

"Can't miss what I didn't have!"

Austin took her time putting her clothes back on and Zander was losing patience with every moment that passed. "Finally!" Zander thought.

"It could have been special. Whoever your significant other is, I hope she knows how lucky she is. I would have given anything to sample what you're packin! I could tell that you know what to do with it! Such a shame!"

As Austin made her way to the door Zander spotted his book and threw a pillow over it. Thank God she hadn't seen it or it would have been curtains.

"Good night Mister Goody Two Shoes, *your* loss."

"Good night" Zander said as he closed the door locking it just in case.

Thirty-Nine

Zander was stepping out of the shower when the phone rang, he wrapped his towel around him rushing to the phone.

"Hello"

"Did I catch you at a bad time?" Gage asked.

"No, I was just coming out of the shower when you rang."

"So what time shall I pick you up..."

"Gage, I'm going to beg off today's festivities..."

"Why, are you okay?"

"Well..." Zander began as he relayed the previous night's activities. He told Gage that he would feel uncomfortable trying to be cordial when he knew that Austin would still be as aggressive if not more so. Gage said that he understood, but that Suzzette would be disappointed.

"Please let her know that I send my regrets..."

"I will but I don't mind telling you that she thinks the world of you!"

"Likewise, I just want you both to be happy!

"I'm trying..."

"Well, try harder..."

"You sure I can't get you to change your mind. I promise I'll run interference."

"Okay, but the minute it's over, I'm out of here!"

"Thank you!"

Zander hoped that he wouldn't regret his decision to stay, but he was determined to make the best of it. Surprisingly, lunch went off without a hitch. Even Drucilla stayed out of the way. Zander looked at his watch, it was time to head home. He found Gage and Suzzette and thanked them for their hospitality and gave final words to his goddaughter.

"Zandrea, keep your parents in line!"

"I'm sure she will," reassured Suzzette.

"And you keep him in line!" he said to Suzzette.

"I'm sure she will," Gage chimed reassuredly.

They all laughed.

"I know you're not leaving without saying good bye to me!"

"Austin, I wouldn't dream of it!"

"What, no kiss for the godmother?" Austin said with a sly smile adorning her face.

Zander smiled, you had to admire her spunk.

"You be good." Zander said shaking his finger playfully at Austin.

"I'm always good." Austin quipped.

"I don't doubt that, but some things are better left unknown."

Austin admitted defeat and hugged Zander trying to get a feel with her leg, but he knew that old trick.

"You never quit do you!?!" he whispered.

"Nope, never..."

"When you speak of this and I'm sure you will, tell them I was a gentleman, okay!" he said with a wink.

Austin couldn't help but smile. Gage offered to walk Zander out.

When the men were out of ear shot Austin asked,"Suzzette, what's his deal?"

"What do you mean?"

"I practically served it up on a silver platter and he didn't budge!"

"Have you ever thought that maybe he was being a gentleman?"

"Or maybe he's gay!" Austin said with a frown.

Forty

The choir was singing a contemporary version of " *Yes Jesus Loves Me,* "as the pastor was preparing to conduct the christening ceremony. He called Gage and Suzzette along with Zandrea up to the front. They were quite the family portrait; Suzzette was stunning in a white raw silk suit and wide brim chapeau, Gage was quite dapper in his black, pinstripped, vested, wool crepe four-button suit and Zandrea looked like an angel in her christening gown. He then asked that the godparents take their place to the parent's left and the grandmother to the right. Zander had selected a gray three button suit with a gray shirt and tie, after all monochromatic was his look. Austin wore a navy suit that was surprisingly conservative. Both Marlena and Drucilla wore white suits and small hats with nets that draped to their chin; for widows they both looked like a million bucks. The ceremony was short and sweet. At the close the pastor asked that they all join hands. They formed a circle around Suzzette, Gage and Zandrea. As he prayed Zander felt Austin squeeze his hand, she then proceeded to take her finger and begin sliding it across his palm. Zander peeked out of one eye and saw Austin licking her lips and winking. He was appalled, but what could he do? He closed his eyes shaking his head at both the brazenness of her actions and her dated attempt at conveying that she still wanted him. He prayed even harder because only God could deliver him from the clutches of this modern day Jezebel.

After the benediction everyone made their way to the fellowship center of the church. They were was marveling over how quiet Zandrea was during the service, that is until the pastor handed her to Austin and she began to cry. Zander took her and she quit instantly.

"You have quite a way with women, I wonder if you would have the same effect on me."

"Austin, I thought we settled this when you made your unannounced visit to my suite."

"Zander relax..."

"Look, I'm asking you as nicely as I can, back off!"

"When I see something that I want, I go after it..."

"Cool, and when I say no? I mean no!"

"That's what your mouth is saying, but you know that deep inside you want me..."

"If that makes you feel good about yourself then fine, but know the truth...for the very last time I don't want you!"

Gage could see the tension on Zander's face and thought the he needed to rescue his friend.

"Austin, did I tell you how lovely you look?..."

"Why thank you Gage. At least one man here appreciates a sister who takes care of herself..."

"What man wouldn't appreciate and celebrate a sister like yourself..."

"Your boy for one! Maybe he's into white girls..."

"I don't think that Zander..."

"No my sistah, thats where you're wrong! It is because I respect you that I am not treating you like some sl..." Zander remembered where he was, "cheap one night stand, got it... good!"

"Whatever?" Austin said as she walked away. Gage looked at Zander. They both shrugged their shoulders and said it in unison, "women!"

"I think I'm going to head out. I really want to get home."

"You're leaving? We didn't have any time together." Gage said sounding so disappointed.

"I know, but at least we did see each other and I got a chance to meet my adorable goddaughter and your lovely wife.."

"Z, can't you stay through lunch?"

"I appreciate the offer, but I think its best..."

"Okay..."

"Have a wonderful time and kiss my goddaughter and Suzzette for me.."

"What should I tell Austin.?.."

"Don't even go there..."

"Bye.."

Zander felt bad about not attending the barbecue, but it was best for everyone concerned.

"Especially me," he said to himself.

Forty-One

"Hello, this is Mr. Lowe!"

"Bristah, wassup?"

"Nuttin much, what about you?"

"The same!"

"So how was the christening?"

"It was interesting to say the least!"

"What?"

"Where should I start?"

"I always like the beginning!"

Zander filled Desmond in on the details from his trip to Seatttle and the encounter with Austin.

"Uugh, she was naked?"

"As a jay bird..."

"Can you still see?"

Zander laughed, "Of course I can!"

He continued to share his misadventures while on his trip with Desmond who was shocked that Zander had endured the clutches of femininity.

"In church? You are lying!"

"I am telling you the truth!"

"And she is still standing, Miss Thang is too much!"

"She is... and then some!"

"I am shocked! She gives finer womanhood a bad name!"

"As my mother would say, 'that girl doesn't have any shame to her game'..."

"Miss Rita is right! Speaking of Diva number one..."

"You'll never guess..."

"What? "

"Mr. Oscar Lee has asked my mother to marry him!"

"Go Momma! When's the wedding?"

"Don't get your bridesmaid dress out yet..."

"Matron of honor or I'm not coming.... "

"Excuse me, I forgot you are married these days, there are some things that you just can't get used too...sniff, sniff...My bristah... a married wo..man..." Zander said laughing at his own joke.

"N-knee-way! When is the..."

"There is no date yet! Mama is praying about it..."

"She better call Ms. Esther 'Damn, Damn, Damn' Rolle and her spiritual friends."

"It ain't gonna happen..."

They both laughed at the idea of Rita calling a psychic.

"Back to the upcoming nuptials.."

"She says she wants to make sure and she's waiting on God to give her the answer..."

"I hope he don't take too long, we need a new daddy!"

They both laughed with the hopes that whatever Rita's decision was they just wanted her to be happy.

"How are you and Eli doing?"

"Couldn't be better, how are you and Jordan doing?"

"We're doing great! His show premiered with the best ratings the station has ever seen in day time or original programming, even the soap's ratings have increased with him as the lead-in."

"Watch out Montel!"

"More like move over..."

"Si!"

"I miss you Desi, I wish we lived in the same city!"

"Me too! Who knows? We are talking about a change of venue...and you're on the list."

"Really!"

"What did I just say!"

"Yes ma'am..."

"Excuse me..."

"I mean sir..." Zander said laughing. He knew how Desmond hated when he did that...

"If memory serves me, I'm the one that's..."

"Don't even start that..."

"Just puttin' you in check..."

"N-knee-way! Besides it's not the size of the pencil, it's what it writes..."

"Wha..."

"Never mind..."

"I didn't think so..."

"Whatever..."

Desmond started laughing; he loved getting the best of Zander. These times were rare but when he did, it was a true victory.

"And what is so funny?"

"Oh nothing..."

"Whatever..."

Desmond started laughing again. He had won this battle of wits.

"Well I'm gonna get off this phone and I'll drop you an email later..."

"Okay..."

"Steadman, I mean Zander..."

"Ha, ha, ha! you know that's getting old already."

"Okay, I'll stop... for the record I think that you did the right thing in going to the christening..."

"You do?" Zander said. He was truly surprised.

"Yeah, I think that it helped put closure on the Gman and you deserve to be that baby's godfather..."

"Thanks Desi, your support means a lot, you know that, but for the record..."

"Yes..."

"I put closure on that the day Jordan walked into my life..."

"Work it out!"

"And you know this..."

"Peace, Z baby!"

"Ditto, Des..."

Forty-Two

"Hello,"

"Mrs. Adams please.."

"This is she, may I help you?..."

"Mrs. Adams, my name is Miles Robertson and I've been counseling your son, Hakiem..."

"Hmmph, it's about time..."

"Why do you say that?"

"He's needs help, maybe you can help him be a real man!"

"A real *man*? What do you mean?"

"You know ain't no *fag* a real man..."

"Is that so?" Miles said feeling his entire body temperature rise. He knew that he had his work cut out for him, maybe this wasn't a good idea. He was at a loss; he had to summon every ounce of professional fortitude not to go off.

"Hakiem was such a special little boy..."

"And he's a special young man who wants his mother, his family, his life back!"

"Well when you fix him, maybe I'll take him back!"

"Fix him?" Miles said totally shocked at her last comment,"Mrs. Adams, I have an opening this afternoon, could you come by and see me this afternoon?"

"Why, I don't need no any counseling! Besides I don't believe in counseling. When I have a problem I talk to Jesus...praise the Lord.."Mrs. Adams said in a no-nonsense tone.

"I'm not suggesting that you do, but I would really like to talk with you about Hakiem..."

"I'm really busy..."

"Too busy for your own child..."

"Pardon me..."

"Hakiem is your son..."

"And you said that to say what Mister?..."

"Mrs. Adams, I really would like for you to come and talk with me..."

"Let me see if I can get a babysitter..."

"I have an idea, why don't you bring the children with you and Hakiem can watch them while you and I talk? Pooh is dying to see him anyway..."

"I don't know..."

"Mrs. Adams, if I didn't think that this was important, I would have never called..."

"Let me think about it..."

"Mrs. Adams..."

"Yes sir..."

"Please come..."

"Give me the address and if I decide to come I'll be there..."

"I need to call Hakiem ma'am so he can be here..."

There was silence.

"Mrs. Adams..."

"I'm thinking, I'm thinking..."

"Mrs. Adams, I have a patient waiting so I have to run, but I'm going to call Hakiem and ask him to be here... I hope you will. He really wants to see his brothers and sisters..."

"Step..."

"Pardon me..."

"Stepbrothers and stepsisters"

"Hopefully, we'll see you at three Mrs. Adams...."

"We'll see..."

"See you then, goodbye..."

Miles hung up the phone and closed his eyes, praying that this would work. If Hakiem ever needed his family; it was now. "God please touch the mother in Mrs. Adams..." he prayed. Then he took a cleansing breath and placed another call.

"Hello, and thank you for calling the Kendricks, we're not available right now, please leave a message and we'll get back with you as soon as possible..."

"This message is for Hakiem, please call Miles Robertson as soon as possible, thank you!"

"Sugar!" Miles whispered. "Hakiem where are you?"

Miles looked through his rolodex to see if he had another number for Hakiem...the only number was Zander.

"Thank you for calling The PRDesign Group, how may I direct your call?"

"Zander Eady, please."

"He's unavailable at this time may I take a message?"

"No thank you, I'll try to reach him by cell phone..."

"Have a good day!"

"You too!" Miles said as he disconnected the call holding the receiver to his chin.

"Sugar!" Miles said again outloud as he looked up Zander's cell phone number.

"Hello, This is Zander Eady of The PRDesign Group. I'm unavailable, please leave me a message and I'll call you back.."

"Where are you, Zander?" he said putting the phone back on the cradle. He was getting nervous; maybe this isn't going to be as simple as he thought. He would have to turn this over to his assistant, he had a patient waiting. He paged Katrina and asked her to show in the next patient. As the patient settled in he gave her the numbers and told her that this was priority.

The hour passed so slowly, he would have to credit this session because he really hadn't heard a word that his patient had said. "Thank goodness for a tape recorder," he thought At least he could listen to it later and make an assessment.

"Any luck?"

"No sir, I've left messages with Mr. Eady and tried Hakiem again..."

"Any word from Mrs. Adams?"

"No sir..."

"Okay, thank you..." Miles said totally frustrated as he released the intercom button.

Miles sunk down in his chair, swiveling from side to side. What was he going to do? He had less than two hours to have everybody in place.

"Dr. Robertson..."

"Yes, Katrina?"

"Mrs. Adams on line one."

"Thank you."

Miles looked towards heaven and mouthed "I owe you one..."

"Mrs. Adams..."

"I'll be there, but don't you even think that you're going to counsel me...I don't need it. I'm only coming to talk about my so...Hakiem...you got that?"

"Yes ma'am..."

"So is he going to be there?"

"He... you mean Hakiem..."

"Yeah, him..."

"Yes ma'am..."

"Well I'll see you at three..."

"Mmmmm huh..."

"Until then!"

There was no response just a loud click in his ear.

"One down and one to go!" he said to himself as he dialed Zander's cell phone again.

Forty-Three

"Dr. Robertson..."
"Yes Katrina..."
"Hakiem is on line one."
"Thank you..." Miles said as he pressed line one.
"Man, you are one hard brotha to find...."
"Wassup Miles, did I miss an appointment or something?.."
"No, but I've been trying to reach you all morning..."
"Wassup, I was hanging out with my boo!"
"Oh... well what are you doing around a quarter to three?..."
"Nuttin..just chillin...maybe watch some videos..."
"Well I need to see you..."
"What I do now?"
Miles laughed, "You didn't do anything... can you make it?"
"Yeah, what's this about?"
"Just be here..."
"Okay, if you say so..."
"And I do..."
"See you then..."
"And Hakiem..."
"Yeah..."

"Yes..." Miles said correcting Hakiem.

"Yes...excuse me..."

"Don't be late, okay..."

"Yes sir!..."

Miles smiled as he hung up the phone.

"Whew," he said as he settle back in the chair. He swiveled in a full rotation as he looked up towards heaven and mouthed, "You the man!" as he gave God a thumbs up.

Miles checked his watch, it was two-thirty. He took a deep breath and continued working on his script for the PSA campaign that he and Zander had discussed. He hoped that Zander and Elle would like his concept. He made a note to see if there were any singers or rappers in the Youth Group that might be interested in doing the video. He wanted this to be hip, but not so much, that the message got lost.

"Dr. Robertson..."

"Yes..."

"Hakiem is here..."

"Send him in..."

"Wassup Miles..."

"Just you my lil' brotha..."

"So what did you want to see me about?"

"Two things..."

"Okay! shoot..."

"Well you know that I'm working with Zander on this AIDS Prevention Campaign..."

"Yeah, I mean yes..."

"Can you sing or rap?"

"I can do both, I'm in chorus, remember.."

"Yes I do..."

"So would you be interested..."

"Only if I can be the star..." Hakiem said jokingly...

"No problem.."

"Hey Miles, I was just joking..."

"I'm not... I think you would be perfect..."

"You serious?"

"As a heart attack..."

"Cool! Move over Will Smith, Hakiem is in da house..."

"Well I'm glad to see you're confident!"

"Ain't nuttin to it but to do it!"

"Okay then its settled, I'll have to talk with Mrs. Kendricks and get her to sign the release.."

"Cool, but she's not my legal guardian... I just stay there... you have to talk to my moms...and knowing her...my rising star has just become a falling one!"

"Well I'll talk to her and see what we can work out, okay..."

"Okay, good luck... you need the number again.."

"No, actually she's going to be here in about five minutes so I'll talk with her then..."

"What you mean she'll be here in five minutes?..."

"Just what I said..."

"Why, how? "

"I called her... "

"Did you tell her about the AIDS and sh....I mean stuff?"

"No, I couldn't do that without your permission, there's a thing called doctor-patient confidentiality..."

"What's that?"

"It simply means that I can't tell anyone what we talk about in your sessions..."

"Really..."

"Really..."

"Okay cool... Miles..."

"Yes, Hakiem..."

"Can you tell her?..."

"About...."

"My HIV..."

"Hakiem..."Miles said taking a deep breath, "I don't know about that..."

"I mean you said that you could if I gave you permission right."

"That's not what I said..."

"Please Dr. Robertson..."

Miles knew that Hakiem must have been serious if he was calling him Dr. Robertson.

"Hakiem..."

"Please..."

"Hakiem, I can't ethically do that....."

"Man, fu... forget etiquette..."

"Ethics..." Miles said trying not to laugh.

"Whatever..."

"No, not whatever... if you'll let me finish. I was about to say that while I can't ethically do what you've requested, I can be there when you tell her..."

"Dr. Robertson, Mrs. Adams is here to see you..."

"I'm outta here.."

"Hakiem, are you sure about that?"

"Yeah... I mean.. yes... I mean... I don't know what I mean..."

"Dr. Robertson..."

"Katrina, I'll be out in a minute..."

"Yes sir!" Katrina, said somewhat stunned at his tone.

"Hakiem, your mother is here because I asked her to come. She still has a responsibility legally to be your parent...and as your counselor and friend I have to do everything in my power to see that you and your mother began repairing this relationship. There may come a time when you really need her..."

"Good luck..."

"From what you've told me, I'm going to need it! But I feel that it's worth it...that you're worth it," Miles said smiling at his young patient. "Now you're brothers and sisters are here as a part of the bargain with your mother. I promised her that you would watch them, now I can't go back on my word...so you gonna help a brotha out?"

"You don't have to ask me twice..." Hakiem was beaming, his smile literally lit up the room.

He was half way out the door by the time Miles put on his jacket.

"Hey Ma!" Hakiem said hugging her. She just stood there not even returning his hug.

"Hakiem..." Pooh exclaimed as he leaped onto his brother's back.

"Mrs. Adams, I'm Miles Robertson, thank you for coming..."

"Dr. Robertson..."

"Hey Nadine...girl you getting so big..." Hakiem said as he hugged his little sister, "and Pop what size shoe do you wear now? You're feet are so big!"

"10½ and they don't call me Pop no more, they call me DJPlaya"

"They don't call you Pop any more," Hakiem corrected. "DJ Playa, huh, you still Pop to me..."

Pop just smiled. He didn't care what his brother called him, he was just glad to see him.

"And...Dionne, you're turning into a young lady...gee I have been gone a long time..."

"What about me?" Pooh asked.

"What about you..." all of the other sibilings asked. Pooh was hurt.

"lil' man you know you my boy, I love you!" Hakiem said giving his little brother, who was still on his back, dap. "So where y'all wanna go..."

"McDonalds, McDonalds..." Pooh said jumping up and down on Hakiem's back.

"Don't nobody wanna go to no Mickey Dee's, thats all you know," Pop and Nadine said almost at the same time. "We wanna go to the mall!" they added.

Pooh looked like he had lost his best friend.

"And what about you Dionne?" Hakiem asked.

"I don't care, just as long as I'm with you..." Dionne said smiling at her big brother.

"Tell ya'll what! There is a McDonald's at the mall so we can all do what we want, cool?"

"Yeah!" Pooh cheered as he started to sing "McDonald's is my favorite place..."

Hakiem laughed at his little brother who was now off his back and doing a little dance around the office. The other kids laughed too, but Pooh didn't care, he was going to McDonalds

"Now that thats settled, here Hakiem..." Miles said as he handed Hakiem some money, "my treat!" "That's okay Miles, I got it! Just got paid"

"You sure..."

"And you know this.." he said winking at Miles.

"Be back in about two hours okay...and Hakiem..."

"I know, be on time..."

"And you know that..." Miles said smiling at Hakiem.

With that Hakiem ushered the noisy gang of kids out the door to the elevator. Pooh could be heard saying, "Can I get a cheeseburger Happy Meal?"

Forty-Four

Miles smiled at Mrs. Adams and invited her into his office.

Tabitha Adams was full figured with a pretty face. She was medium brown and had her hair fixed in a French roll and finger waves hairstyle. She wore a gold nameplate and one other chain with a diamond attached. Surprisingly, she was much younger than she looked. She had rings on both hands, including a mother's ring with five birthstones inlaid and her nails were done in French tip.

"Thank you again for coming Mrs. Adams..."

"Tabitha..."

"Pardon me?"

"You can call me Tabitha..."

"Oh...kay Tabitha it is..."

"And what you want me to call you..."

"Miles is fine..."

"Oh okay..."

Miles noticed her body language, it was saying, "don't bother with me, I am not having it."

"Mrs. Ad...Tabitha... let me ask you a few questions so that I can better assess the situation, if you will..."

"Could I stop you?"

"If you really wanted to, yes..."

"Okay ask away!"

"Oh...kay, Tabitha how did you feel when you were told Hakiem was gay?"

"I was pissed, I mean po'd"

"Pissed is fine..." Miles said, "and you threw him out..."

"Is that what he told you!"

"We're not discussing Hakiem, we're talking about you right now..."

"Well yeah, my husband and I thought that it would be best if he wasn't around the children.."

"And why was that?"

"We didn't want him messing around with them....you know what I mean!"

"No ma'am I don't..."

"We didn't want him touching them..."

"You mean molesting them?"

"Yes..."

"Had Hakiem every exhibited this kind of inappropriate behavior before?"

"What do you mean by that?"

"Did you ever witness or hear from any of his siblings that Hakiem was touching them or making them do things that he shouldn't have?"

"Well, no but.....

"Well, then what would make you think that..."

"Well, he was a fag!" she said.

Miles knew where this was headed so he discretely took a deep breath and braced himself for what was to come next.

"Then he probably would be trying stuff out on his brothers..."

"And why do you think that?"

"Because that's the way they are..."

"They who?"

"Fags!"

"If she said that one more time," Miles thought, "he would scream." She did, he didn't.

"They like lil' boys..."

"Mrs. Adams, it is a known fact that most pedophiles are not gay men, but heterosexual males,"

Miles said trying not to loose his professional manner.

"Is that a fact?"

"Yes, ma'am.."

"Well, I'll be damned!"

Tabitha continued to explain how she thought that Hakiem would be a negative influence on the boys. She talked about how he had always been an artistic child and she knew that he was different from an early age because while the other boys in the neighborhood were asking for footballs and bikes, her son asked for piano lessons and sketch books. She said her husband tried to get his to play baseball and football in the youth athletic league, but Hakiem cried when it was time to go to practice, but would play for hours when it was time to practice the piano. Her husband had sold the piano to try and make a man out of Hakiem, because he said he didn't want no queer church musician for a son.

"So you mentioned Mr. Adams, I take it that he is Hakiem's step father..."

"Yes, Hakiem's daddy and I never really got any further than a first date, if you could call it that."

"Please explain..."

"Hakiem was the product of a college date gone bad..."

"You mean date rape..."

"Yes.." Tabitha said as the tears swelled in her eyes.

"I'm sorry..." he said handing her the box of tissues next to his chair.

"You know, you the first person I ever told that to..." she said blowing her nose and wiping her eyes as she continued. "When I found out I was pregnant I thought about aborting the baby, but my parents wouldn't let me. They said that this was God's way of punishing me for being promiscuous."

"You know that isn't true now don't you..."

"I really don't know what I believe, I carried the guilt around for so long..."

"But this was a nonconsensual act, correct?"

"If you mean did I give it to him, the answer is no..."

"Then why the guilt?"

"I was raised in a Christian home and any kind of sex before marriage was wrong, con..."

"Consensual..." Miles added seeing her difficulty with the pronounciation.

"Thank you, con-sen-sual or otherwise..."

"So did you consider your options?..."

"You mean abortion? My father would have killed me..."

"Or adoption...."

"My mother suggested that, but my father said that was the easy way out and that I would have to raise this baby..."

"And you did, so does your husband know how Hakiem was conceived..."

"Yes..." she said with a sadness on her face, "and that's one of the reasons he resents Hakiem..."

"And what about you..." he asked with concern.

"I know Hakiem didn't ask to be born and he couldn't help how he got here, but there are days when I wished that he hadn't been born..."

"At least you're honest. But do you think it's fair that he be punished for something he had nothing to do with for the rest of his life..."

"No, but now he's a sissy and my husband says ain't no "funny folk" gonna live under the roof that he provides for..."

"Not even your son?..."

"Well... "

"So do you want him to come home?"

"I don't know what I want, my husband said he would leave us if I ever even talked to Hakiem again..."

"And you would sacrifice your son?" Miles said realizing that he had to maintain an unbiased opinion.

"I don't want to, but at least he has a place to stay and he seems to be happy"

"Yes he does have a place to stay and he is okay with where he is. He likes the Kendricks, but it's not his home, you know that..."

"Well what do you want me to do, if I take him back in, my husband will leave me and then what..."

"I'm not here to tell you what to do..."

"I love my son, but my husband is a good man..."

"Who are you trying to convince Tabitha, me or you?"Miles asked."I go back to my initial question, do you want him home with you?"

"Yes, but I need some time..."

"Would you like to talk to him?"

"Hakiem..."

"Yes, it's been two years and a lot has changed, he's had to grow up a lot in that time..."

"Would you be there?"

"I can be..."

"I would like that..."

"When he gets back, I'll have Katrina take the children to the movies or for pizza and we can talk..."

"Ohhhhka,y..."

"Are you sure you're ready? I don't want you to feel pressured, we can always schedule another session.."

"No, it's now or never," Tabitha said with a nervous smile on her face.

Forty-Five

"Dr. Robertson, you asked me to let you know when Hakiem and the kids returned."

"Thanks Katrina, could you please send Hakiem in?"

"Will do, I guess you'll page me when you're ready for us to come back..."

"Yes I will, get forty dollars out of petty cash, better yet use the company credit card..."

"Will do."

"Hey Miles... Moms...wassup?"

"Sit down Hakiem, I think it's time to have a talk..."

"Okay..."

"Moms why you crying?"

"Hakiem your mother has something she needs to say. Tabitha go ahead..."

"Son, first I want to apologize to you for letting Matthew talk me into throwing you out the house..."she said as she began to weep. "I know you must really hate me... "

"Moms I could never hate you! You are my moms, hate ain't even apart of the picture, I'm only sad that you hate me!"

"I don't hate you..."

"When Mr. Adams told me to get out because God didn't allow sinners like me in his presence. You didn't say nothing...I mean anything...you took his side..." Hakiem said as the tears fell from his face. "I begged you to help me and you just picked up Pooh and walked into your bedroom and shut the door."

"I didn't know what else to do. If he kicked us all out where would we have gone, I thought he would calm down and I thought that I would be able to talk him into letting you come back when he calmed down..."

"Really why didn't you tell me that...you just let him call me faggot, sissy, punk and queer. He kept saying that I would bus hell wide open and that God hated me. He told me that if and when I got AIDS that I deserved it and this would be God's punishment and that I would be better off dead..."

Then it clicked. Miles now understood why Hakiem wanted to give up all on life.

"I didn't know he said that to you..."

"Yes ma'am..."

"He had no right to say that to you.."

"He even told me that my father raped you and that you hated me from the day that I was born..." Hakiem said trying not to cry. "If that's true then I don't blame you for not wanting me. I can understand, I think that I would hate me too..."

"I never wanted you to find out about that, but I don't hate or blame you Hakiem..."

"Then why didn't you come to the phone when I called?"

"Because I didn't know what to say"

"Hello would have been a start, but instead you sent my baby brother back to tell me that you weren't home."

"I know that was wrong..."

"Mama, I called you because I need you and love you...

"Baby, I love you too! I never stopped and I'm sorry for all the things that you've been through. I'll spend the rest of my life trying to make this up to you..."

"We may not have that long..."

"What is he talking about?..."

"Hakiem, it's time..." Miles said

"Mama, I have full blown AIDS..."

"No, you can't..."

"Yes mama, I do..."

"No God, not my baby... no.... "

"Mama, please don't cry...."

"Tabitha, Hakiem doesn't want your pity, he needs your support and most of all your love..."

"He can have it! Lord take me instead of my baby... I deserve it... I've been a awful mother I deserve to die..."

"Mama, no you don't, its my fault... all mine..."

"Baby..."

"I don't think that either of you blaming yourselves is going to do any good..." Miles said.

He advised Tabitha and Hakiem to continue their counseling sessions and join a family support group like PFLAG or the local PWA Coalition. They both agreed that if it would help them get back on the right track they would go to the next meeting. He also cautioned them that it was going to be a process and that they needed to move forward taking it one day at a time. Miles knew that his approach to getting his young patient and his mother back together was not the most practical, but he told himself that desperate times called for drastic measures.

At the end of their session Tabitha hugged Hakiem with every ounce of strength she had. You would have thought that she was trying to get in two years worth of hugs at the same time.

"Ma! I can't breathe..."

They all laughed. Hakiem tried to catch his breath. For the first time in a long time he felt like life was really worth living.

"Son you wanna come home?..."

"Do you want me to come home?..."

"I wouldn't be asking if I didn't!"

"What about Daddy?..."

"You leave him to me..."

"Miles maybe you should come to dinner..."

"No, I think that your mom will do fine all by herself..."

The two of them hugged for what seemed like an eternity and then they were joined by the rest of the family for a group hug. Hakiem could feel Pooh grabbing him at the waist. Yep, he was home.

Forty-Six

"C'mon in..." Tabitha said as she opened the door, "Are you nervous?"

"A lil' bit..." Hakiem said as he looked around, everything was pretty much like he remembered.

"I left your room the way you left it, except I cleaned it..."

"Now I won't be able to find anything.."

They both laughed.

"Who's been sleeping in my bed?"

"Me..." Pooh said with pride.

"Yeah and he peed in it to..." Pop said.

"Matthew Zachary Adams, leave your little brother alone!"

"DJ Playa..."

"Whatever, you better do what I say boy.."

"Yes ma'am," Pop said knowing that his mother meant business.

"Pop's gonna get it!" his sisters chimed in...

"And so will you, if y'all don't stop it right this minute..." Tabitha warned, "You sure you want to move back in here..."

"This is like music to my ears..."

"Let's see if you say that next week this time..." Tabitha said smiling.

"Momma, it's good to be home..."

"It's good to have you home Hakiem..."

It was about seven when Deacon Matthew Zachary Adams, Sr., arrived at home. He was the chairman of the Deacon Board at Mount Moriah Baptist Church. A tall man, he was light in complexion with freckles that decorated his face. His arms were laced with veins, badges from the manual labor he did years prior to making foreman with the custom home builder that he worked for. He was balding and most recently decided to shave off all of his hair. He thought it added character and made him look more like a man. His eyes were light brown but were more often red from irritation. He had a booming voice that seemed like a roar when he talked. Deacon Adams was a God fearing man who loved his wife and family, but when he believed in something it would take an act of Congress to change his mind.

"Tabby, I'm home..." he said as he put his briefcase in the small home office.

Hakiem's heart rushed to his throat hearing his stepfather's voice.

"Hey baby, we're in the family room..."

He was ambushed by the his two younger children as he crossed the threshold of the family room,

"Daddy look who is here!" Pooh said with excitement

"Hello Daddy," Hakiem said with barely any volume.

"What the hell is he doing here?"

"Matthew!!" Tabitha exclaimed, "not in front of the children."

"You guys go to your rooms...I'll be in to say good bye before I leave," Hakiem said trying not have a major scene in front of his younger siblings.

"Daddy, don't make Hakiem leave again" they all begged.

"C'mon kids..." Tabitha said scooting the kids out, "don't you dare say anything until I get back Matt.."

"Daddy, if you make Ha..Hakiem leave, I'm going too..." Dionne said with tears in her eyes.

"Dee Dee, go! I'll be fine.."

With the children out of ear shot, Tabitha came back into the room.

"I hope you're happy!"

"What are you talking about?"

"The kids haven't been this happy in a long time and now they're afraid that you're going to kick their big brother out again..."

"Well, they're right...I don't allow the likes of him in my house!"

"I'll go mama... thanks for trying!"

"No son, wait..."

"No let him go, before I kick his gay behind out!"

"It that really what this is about Matthew or do you have other issues with my son?"

"What are you talking about? Issues, you been watching Oprah again haven't you?..."

"Don't try to be cute with me, it isn't going to work,"she said giving her husband one of those "if looks could kill you would already be dead" stares. "Why do you hate Hakiem so much, is it because he's gay or because of the way he was conceived?"

"What does it matter? He's a misfit anyway!"

"You wait one damn minute!" Tabitha said shocking herself, "this is my son! For three years it was just the two of us and we did just fine...and when you came into our lives you promised to be his father and you were a good father until you found out that he was gay..."

"Mom..."

"You just sit there and let me handle this..." she said to Hakiem. "Now you call yourself a Christian. I never knew that you told Hakiem all of those awful things about him getting AIDS and deserving it. How dare you!?! The last time I checked God still was judge.."

"Tabitha, I think you've said enough..."

"You think so, I'm just getting started,"

"Tabby..."

"Don't Tabby me... I stood by and let you kick my own child out because I was afraid. Well, Deacon Adams you can have your house, your fancy car and anything else, but me and my five children will walk out of here and never look back. Here me loud and clear, nothing, and I mean nothing will ever separate me and my son again. In fact, if anybody is leaving here it'll be you. I am tired of you bullying me and my son and hiding behind the Bible to do it! He is a part of me, you see him.You see me! You mess with him; you have to come through me. You will *Never, Ever Ever* talk to him like you did two years ago! So what's it gonna be? Either he stays or..."

"He can stay!" Matthew said still in shock.

"And another thing, he is not a fag, queer, sissy or "funny" in case you've forgotten, his name is Hakiem. He is our son! No more names!"

"No more names!" a bewildered Matthew said.

"Thanks mama!"

"No thanks needed."

Hakiem sat with tears streaming down his face. His mother actually stood up for him. He was home.

Forty-Seven

"The building that sparked controversy goes up in flames..." the reporter said as video of the burning buildings was shown. "as firemen, EMS and our city police are now on the scene. A very ambitious and unsuccessful attempt was made to bring the burning building under control," she continued. "The charred remains of the building that you see behind me in our live pictures are all that is left of what was to be the new Center City Gay and Lesbian Resource Center. The building next to it, the Mount Moriah Baptist Church, was not without it's share of damage. It it estimated that over five hundred thousand dollars in damage was done to the main sanctuary of one of the city's most popular African American churches."

"Regina, what are officials saying about the fire?" the anchor asked.

"Well they're not saying much, but we have learned that the fire is being called suspicious at this time. We will have more team coverage for you in the noon hour now back to you in the studio.."

"Thank you Regina," the main anchor said as he turned back to address his camera, "so there you have it! In this late breaking story, the building that was slated to be a place of where the cities gay and lesbian community of color could come together has been burned beyond repair and costly damage has been done to one of the city's largest and most popular African American churches, as well. There is no word on what caused the fire, but officials are calling the fire "suspicious" at this time.. We'll have more for you in our noon newscast," the anchor said as he signed off.

"The Jordan Jacobs Show"

"May I speak with Jordan please?"

"Hold on please..."

"This is Jordan..."

"Did you see the news?"

"Hey baby, yes I did... "

"Did you call your father?"

"I spoke with my mother? My father is shook up, but he's okay!'

"And how are you?"

"Me, I'm fine"

"Are you sure? "

"Well call me if you need me..."

"I always need you!"

"Same here..."

Zander and Jordan talked for a few minutes more when a breaking news story came across the television.

"Hold on babe, there's a breaking news story," Jordan informed Zander.

"I'm watching...."

"We interrupt your regular programming to bring you this breaking news story," the anchor said. "Earlier this morning we brought you the exclusive story of the fire at the Central City Gay and Lesbian Resource Center and the Mount Moriah Baptist Church. Officials are saying that the fire is no longer suspicious, but is now is confirmed as 'arson.'

"Arson, well I'll be..." Jordan said

"But who?" Zander added.

"Officials say that a group known as the "Aryan Protectors" are said to be claiming responsibility for the double arson. Officials say that no one member is a suspect at this time. Eyewitness News has learned that there is a note from the separatist group and that investigators are still examining it for prints and any other clues that may be available. No plans at this time are being released as to when we will know the contents of the note, but as soon as they are available, you can be sure that the Eye Team we will bring them to you, first, fast and factual. We now return you to your regularly scheduled programming."

"Those bastards..."

"Sick, sick, sick..."

"I grew up in that church..." Jordan said.

"Babe, I'm so sorry..."

"Hey! Those mofo's didn't care, they got two for one. They destroyed the dreams of niggers and queers with one match."

"Jordan..."

"Z, I can't help it. I'm pissed! Not only is the church gone, but the center too. We've put the last six months into the Center. You, me, Miles, Hakiem and even Tabitha worked to make this vision a reality. We all wanted a place where gay people of color could come and feel safe and grow. But it's all gone now. It's not fair, dammit, it's not fair."

"Jordan, calm down baby. Who said life was fair? And as far as the vision, it's still in each of us. We'll just start over and build it even better..."

"They'll probably just burn it down again..."

"And we'll just build it again, this time with a working moat..."

The last comment made Jordan laugh.

"I think you need to do a show about what has happened..."

"You think?"

"Yes I do, that I think people will want to know more about why this happened and who are the players involved..."

"I don't know. Maybe I'm too close to the issue..."

"If you don't do it, who will? I think that people will want to hear more about the fires..."

"We'll see, thanks for the suggestion...way to look out!"

"Hey, somebody's got to watch your back.."

"Is that all you're watching?"

"You are a mess boy.."

"You got that right!"

"So let me know if I can help you..."

"I'll talk with you later..."

"Okay, hey!"

"Yes?!?"

"I love you..."

"I love you more..."

"Says you..."

"And you know this..."

Jordan smiled as he put down the receiver. He didn't know what he would do if anything happened to Zander. In the months they had been together, he had come to depend on him a great deal. He was often his voice of reason and he was glad that he was in his life. He hung up the phone and decided to give Zander's show suggestion some thought.

"To the ground?"

"the ground..."

"Lord, what has the world come to?"

"I don't know, but it ain't nothing nice."

"So what are you guys going to do about it..."

"Well luckily, we were heavily insured, but that doesn't negate all of the hard work..."

"But it helps..."

"True.."

"Des, you should have heard the hurt in his voice..."

"He really took it hard..."

"Yeah..."

"So what are you guys going to do?"

"Start over..."

"Well you know that you can count on our money..."

"But you gave quite a bit before..."

"And we'll give again..."

"Thank you guys!"

"Hey, what are bristahs for?"

"Thanks Desi! I don't know what I would do without you..."

"This is true. Bye Z baby.."

"Talk with you later, love you..."

"Me too..."

With that Zander hung up the phone and sighed. He was worried about Jordan, he had never seen him like this, not even when he and his father had an argument. This project had been something that Jordan had dreamed about doing every since he started working with Brother's United. Now, it was gone. But Desmond was right, all they could do was start over. He sighed, that was easier said than done.

Forty-Eight

The station had decided to do a town hall meeting after the burnings. They wanted it to be a special Saturday night version of Jordan's show. He had already really decided against covering the issue especially since his father would have to be one of the guests. His first mind was not to and he tried to convince them to let someone else do it, management insisted. So what was he to do, call in sick?

The audience applauded as Jordan made his was down the steps center stage to the set. He looked so handsome. He was wearing the navy three-button suit that Zander had given him for his birthday. He welcomed the audience both in studio and at home. As the applause died down he informed them of show's topic.

"'A House of God and House of Hope are Burned to the Ground: Hatred's Burning Question,' that's the focus of tonight's Special Edition. It's gonna be a hot one, no pun intended. Stay with us..."

The floor director cued the audience to applaud, the show's theme swelled and the show's open was up on the screen. As it dissolved, Jordan was now in the audience as he began his introduction of today's topic and his guests.

"A week ago we all watched in horror, as two building burned as a result of hatred. The destruction of these two buildings sent a clear message to this community, hate is alive and well. But these were more than just buildings, they were symbols of good and hope. Each of our guests have defined interest in what happened on that unfortunate night. Joining us is Miles Robertson, executive director of the Umoja Project, a gay and lesbian support organization. Next, Reverend Hezikiah J. Jacobs, pastor of the burned church, Mount Moriah Baptist, also joining us is David Mayes, the founder and city director of "Straight Laced," an anti-gay rights organization and Howard Metzger, leader of the Aryan Protectors, a local separatist organization. Please help me welcome them to the show."

As the applause died down Jordan purposely began his questioning with Miles. He knew that if he didn't the show would get off on the wrong foot.

"Miles, let's start with you...where were you when you learned that the building had burned?"

"I was at the hospital visiting a friend, we were watching "The Price is Right" and it was interrupted," Miles said with a faint reminiscent smile. "He loved that show...I would go by everyday and watch it with him..."

"And what was your first thought when you saw the Center going up in flames..."

"I couldn't believe it... and I tried to turn the channel..."

"And why was that?"

"The friend that I was visiting was to be a patient in the center's hospice program, his last wish was to die at home..."

"At home?"

"Yes the building had been donated by the friend I was visiting. Previously, it was his home slash office. After he became ill, he said that it was too big for just one person. He could no longer keep it up, so he gave it to us, he said he wanted to share it. He wanted it to be a place for people to come and be a family! Like it had been when he was growing up..." Miles said as the tears began falling from his eyes.

"And how did your friend react when he saw his gift and vision go up in flames?"

"He cried...and kept asking who would do such a thing..." Miles said becoming more emotional.

"And how is your friend doing today?"Jordan asked already knowing the answer.

"He died shortly after..." Miles said breaking down.

"We'll be right back..." Jordan said as he went on set to console Miles.

The show's slow and more somber version of it's theme played as a picture with the name Kenny Cox and the dates of his birth and death appeared and then the picture faded to black.

"Are you going to be okay?" Jordan asked concerned about his friend. "If you don't want to continue, you don't have to..."

"Yeah cry baby, you can go home, ooops! All gone," chimed in Metzger.

"Shut up..." Miles said.

"Nigger, who are you telling..." Metzger said jumping out of the chair.

Jordan turned to Metzge and looked him straight in the eye.

"I think that you need to sit down..."

"Who the fu..." Metzger said with a look of disgust on his face.

"You..." Jordan said not moving a muscle.

By that time security was on stage.

"Is there a problem?" they asked.

"Nothing I can't handle,"Jordan said still looking at Metzger, "and this is your first and last warning, If the word nigger comes out of your mouth one more time on this show, I'll have you removed from the set."

"Quiet on the set, Jordan we're back in ten," the floor director shouted.

Hearing that, Jordan made his was back to his mark to begin the next segment. The floor director cued the audience to began applause.

"In three, two, one," counted the floor director.

"Welcome back,..." Jordan began as the applause died down. "Hatred's Burning Question' is the focus of today's show. When we left, Miles was telling us about the generosity and vision of Kenny Cox whose hopes and dreams went up in smoke when the Resource Center was torched. So, Miles did you talk with Kenny after the fire?..."

"Yes, he was quiet and not very talkative. He had lost his will to live. Seeing the Center open was the only thing keeping him alive."

"And now with the Center gone..."

"Kenny said he didn't have anything to live for..."

"One less nigger fag to worry about..." Metzger said looking at Miles.

"Hold up Howard. Since you're joining in the conversation let me reintroduce you to our viewers... ladies and gentleman, meet Howard Metzger, leader of the Aryan Protectors, a white separatist group who believes that sometimes you have to take matters into you own hands, by any means necessary. Please welcome him at this time..."

No one in the audience applauded except for these three white guys on the front row. To look at them, they were obviously followers.

"Your ignorance is showing my brotha..."

"I ain't you brotha..."

"Like it or not, we're all apart of the same race, get over it..." Miles answered.

"Don't start that human race crap, the only true race is white race..."Metzger shouted.

"Okay... Howard, let me ask you this..." Jordan said trying to maintain control of the show, "where does all the hate come from?"

"Hatred! Is that what you people call it. I call it keeping the race pure..."

"Then why burn down the church and the center?..." Jordan asked.

"Who says that my group burned down anything?"Metzger recanted.

"The mayor's investigative task force has received correspondence from people identifying themselves as part of your organization and claiming responsibility for the burning..."Jordan said with intensity.

Metzger was silent as the audience booed him; he just sat with a smug look on his face. Jordan asked him again if his organization had anything to do with the burning. He just stared at Jordan.

"Earlier in your introduction, I quoted you as saying that you would get your point across, by any means necessary..." Jordan said since it was evident that Metzger wasn't about to admit his guilt. "And your point is..."

"My point is, do those means include burning down a building and desecrating God's house to get your point across?" Jordan asked staring Metzger in the face.

"No, but I would kill a nigger like you..."

"I think this is a good place to take a break!" the producer told the floor director in his headset. He tried to give Jordan the break signal, but he had some unfinished business to take care of.

"That's it! You know I let the first one slide because I wanted to let you get the point out, but I warned you about calling anyone here a 'nigger'...I'm asking, no make that telling you to leave Mr. Metzger..."

All of the audience applauded Jordan taking a stand, all except Metzger's cronies who started chanting "White is Right, Black go Back!"

Needless to say security ended that real quick.

"Nigger you better watch you back..." Metzger shouted as security escorted him away and the audience broke out into thunderous applause, as he was taken out.

"We'll try to get this conversation back on track and let the rest of our guests speak when we continue, right after this."

The floor director didn't have to cue the audience to applaud, they already were.

"Jordan, I'm proud of you!" Miles said winking at his friend.

"Just doing the right thing,..."

Jordan's producer came out of the booth to check on him.

"You okay?" the producer asked.

"Yep! Sorry about that, but I couldn't let him continue or we would have been"Geraldo" all over again, I don't want to make a name for myself like that."

"We're here my brotha?" The producer said trying to break the intensity of what had just occurred moments before.

Jordan had to laughed at his producer's attempt at cool, especially since Megan was blonde and blue-eyed.

She briefed him on the upcoming segments and had the stage hand move the vacant chair off the set. The audience was buzzing with excitement and people were commenting on what had just happened; they were ready to say their piece. Jordan informed the balding, slightly overweight gentleman from "Straight Laced" that he would be coming to him first in this segment.

"You okay?" Jordan asked all of his guests.

"I'm ready as I can be sir," David Mayes said eagerly as the other guests just nodded.

"Okay stand by..." the floor director shouted cuing the audience. When the show came back on the air, Jordan was sitting in the midst of the empty seats where Metzger's followers had been sitting.

"Welcome back, the room seems a little brighter don't you think?"

With that statement the audience stood applauding, chanting Jordan's name.

He smiled and told them to have their seats.

"Where do you think you are, *Springer*? Just kidding Jerry!"

Everyone laughed including Jordan, He thought that everyone could use a tension breaker including himself. But he quickly regained his composure and prepared to ask the next question.

"Let me go the guest that we haven't heard from..." Jordan began."David Mayes is the founder and city director of "Straight Laced," the organization that opposed the opening of the Center. Please welcome him at this time."

As the audience began to applaud, a few members of a gay rights organization decided to boo!

"C'mon guys! You haven't even heard what he has to say!" Jordan interjected, "so let's give him a chance to bring his perspective to the discussion."

"Thank you!" Mayes said nodding to Jordan.

"You're welcome, so let's start here. Mr. Mayes, you opposed the Center's opening and were very vocal, correct..."

"Yes, sir! We believed that this Center was actually going to be nothing more than an orgy house for those people..."

Some of the audience members snickered at his comment.

"And what made you think that?" Jordan asked surprised at Mayes' answer.

"You know that when *those* people get together all they have on their minds is sex..." Mayes said as if he knew this to be a fact.

"Oh really? Is that so?" Jordan said questioning the primitive thinking of his guest.

"Yes sir, it's a fact!"

"Let me ask the counselor on the panel," Jordan said directing the next question to Miles.

"Miles you counsel gays and lesbians, is that all on their minds?.."

"It's really the last thing on their minds. Most of the gays and lesbians that I counsel are more concerned with being estranged from their families and coping with the loss of friends or a partner."

"To AIDS most likely," Mayes blurted out.

"It's no secret that AIDS infected and affected gays first, but thats not the case as much anymore and..." Miles said.

"See I told you, even he has to admit it..." Mayes interrupted.

"May I finish..." Miles said, "but they also are mourning the loss of relationships..."

"Psychobable..." Mayes mumbled

"Point in case, have you never been in love and you were dumped?" Miles asked Mayes.

"No, never, I married the first and only woman that I loved," Mayes said. "Stand-up baby and let them see my beauty queen for the past twenty years."

Mrs. Mayes stood blushing and waved to the audience like she was Miss America; the audience applauded.

"That's wonderful, especially in this age of divorce. But Mr. Mayes, you do understand that you are the exception to the rule, right?" Miles asked.

"That's because I have a normal life!" Mayes responded.

"Normal?" Jordan asked with a puzzled look on his face and tone in his voice.

"Yes! There is nothing normal about homosexuality..." Mayes said in a aggressive tone.

"Says you..." Miles interjected.

"Well, you're one of them so.." Mayes said accusingly.

"Exactly, and I'm "normal!" Miles said exasperated with Mayes.

"Says you, but according to psychological studies gays are not normal people..." Mayes said with a somewhat disgusted tone..

"And what studies are those?" Miles inquired.

"Numerous studies, including the Religious Observation of Deviant..."

"Stop right there, this is one of those studies that are bought and paid for by organizations such as the one your head.."

"Well, yes it was, but..."

"You bring me scientific data and real psychological studies regarding homosexuality and we can talk!" Miles said.

"Mr. Mayes, can you produce the data that Dr. Robertson is requesting?" Jordan asked, waiting for Mayes to hang himself.

"Hold on Mr. Mayes. Let me take this one!" Reverend Jacobs interjected. "Dr. Robertson, I've got proof and here it is..." he said holding up a rather large Bible.

"Reverend Jacobs, you say that you have proof?" Jordan said addressing his father.

"Yes, in the word of God it says...." Reverend Jacobs began.

"Nope, nope, nope! Hold on! I can see where this is going and we're getting too far off the subject," Jordan said interrupting his father.

"In Leviticus it says..." Reverend Jacobs said trying to continue.

"Reverend with all due respect, I said 'no,'" Jordan said as politely as he could.

"How can you say no to the word of God?" Reverend Jacobs shouted.

"Reverend Jacobs, I am not saying no to the word of God, I'm saying no to you!"

"How dare you? I raised you better than this! I can't believe that you would bring me on television and disrespect me! You see Mamie, this is what we raised!" his father said directing the comment to his mother who was sitting in the audience.

Mrs. Jacobs put her finger up to her mouth trying to get Reverend

Jacobs to "hush up."

"I never did get a chance to introduce our last guest. This is Reverend Hezikiah J. Jacobs, pastor of Mount Moriah Baptist, the church that was burned as a result of the fire at the Resource Center and if you haven't guessed by now, my father," Jordan said in his introduction of his father.

He should have listened to his first mind; this show was not a good idea.

"And right about now, I am ashamed to call you my son..." Reverend Jacobs added at the conclusion of the introduction.

"Hezikiah! You, hush this instant! Don't embarrass yourself or me for that matter.You are on live television" Mrs. Jacobs shouted from the audience.

The audience couldn't help, but laugh at the Jacobs', even Jordan had to laugh at his mother's last comment.

"Okay, let's settle down before my father sends me to my room!" Jordan said trying to humorously regain control of the show. He only prayed that he could. "Pop, I mean Reverend Jacobs, I meant no disrespect, but we're not here to debate homosexuality, that's a whole other show." The audience applauded, most of them feeling for Jordan right at that moment.

"We're hear to talk about the burning of the church and the Resource Center." Jordan said trying to get the show back on the topic.

He took a deep cleansing breath before asking his next question,. He thought that he would go Miles with the next question giving his father a chance to cool down.

"So what happens now? Are there plans to rebuild the center?"

Miles talked about the plans to rebuild and a candlelight vigil that was being planned in Kenny's memory.

"We would also like to extend an invitation to Reverend Jacobs and the Mount Moriah church family and anyone else to join us in a show of solidarity, sending out the message that even hate can't keep us down."

"So Reverend Jacobs, will you and members be attending the vigil?" Jordan asked with hope brimming from his voice.

"Son, you know that Mount Moriah means the world to me, I built that church up from a storefront to the church it is today. It was like seeing all of my children killed when I watched it burning. It was like someone sucked the life out of me. So to answer your questions, yes I'll attend the vigil..."

Jordan was shocked. "Was his father coming around?" he asked himself.

The audience erupted into a thunderous ovation.

"When..." Reverend Jordan continued, "when hell freezes over. I would rather skate through Hell in gasoline drawers than honor some homosexual that was partly responsible for what happened to my church. I would march with Metzger and his crew or the KKK before I would join hands with a bunch of deviants and diseased fags." he concluded.

You could hear a pin drop. Everyone was shocked, everyone except Jordan.

Forty-Nine

"Amen."

"You bettah sing that song!"

"Halleluia!!"

"Praise Him!"

"C'mon choir!"

The choir had the church on it's feet. Harrison was sweating so much that his robe was drenched. Sister Brooks had shouted her wig lopsided and the ushers were trying to contain her. You would have thought that the church orchestra was playing back up to one of the hottest musical acts in the country, their sound was crisp, so clean, it was all that. The choir finished their selection and the church gave them a standing ovation. You could tell they wanted more, so they gave it to them. This time they threw in a little choreography which frenzied the congregation. Sister Brooks was up and shouting with a new found energy, but this time the wig stayed on straight.

Since the main sanctuary was now under renovation, services were being held in the the Family Life Center and it was packed to capacity. Both Jordan and Zander were surprised at the number of people who were in service, especially after his father's rather revealing appearance on his show. It was almost as if no one had seen the show last night.

The choir was about to finish their encore as Reverend Jacobs approached the podium with his usual dignity; that had been one of Jordan's favorite moments as a child. His father's approach was always so reverential, it was as if he received power with ever step he took.

"Let everybody say 'praise the Lord!'" Reverend Jacobs shouted with effervescence

"Praise the Lord!" the congregation responded.

"For this is the day that the Lord has made," Reverend Jacobs began.

"And we shall rejoice and be glad!" the congregation replied with enthusiasm.

"If you're really glad, stand to your feet and give the Lord some praise!"

The church stood to its feet and you could hear people praising God all over the building. Sister Brooks was like a jumping jack, this time the ushers just let her jump. Jordan smiled as he remember the time Sister Brooks got so caught up in the spirit that she shouted her wig off.

"That's right church, give him some praise!" Reverend Jacobs encouraged the congregation to really offer up some praise.

"Did he wake you up this morning? Did he start you on your way? Was there a roof over your head? Food on your table? "Reverend Jacobs asked the congregation as the sweat poured from his brow prompting them to praise God for His goodness and blessings.

"Who wouldn't serve a God like that?" he asked rhetorically.

With that said the church went into fifth gear as the church orchestra started playing a vamp and you guessed it, there went Sister Brooks. Before you knew it she was in the aisle doing her dance. The ushers looked one to the other to see who was going to tend to her that time. This time the "Go Git It Committee," you know, the sisters in the church that form a circle around the people shouting all over the place, lay clothes over people that have shouted themselves unconscious, or help them back to their seats were up and in formation. Sister Brooks just shouted even more, she wasn't coming down anytime soon.

"That's right praise him daughter" a sister with this hat covered in feathers shouted encouraging her to get her praise on.

"Let the Lord use ya!" the sister with the oversized pillbox shouted.

"Give it up, Give it up, Give it up!" the little lady with the sequin covered beret.

And shout she did.

"Shout Halleluia!" Reverend Jacobs instructed the crowd.

"Halleluia!"they shouted back.

"Shout Glory!"he continued

"Glory!" they replied

"Tell Him Thank Ya!"

"Thank Ya!"

"Ain't God good church!"

"Yes, he is!" they answered.

"Say Amen!"

"Amen!"

"Say Amen again!"

"Amen!"

"One more time..."

"Amen!"

"One for the Father! One for the Son and one for the Holy Ghost!" Reverend Jacobs said motioning for the congregation to take their seats. By this time even the "Go Git It Committee" had given up, so he signaled for one of the ushers to help Sister Brooks to her seat. The usher nervously approached and helped her to her seat. As she sat you could see her feeling to see if her wig was in place tugging on it just in case.

"Shall we pray..." Reverend Jacobs began. In the course of his prayer he mentioned the sick and shut-in, the bereaved families, the ministries and the homeless. He thanked God for allowing it to be as well it was, for bringing him through dangers, seen and unseen. He even prayed for the people that had burned their church. But much to Jordan's dismay there was not one mention of the Center or Kenny Cox; he squeezed Zander's hand for strength. He too was praying his own prayer that his father would come around and apologize for his comments on last night's show.

"And the people of God said amen."

"Amen!" the congregation responded.

"Didn't this choir sing out of their souls this morning!" Reverend Jacobs began, "I am so blessed to have one of, no make that the best choir in this city, maybe even the country. Many pastors would give their eye teeth for such an anointed choir. Church give it up for Minister Delaney and this fine group of musicians. You all are awesome! Simply awesome." The congregation gave the music ministry a standing ovation.

"I know that Sister Jacobs would have been so proud of you all this morning. She's under the weather today, so keep her in your prayers."

"She was probably too embarrassed to even show her face after last night..." Jordan whispered to Zander.

"Si!" Zander whispered back.

"What you wanna bet that he's going to pretend like nothing happened..." Jordan whispered.

Sister Brooks turned back looking over her glasses at Zander and Jordan with a disapproving shake of head. They both smiled like guilty school boys.

"This morning we won't worry you long! We thank God for another opportunity to lift His name and share His word with His people. Beyond a shadow of a doubt, I know that God has a word for us today. My brothers and sisters, we are living in perilous times and God is not pleased."

Jordan's heart began to beat with each word that his father spoke, he knew where this sermon was going. He and Zander looked at each other and took a deep breath. They had a feeling that this was not going to be a feel good, going up yonder kind of sermon.

"Most recently, we suffered the loss of our home..."

"Yes," members of the congregation moaned in agreement.

"We fell victim to the hands of hatred..."

"Yes, sir," the deacon's chimed in.

"To no fault of our own, we were the innocent party!"

"Yes, we were..." people responded all over the congregation.

"I don't know about you, but when the fires lashed out at us I became angry..."

"Help yourself preacher!" the deaconess corner sang.

"Here goes..." Zander whispered to Jordan.

"Ready or not!" Jordan whispered back.

"Not!" they both mouthed.

"We didn't do anything to warrant this..."

"No, we didn't" the congregation answered.

"And now my brothers and sisters, the real reason behind our troubles is asking us to hold hands with them. Are we going to hold hands with sin itself?"

"No, we won't" the congregation answered back.

"They want us to condone sin and we can't. Are we suppose to turn our heads and pretend we don't know who and what they are?

"No, sir!" the congregation shouted.

"I don't believe this!" Zander wrote to on the church program and slipped it to Jordan.

Jordan didn't respond, he just sat with tears streaming down his face.

"I know the Bible says love thy neighbor, but how can you love the likes of them..."

"Well," the deacon's chimed in.

Zander sat quietly praying for this to be over soon; he could see the pain on his partner's face. Jordan sat still and silent, he knew that his father hated homosexuals, but he never thought that he hated him too. He asked himself how could his father go on a tirade like this one or the one he went on the night before without even giving his son the slightest consideration. Knowing how he felt was one thing, but to actually witness him spewing hatred from behind the sacred desk really was more than he could bear. He was reared to respect the pulpit and its sanctity. "I guess all of that goes out of the window today.." he thought to himself. He could feel himself getting sicker with every word. This was his father doing this; not some white televangelist, but the man who gave him life, the man that he loved and thought loved him in return."How?" he asked himself as his father continued his sermon of hate.

"Last night if you watched the television show that I was on, you heard the story of how the building next door was going to be used as "Resource Center" for gays and lesbians. A place where they could be healed, nurtured, a place where they come for support. Well my dear brothers and sisters, I say to those who say that they need healing, seek Jesus..."

"Amen," the congregation shouted as several members stood to their feet in support of the pastor's statement.

"The Bible says that if they would turn from their wicked ways! He would heal them...didn't He say it!"

"Yes, He did!" the amen corner chinned in.

"Nurtured, is that what they call it when two men are all hugged up, one trying to be a man and the other taking on a role that God meant for the woman?" Somebody tell me what kind of sick behavior is that? God made Adam and Eve..."

"C'mon, Adam and Steve again, can't he be more original?" Zander thought to himself.

"And not Adam and Steve..."Reverend Jacobs continued. "That's taking loving your brother a little too far!"

"You better preach today!" could be heard all of the building.

Zander looked at the members of the music ministry and he could see the hurt on the faces of those he knew were gay. Some had tears in their eyes, others looked like they had just lost their best friend. He looked at Jordan, and his heart broke. His partner sat quietly hurting, but the pain on his face told it all.

"I know that there are some of you here today who would say 'Brother Pastor, we need to love everybody, maybe they were born that way, or maybe there was no male figure in the home or maybe something tragic happened in the their childhood...' And while I'm sorry for anything that happens in the life of a child, you can't make me believe that this is the case with most of these people. I don't buy it and if you do somebody's selling you a bill of goods and I've got a couple of bridges and some swamp land to sell you!" Reverend Jacobs said as he stopped to take a sip of water from the glass that rested on the podium. He wiped the sweat from his brow and took a moment to catch his breath while the church clapped and said amen to his last comments.

"All you have to do is turn it over to Jesus and He'll make everything all right. Won't He do it church? "Don't you know He will!"

"Yes He will!" Sister Brooks stood up shouting back in agreement.

"Fix your wig, your kitchen is showing..." Zander thought to himself. He thought about sharing his thought with Jordan to make him laugh, but he could see that even humor wasn't going to help at that moment. While he was hurting too, he knew that his pain paled in comparison to his partner's.

"I'm sick and tired of people showing up on these talk shows and crying about they were abused as children and that this is why they abused drugs and became sexually addicted..." he said as he wiped his brow again. "Oprah is to blame for a lot of this. She blamed being fat on her being abused. She sat on TV weeping and crying and America bought it! I blame it on her not knowing when to put the fork down!" The church chuckled at his observation.

He continued, "No man in the household, they were raised in a house full of women, his mother was domineering-all excuses. So what? A lot of people were raised by the single mothers who had to be strong, but you don't see them finger snapping and switching all over the place. Let a man be a man and a woman be a woman." With that said a contingency of the single sisters stood giving each other high fives.

"And just like God destroyed Sodom and Gomorrah, he destroyed that building. It's time for a change, God tried to warn the gay community, but they wouldn't listen. So AIDS is their destiny! If they hadn't been abusing their bodies and sleeping with anything that walked, a lot of them would be here today!"

The sermon continued for what seemed to be an eternity. Jordan thought about walking out, but he knew that this would only cause more confusion. So he and Zander sat through the rest of his father's sermon. He looked at the gay men and women in the choir and the joy that had graced their faces just a few short minutes ago was now replaced with hurt and even shame.

Finally the sermon was over and as Reverend Jacobs finished his hate filled sermon most of the congregation stood applauding their pastor. Several of the closeted and married men in the church were up giving each other high fives and applauding the sermon with zeal. Jordan thought he was going to be sick.

After service Reverend Jacobs was in the back of the church greeting members; there was a line of people waiting to greet him and shake his hand. The mere sight made Jordan feel even worse, especially since several of the choir members were in the line also. While he and Zander were waiting on several of the members of the choir to go out for lunch, Mrs. Clay, a petite, gray haired woman wearing pointed spectacles, made her way to Jordan. Her steps were short but deliberate. Jordan began smiling as he saw her approaching.

"How my boys doing today?" she said speaking to Zander and Jordan.

"Fine," they both said trying to mask their hurt.

"You wouldn't lie to Mrs. Clay would you?"

"No, ma'am," they said like little boys back in Sunday school.

Zander saw Harrison and wanted to go check on him, he excused himself and made his way through the crowd. As he left Mrs. Clay noticed the look on Jordan's face.

"Son, now tell me the truth," she asked Jordan with genuine concern in her voice as she reached to hug him. Jordan bent down to hug his Sunday school teacher, mentor and favorite member of his father's church.

"Right about now, I'm not sure" Jordan answered trying to fight back tears.

"It's okay baby! You know that I love you no matter what, don't you?" she said kissing his cheek and patting his back.

"Yes ma'am," Jordan said as a tear fell.

"And most importantly never forget that God loves you! He made you just the way you are and He makes no mistakes," Mrs. Clay said still hugging her favorite pupil and protege.

"Thank you Mrs. Clay!" he said smiling.

"You and Zander come by and see me sometime, okay!" she said returning his smile and patting his hand reassuringly, "I'll make a soul food dinner and your favorite, sweet potato casserole. "

"It's a date!" he promised.

"Okay, I'm going to hold you to that or I'll put both of you over my knee and give you a good whipping," she said smiling.

"I promise..." he said winking.

Zander found Harrison; he was visibly shaken by the sermon. He hugged Zander and they talked about what had just occurred. Harrison told him that he had tendered his resignation and that he wouldn't be attending Mount Moriah, anymore.

"Well you know we got your back" Zander assured him, "So are you coming to eat?"

"I'm really not hungry..."

"C'mon, a bunch of us are going to Allie Mae's for gospel brunch..."

"Nah! I think I'm going to go home and just chill, think about what I'm going to do now that I'm not going to be here."

"Hey! We all need some support right about now, especially Jordan. So what do you say?"

"Aiight, I guess you're right! Strength in numbers and all that..."

"And you know this..." Zander said smiling at a rather bewildered Harrison.

Brunch at Allie Mae's was quite different today, they were quiet and played with their food. While it was obvious that everyone there felt like they had been punched in the stomach they all knew that no one could possibly feel as beaten up as Jordan. Maybe brunch wasn't such a good idea after all.

Jordan was quiet all the way home, Zander tried making small talk, but his partner's one and two word answers were an indication that he wasn't in the mood to talk. When they arrived, Jordan said that he needed to be alone.

"I'll be back in a bit..."

"Where you going?"

"Driving, I need to clear my head..."

"I understand."

They smiled and Zander reached in a gave Jordan a quick peck in the cheek.

"Thanks babe..."

"See you when you get back..."

"I won't be gone too long.."

"I love you!"

"Love you more!"

Jordan mustered up a smile as Zander closed the door to the car. As he drove off he didn't have any idea where he was going, he just needed to drive.

Fifty

"What's wrong?"

"What makes you think anything is wrong?"

"Who are you talking to?"

"You ma!"

"Exactly and mother's know their children and I know you!"

"Nothing's wrong, can't a fella call his mother?"

"Any other fella yes! You...no!"

"You act like I never call!"

"I didn't say that now did I?..."

"Well, no..."

"I hear from you all the time, but rarely on Sundays. Now do I have to guess why you called?"

"No, I'll tell you!"

"Baby what's wrong?"

Zander began telling his mother about the past couple of days. He told her about the show and how Reverend Jacobs said he would march with the Klan if they were protesting against gays and lesbians. Rita was dumbfounded. At first she thought Zander was kidding, but soon realized that he wasn't.

"The Klan?"

"Yes ma'am. The first time Jordan told me that I thought he was exaggerating, but I heard it for myself."

"And he said it on live television?"

"Live!"

"Sounds like baggage to me..."

"More like storage..."

"Where is Jordan? Put him on the phone.."

"He's not here...

Zander went on to tell her about the services and how Reverend Jacobs let gays and lesbians have it with both barrels. Rita could hear the pain in her son's voice and her heart went out to both Zander and Jordan. She tried her best to console Zander and let him know that she was in their corner no matter what.

"And when Jordan gets back, tell him to call "Big Mama," I got some love here just for him..."

"Mom, thank you..."

"Chile for what!"

"For being so understanding and supportive..."

"What else am I gonna do? It's my job, boy!"

"What did I do to deserve a mother like you?"

"Just lucky I guess, God knew who you needed...and by the way I'm the lucky one!"

"Ma, you my girl!"

"Now hold on son, I have to be honest..."

"Bout what?"

"It took me a while to get used to the idea, but I had to realize that it wasn't anything I did or didn't do. This is just who you are and the easiest thing to do was to accept it and just be there for you."

"I wish that Reverend and Mrs. Jacobs could be that way when it comes to Jordan..."

"Baby, it takes time...just keep them in your prayers."

"I do and so does Jordan..."

"And that's all you can do...and love em' in spite of.."

"I do and so does Jordan, but they don't make it easy..."

"And nobody said it would be..."

"But Ma, it hurts me to see my partner hurting like this...he's been a good son. He's smart, intelligent, successful...any parent would be proud to have him as their son, except his..."

"Baby, they can't get beyond his orientation, it has them blinded..."

"But being gay is such a small part of who we are and every body else makes it a big deal..."

"To you, but to a parent it is a big deal. Once again it takes time..."

"And with each day that goes by, they push him further and further away..."

"Only if he let's them... remember son, Jesus never stopped loving the people that crucified Him and neither can Jordan..."

"I know that Ma, he hasn't stopped loving them, but he feels like his parents don't love him.I mean his mother still thinks that it's a phase he's going through and his father...well you know how he feels..."

"Baby, that's their problem not Jordan's..."

"See that's why you my girl..."

"And you know this..." Rita said laughing.

"No you didn't steal my line....

"Your line huh? You got papers?"

"Ma! Hold on, I have another call..." Zander said laughing at his mother when the phone beeped.

"I can talk to you later..."

"No hold on Ma, I'll get rid of who ever it is..."

With that said he put Rita on hold switching to the other line.

"Hello!"

"Hello may I speak with Zander please..." the female voice said on the other end of the phone.

"This is he..."

"This is Mamie Jacobs, Jordan's mother..."

"Yes, ma'am if you're looking for Jordan...."

"No son, I'm calling because there's been a horrible accident..."

"What kind of accident?" Zander asked as panic consumed him.

"Jordan has been beaten, very badly...in fact he's unconscious..."

"Okay, ummm let me get my mother off the phone and..."

"We're at Community Hospital in the emergency room. Hurry son, it's really bad..."

Zander could hear the urgency and fear in her voice as she hung up. He clicked back over to Rita.

"Ma, you still there?"

"Finally, I was just about to hang up..." Rita said giving Zander the business about keeping her on hold for so long.

"Ma! Ma..." Zander said sobbing as the reality of what Mrs. Jacobs had said set in.

"Son, Z...what is it?"

"It's Jordan, he's been in some kind of accident..."

"Baby, what do you mean an accident?"

"I don't know, it...that.. was Mrs. Jacobs...she was at the hospital..."

"The hospital..."

"Yes Ma'am...Jordan is unconscious and she says it is real bad and that I need to hurry. It must be bad if she wants me there..."

"Oh Lord Jesus," Rita said almost whispering. "Baby get off the phone and try to calm down. Call Miles and ask him to drive you to the hospital, he's probably the closest and the quickest. I'm gonna get on the next plane coming that way!"

"Okay Ma..."

"And Zander..."

"Yes Ma..."

"I love you..." Those words gave Zander a sense of security and peace all at the same time.

"I love you too Ma!"

"Son,..."

"Ma'am?"

"Pray..."

"Yes Ma'am...bye..." Zander whispered.

Zander pressed the speed dial and Miles answered the phone on the first ring.

"Hello, this is Miles..."

"Miles, it's Zander.."

"Are you okay?"

"It's Jordan.."

"What about Jord..."

"He's been hurt, he's at Community...can you drive me?..."

"I'll see you in 10 minutes...make that five..."

"I'll be outside..."

"Zander hold on, I'm on the way! I love you boy!"

"Me too," Zander said as he hung up the phone. Mamie's words echoed in his head as he got his keys and his wallet. He checked to make sure he had all of the info for the hospital. He set the alarm and locked the door behind him. He paced up and down the driveway waiting on Miles. He couldn't wait any longer, he was in his car when Miles pulled up.

"Hey! I'm sorry it took me so long...accident on Brien and Mitchell..."

"I was just about to leave..."

"C'mon, you're in no shape to drive..."

Zander shut off the car and grabbed his wallet. He hit the car alarm as he jumped in Miles' Jeep. Miles could see the look of panic in Zander's eyes.

"Zander, take a deep breath..."

"Can we go please?..."

"Okay, but you have to calm down...you need to be calm and cool for Jordan...okay?"

"Okay, I'm calm..."

"Yeah right..." Miles said as they sped off to Community. Zander sat quietly whispering a pray for his partner as he stared out the window.

"God, I'm helpless, but you can help. I'm scared, but you are fearless. Speak your sweet peace to my heart now. Lord send an angel of protection to Jordan's bedside. Please Lord let him be okay, I need him to be okay! In Jesus' name..."

"Amen," he said out loud before he realized it.

"You say something?..."

"No, just thinking out loud..."

"You aiight?..."

"I don't know..."

"Hang on...we'll be there in a bit..." Miles said massaging Zander's shoulder.

"Okay..." Zander said trying to muster up a smile for his friend.

He took a deep breath and looked out the window. He didn't know what he was looking for, but what he did know was that it had to be out there some where. Maybe he was looking for a sign, one that said it was gonna be okay.

"Paging Dr. Williams, paging Dr. Williams..."

"Paging Dr. Forde, paging Dr. Forde..."

"I'm looking for Jordan Jacobs..." Zander told the information nurse as he rushed in to the ER.

"He is in surgery at this time..."

"Surgery? For what?" Zander asked panicing

"Sir, please lower your voice..." the nurse said rolling her eyes at Zander. "I don't have that information..."

"Well who does?" Zander asked through clenched teeth.

"The doctor will be out to talk with the family as soon as the surgery is over..." the nurse informed Zander.

"Where is the surgery waiting room?" Zander asked.

"Its on the third floor west..."

"Thank you..." Zander said as he and Miles took off for the third floor.

"Zander slow down..." Miles said trying to keep up.

"Sorry, I just need some answers..."

"Here we are..." Miles said as they found the west wing elevators.

"Third Floor West..." the elevator's automated voice prompt announced.

As Zander and Miles approached the nurses' station, they saw Reverend and Mrs. Jacobs in the surgery waiting room.

"Reverend and Mrs. Jacobs, you remember Dr. Miles Robertson...."

"What in God's name is he doing here?" Reverend Jacobs said staring at Miles.

"I needed someone to drive me and Miles lives in our neighborhood, so he was kind enough... why am I explaining this... how is Jordan?" Zander asked frustrated at the reception they received.

"We don't know anything yet Zander, they just took him into emergency surgery..." Mamie informed him.

"Was it a car accident?" Zander asked trying to make sense of the whole thing.

"No! It was all because of the building again!" Reverend Jacobs said in an angry tone.

"The Resource Center?" Zander and Miles asked, totally confused.

"Yes, that building had destroyed my church and now my son! How much more do I have to loose because of you people?" Reverend Jacobs asked in a hurt and angry voice.

"What does the Resource Center have to do with this?" Miles asked.

Mrs. Jacobs told Zander and Miles that she and Reverend Jacobs were sitting in the living room when they heard someone yelling and pleading for help. It seems that Jordan was driving to see his parents, or so they assumed, when he saw a gang of men vandalizing the Resource Center's remains and he tried to stop them. Instead of running off, they retaliated and started beating Jordan. It was after they had left that he made it to the sidewalk and was calling for help when he collapsed. His father found him lying on the sidewalk in a pool of blood with the words "nigger faggot" spray painted on his clothes and face.

"They beat him so bad that his daddy didn't even recognize him at first..." Mamie said breaking down and collapsing into her husband's arms sobbing.

"This is all your fault! You do know that don't you?" Reverend Jacobs said directing the comment at Miles. "If it wasn't for you and that Center my son wouldn't have been there."

"Does anyone know anything about Jordan's condition yet?" Zander asked ignoring Reverend Jacobs last comment.

"Not yet..." Mamie managed to get out in between sobs.

The next couple of hours seemed more like days. Zander had sent Miles to the airport to pick up Rita. He wanted to go, but he didn't want to leave in case there was any news. Reverend and Mrs. Jacobs didn't say much to him, but then again he really didn't expect them to considering how they felt about gays. The waiting was killing him and so was the silence. He needed to hear a friendly voice... Zander called Desmond to let him know what was going on.

"No!" Desmond shrieked.

"According to his mother he was beaten beyond recognition.." Zander said shuddering at the thought of Jordan being beaten that badly.

"I'm on the next plane out..."

"I would give anything to have you here, but Moms should be here at any moment," Zander informed Desmond.

"That's good, but you know I'll be on the next broom leaving if you need me..."

Zander had to chuckle at the visual that accompanied Desmond's last statement.

"Thanks Desi, how's Eli?"

"He's fine, but we'll talk about that later..."

"Oh, okay..."

"So promise me that you'll let me know anything as soon as you know something, okay Z baby."

"I promise..."

"You know that I'm praying for Jordan and you..."

"Yep! Hey, here comes Mom, so I'll holler at you later. Okay?...."

"Tell Diva, I said hello."

"You can tell her yourself," Zander said handing Rita the phone in their midst of a quick hug.

"Hello?" Rita answered somewhat baffled.

"Moms wassup, its your favorite child..."

"Hello baby and how are you? Long time no talk to. I don't even see you online anymore..."

"I know, haven't been on the computer much these days..."

"You, Miss AOL..."

"No you didn't..."

"Yes I did, now what you gonna do about it? Rita asked with a smile on her face and a twinkle in her eye.

"Not a thang Missy, when you right you right..."

"Well baby, I'm gonna let you speak back to Zander, so you go pick up your face and we'll talk soon," Rita said handing the phone back to Zander.

"See that's what you get for messing with Mutha Nature...."

"You ain't never lied..." Desmond said chuckling.

"Well, I'll talk to you later, be good okay..."

"Only if I have to..."

"Love you Desi, keep Jordan in your prayers, okay?..." Zander said as the serious tone returned in his voice.

"I'll keep all of you in my prayers..." Desmond corrected.

"Peace Des!"

"You too Z baby"

"What, no real hug for your mama?" Rita said with her arms stretched wide.

"How much you got?" Zander said smiling and hugging his mother.

"Ma this is is Reverend and Mrs. Jacobs, Jordan's parents... this is my mother Rita Eady"

"Nice to meet you both even in this unfortunate situation..." Rita said as she shook both of their hands.

"Likewise, I'm sure..." Mamie said patting Rita's hand.

"I'm so sorry that this has happened, Jordan is such a wonderful young man."

"Yes, he didn't deserve this..." Zander said holding on to Rita.

"No, he didn't..." Rita echoed.

"Where is that doctor?...Someone has to know something..." Zander said getting frustrated again.

"Son, calm down..." Rita said hoping that she could get Zander to calm down.

"Your mother is right, getting frustrated isn't going to help Jordan or his parents or you for that matter. So come sit down and try to calm down," Miles said.

"For once he said something that I agree with" Reverend Jacobs chimed in, "why don't you all just go home? After all this is a family matter."

"I am his family! Jordan is my partner. We love each other, we support each other and..."

"And what? If there are any medical decisions to be made I will make them for my son, not you, me! In fact if I wanted you removed from here I could have you thrown out..." Reverend Jacobs said with that look of hate present in eyes.

"You can go to..." Zander said when Rita interrupted.

"Zander Evan..." Rita said giving him her "that's enough, you better quit while you're ahead" look.

"Son, you better listen to your mother..." Reverend Jacobs reassured.

Zander wanted to say something so bad, but he knew that his mother was right. Anything he said would set Reverend Jacobs off and as much as he didn't want to admit it, he didn't have a leg to stand on if anything happened to Jordan. This was one of the harsh realities of being in a relationship that isn't honored in the legal system or by families. He was sure that if anything happened, God forbid, he would not be given a voice in any decisions regarding Jordan's health, especially considering the way Reverend Jacobs felt about homosexuals. Zander felt helpless.

"Is there any word yet?" Zander asked at the nurse's station.

"No sir, at last check Mr. Jacobs was still in surgery," the charge nurse informed him.

"Okay, thank you..."Zander said letting out a huge sigh as he walked back to the waiting room.

"Any word?" Rita asked

"No Ma'am."

Zander sat next to Rita and rested his head on her shoulder. He was glad that Rita was there, he didn't want to face Jordan's parents alone. He thought back over their relationship and smiled, remembering their first date and all of their special moments, before he knew it, tears were falling. Rita noticed them and wiped them away. She thought to herself, "if only she could wipe away the hurt as easily."

"Son, let them fall, no harm in crying..." Rita said reassuringly.

"Mama, I don't want to loose him..." Zander said, finally confronting the fact that this could happen.

"Don't even think like that..."

"I'm trying not to, but he's been in surgery for an awfully long time..."

"Better he be in there a long time, than come out and have to go right back in..."

"You're right Ma"

"And you know this..." Rita said winking and trying to get a smile out of Zander.

"Ma! So am I gonna get a new Daddy?" Zander said wanting to change the subject to try and get his mind off Jordan for just a little while.

"I'm still praying...." Rita told him.

"Well do what you have to do, I only want you to be happy!"

"Oscar's not pressuring me; he knows that I'll give him an answer when I have one. I know he won't wait for ever."

"He will if he knows what's good for him..." he said kissing his mother's forehead.

"Oh go on boy!" she said pushing him away. The two of them sat there giggling in each other's arms.

"Well, I'm glad somebody can find something to laugh about. My son is in there fighting for his life and the two of you are laughing and giggling..." Reverend Jacobs said looking at the two of them, his voice was filled with resentment, "So this is how much you care about him, huh son?..."

"Reverend Jacobs, I have had just about enough of you talking to my son like this..." Rita began.

"Ma..." Zander said trying to calm Rita down.

"No son, he started this and now I think it's time for me to finish it! Now your son is in there fighting for his life and all you can do is blame everybody else for your pain. Well don't look this way. Try a mirror Reverend Jacobs. My son loves Jordan, can you say the same? Now you may not understand or accept their loving each other, but the reality is they do. So now either accept it or get over it. You call yourself a Man of God, a Christian, a Father. Well, from where I stand, you aren't much of any of those, each requires one common denominator and that's love."

"Madam, how dare you talk to my husband like that?" Mamie squawked.

"And you, his mother... how could you let your husband talk to him and treat him like that. Jordan doesn't think that either of you love him! He needs to know that!"

"I do love my son!" Mamie protested.

"Actions speak louder than words..." Rita said, "...when was the last time you told him?"

"You mean to tell me that you are okay with a gay son?" Mamie added whispering the word gay.

"With time, yes, I did, and I have grown to love Jordan, too." Rita said smiling at Zander."...time heals all wounds, even when the wound is self inflicted. I honestly believe that God knew what he was doing when he created Zander and Jordan. He knew that they were strong enough to endure whatever was thrown their way. He loves them and if their good enough for God to love then guess what, it's good enough for me." she said with tears in her eyes as Zander massaged her shoulders in support.

"Well, what you choose to do is your business, but I know what the Bible says about those people and..." Reverend Jacobs barked back.

"And I know what the Bible says too, look at Psalms 100:3, It says that, it is He that has made us and not we ourselves..."Rita shot back.

"That's one scripture compared to the many in Leviticus and and Romans and..." Reverend Jacobs began just as the doctor walked in.

"Sounds like to me that you're so heavenly minded that you're no earthly good reverend!" Rita said as the doctor approached.

"Hello, I'm Dr. Wintons, your son's surgeon...."she said as she removed her glasses to rub her tired eyes, "He made it through the surgery."

A unanimous "Thank you Jesus!" was heard all over the small waiting room. Mrs. Jacobs began to cry and Rita comforted her, rubbing her back and whispering, "Its okay."

"The next forty-eight hours are the most crucial, he's not out of the woods yet. I know that he's a fighter because we nearly lost him there twice and he came back like a champ" Dr. Wintons informed them.

"That's my boy" Reverend Jacobs said with a look of pride on his face. The comment shocked everyone else in the room.

"He had some major internal bleeding.." Dr. Wintons continued, "and he has three broken ribs. His heart stopped while we were operating on him and he has a really bad concussion. He is conscious and semi alert. He's in recovery and should be in a room in about an hour."

"Can I see him?" his mother asked.

"Yes you can, in the morning..." Dr. Wintons said to be as sympathetic as possible.

"When can I see him..." Zander eagerly asked.

"You must be Zander..." she said smiling.

"Yes, I am..." Zander said smiling bashfully

"He's been asking for you ever since he came to." Dr. Wintons said knowing that Zander wondered how he knew who he was, "You can go in as soon as he's settled but don't stay too long. He needs a lot of rest."

"I won't I promise." Zander said breathing again.

"Did he ask to see us?" Reverend Jacobs asked almost pleading for an answer.

"No, he didn't, but he was very groggy," Dr. Wintons said smiling empathetically at Reverend Jacobs; she could see the disappointment on his face.

"I'm sure Zander will give him your regards. Won't you son?..." Rita asked

"Sure will..." Zander said wanting to feel vindicated, but he couldn't help but feel a little sorry for Reverend Jacobs.

The minutes seem to drag on until Zander could see Jordan. He tried to prepare himself for whatever he would see, but nothing prepared him for the hurt he would experience when he entered the room. Jordan was hooked up to machines and there were tubes coming from everywhere. Zander tipped in quietly and sat next to Jordan.

"Hey Z!" Jordan struggled to say.

"You're not suppose to be talking" Zander said

"Where am I?" Jordan asked almost whispering.

"You're at Community, now stop talking!" Zander said lovingly scolding Jordan.

"K..." Jordan said sighing and trying to smile at his partner, but even smiling hurt.

Zander returned the smile and tried to hide his concern. He felt himself tearing up, but he managed to fight back the tears. Jordan looked so helpless and you could tell that he was in pain. His eyes were blackened and swollen. Jordan drifted in and out, but Zander didn't care, he was just glad to be there with him. Jordan seemed to be able to rest better with him there.

"Jordan, I need you to know that I love you! I need you. When you came into my life, I started to breathe again and life had new meaning. You've got to get better, you've just got to. Take my strength and drain it if necessary, but don't leave us...don't leave me! Whatever comes we can face it and conquer it, but I don't want to, no make that I won't make it without you. I love you, baby be strong...fight for you.. for us..."Zander said pleading with his partner to fight for his life, "I love you" he said kissing his partner on his forehead.

"I love you too Z and know that whatever happens.. I always will." Jordan whispered, as he began to fade away. Eventually Jordan drifted off, but not before telling Z that he loved him and that he wanted to see his father. Zander waited until Jordan was sound asleep. He tip-toed out just as quietly as he tip-toed in.

"How is he?" Mamie asked

"He's Jordan..."

"What does that mean?" Reverend Jacobs asked.

"He's tired, he's hurting, but he's fighting and I can see the will to live in his eyes...." Zander said looking at Reverend Jacobs"...and he wants to see you."

"He does!" Reverend Jacobs screamed.

"Yes he does, but I need to warn you..." he said to Reverend Jacobs, "he doesn't look anything like himself and there are tubes everywhere.

"Thank you for telling me..." Reverend said in an almost civil tone, "but he can't look any worse than he did when I found him."

Reverend Jacobs walked slowly down to Jordan's room. He peeped in the door to see if he was sleeping. He stood in the door wondering where he went wrong. He asked himself how he could raise a gay child.

Fifty-Three

"Pop is that you?"Jordan asked.

"Yes son,'it's me' I was here earlier, but you were sleeping so peacefully that I thought I would come back later..." his father informed him.

"You could have..."

"I thought it best to let you rest. So how are you feeling?"

"Feeling a little beaten up, right now!" Jordan said trying to get a smile out of his father.

Reverend Jacobs failed to see the humor.

"Son why can't you be serious?" Reverend Jacobs.

"Pops lighten up!"

"Lighten up? Why is everything such a joke with you? You haven't even been out of surgery six hours and you're cracking jokes. We nearly lost you!"

"Pops, I didn't mean to upset you! I know that I'm not out of the woods yet, but I refuse to lay here and just wait to die!" Jordan said coughing at the conclusion of his statement.

"Son are you all right?" his father said with a tinge of concern in his voice.

"Yes..."Jordan said still coughing.

"Your friend said that you wanted to talk with me..." Reverend Jacobs said.

"You mean my partner, Zander..." Jordan said correcting his father.

"Whatever..." Reverend Jacobs said annoyed at being corrected.

"No Pops, not whatever... this is the man I love..."

"The man you love, listen to you... "Reverend Jacobs said with a venomous disgust.

"No! you listen...Zander and I have been together for nearly nine months and he's been my rock. I have waited a long time for someone like him. Someone that wanted me for me..." Jordan said amidst trying to catch his breath, "someone that loves me for me, Can you say that?"

"Son, I love you, but I hate what you've become..."

"Then you don't love me..." Jordan said as hurt consumed his voice

"How can you say that?"

"How can you say that you do?" Jordan said as his breathing became a little bit more rapidly.

"Homosexuality is wrong..."

"Says you..." Jordan said almost whispering.

"Says the Holy Bible!"

"Pops, God loves me...why can't you?" Jordan asked trying to catch his breath.

"Don't bring God into this...how can he love you?"

"You're a minister you tell me..." Jordan said, settling down now that he was able to catch his breath.

"I can't talk with you when you're like this..."

"Like what? I'm the same Jordan that I've always been. It's time for you to accept the realities that I am who I am..." Jordan said as he started to cough a little bit more. You could tell that he was taking short breaths.

"I will never accept this lifestyle of yours, it's sin...plain and simple..." Reverend Jacobs said

"It's not that simple...I had hoped that we could talk, but I see..." Before he could finish his statement, Jordan began choking as blood started to trickle out of his mouth.

Reverend Jacobs went to the hall and called for a nurse.

"He's having difficulty breathing and he started bleeding... help him..."Reverend Jacobs shouted.

"Sir, you're going to have to leave, you're upsetting the patient," the nurse ordered.

"I will not, this is my son...." Reverend Jacobs protested.

"Sir..." the nurse said looking up over her glasses.

"Paging Dr. Wintons... paging Dr. Wintons"

"Oh my God, that's Jordan's doctor..." Mamie said

They all rushed to Jordan's room only to find Reverend Jacobs in the hallway leaning against a wall crying.

"What's going on in there?" Zander demanded to know.

"He's bleeding again...." a shaken Reverend Jacobs told them.

"What happened?" Zander said pumping the reverend for answers.

"We were arguing..." Reverend Jacobs began...

"Arguing about?..." Zander asked about to lose his cool when he caught Rita's eye.

"You and your deviant lifestyle..." Reverend Jacobs said with a defensive tone growing in his voice.

"I don't get you..." Zander said with a bitter tone, "Your son is fighting for his life and you get into an argument about his orientation... what planet are you from?"

Zander wanted to read Reverend Jacobs the riot act, but he knew that this was not the time nor the place. His concern and energy had to be directed to Jordan. Rita walked over and put her hands around Zander and whispered, "Pray..."

"I think its best that you leave now..." Reverend Jacobs said to Miles, Rita and Zander.

"Hezikiah, get over yourself, these people aren't going anywhere... I've had enough of this. You say that you're a man of God, then talk to God about our son. I don't know what happened in there, but if anything happens to that boy, I will never forgive you," Mamie said breaking down.

Rita left Zander and took Mrs. Jacobs into her arms and rocked her, rubbing her back and whispering words of encouragement to her sister in motherhood.

"Just lean and depend on him Mamie, God is able..." Rita reassured Mamie, "God is able" she repeated.

They all stood waiting on Dr. Wintons. The emergency doors flew open and two orderlies came rushing through and into Jordan's room. Moments later, the door opened and they saw Jordan being rolled away. Zander's heart began to beat so rapidly that he thought it would jump out of his throat.

"What's happening?" Reverend Jacobs asked.

"Your son has started hemorrhaging and we're taking him back to surgery. He lost consciousness again and we haven't been able to resuscitate him. It doesn't look good...all I can say is... pray. Now if you'll excuse me..."

"Lord Jesus..." Reverend Jacobs whispered exasperated.

"I hope you're happy now Hezikiah.... our son may die because of you..." Mamie said leaping out of Rita's arms and pounding on her husband's chest."

"Mamie...that's not going to do you or Jordan any good..." Rita said grabbing her arms and hugging her.

"Mamie..." Reverend Jacobs said hurt at his wife's last words.

"Don't Mamie me... you just don't get it do you? You just don't get it!" Mamie shouted at him, burying her face in Rita's shoulder.

"But Mamie..." Reverend Jacobs said trying to get his point across. Seeing that his wife didn't want anything to do with him, he walked away with his head hung low. He didn't know where to go, but he knew that he wasn't welcomed there.

Zander found his way to the chapel. He needed to get away and just think about what was going on. As he entered he heard a familiar voice, it was Reverend Jacobs.

"....and God help me to understand the things that I cannot change. I know for myself that none of us are perfect, but God I'm having a real problem accepting my son and his lifestyle. Could it be that I am so blinded by my hate that I can't love my son? Help me Lord, I think my son's recovery depends on it. He asked me if I loved him and I've always said yes, but the truth of the matter is that I don't think I know how to love him. teach me how, show me, tell me. I know that all of this is my fault. I've pushed him away with my hatred and holier than thou ways. Please Lord, let me have the opportunity to tell him that I'm sorry and that I love him... please let me hold him one more time." With that said Reverend Jacobs began to sob. Zander was so moved by Reverend Jacobs plea. For the first time he saw a side of Jordan's father that he had never seen. His heart broke for him as he pleaded with God to give him one more chance. Zander prayed that he would have that chance.

"Reverend Jacobs..." Zander whispered.

"Yes son..." he answered startled by his presence, trying to wipe the tears from his eyes.

"I heard what you said..." Zander said in a peaceful voice

"So..." Reverend Jacobs said regaining his composure

"So... I think that God is going to honor your prayer..." Zander said offering his support.

"I hope so..." Reverend Jacobs said in a doubtful tone.

"I know so...and so do you" Zander said reassuringly.

"I just hope it's not too late..." Reverend Jacobs said with his voice being overtaken with remorse and sadness. "Son, I know you may not understand, but the word of God says that your lifestyle is wrong. I will never accept it, but I have seen the love that you and my son share and I must admit that I'm jealous. The two of you have something that he and I never had. I just hope its not too late to try again."

"Faith...Reverend...you gotta keep the faith!" Zander reminded him.

Zander and Reverend Jacobs were coming off the elevator when they saw Dr. Wintons talking to Rita, Mamie and Miles. They approached quickly and could see that the news wasn't good.

"Jordan hasn't regained consciousness yet and that worries me..." she said with a look that worried everyone listening. "He's lost a lot of blood and so if any of you are his type please go to the blood bank and donate. I can't tell you much more except that he's going to be in for the fight of his life and we're far deeper in the woods than we were before. We're putting him in ICU and we'll watch him very carefully."

"Is there anything we can do?" Miles asked.

"Pray..." Dr. Wintons said.

Zander took a deep breath. He wanted his partner back. He wanted the life he'd come to know and love back. He wanted things like they were... when everything was like breathing. All he really wanted to do was breathe again.

A Sneak Preview just for you!

The First Chapter

of

Breathe Again

(the sequel to *Like Breathing*)

Courtesy of

One

Zander stroked Jordan's forehead in hopes that his familiar touch would revive his partner. He wouldn't allow himself to believe that Jordan wouldn't pull through this. He had prayed a greater portion of the night. "Jordan, can you hear me? Come back to me... I need you! Open your eyes, come on babe, if you can hear me squeeze my hand." Nothing. Zander took a deep breath and whispered another prayer.

Sister Brooks had stopped by to offer her support and to see if her pastor and first lady needed anything. Mamie filled her in on Jordan's condition as Reverend Jacobs continued to pace the floor.

"So all we can do is pray..." Mamie told her best friend.

"Sistah Jacobs you took the words right out my mouth." Sister Brooks said patting Mamie on the hand. "Pray with out ceasing, God never slumbers nor sleeps." She said lifting here hands towards heaven.

"And that's what we're doing, Francenia. That's what we're doing." Mamie reassured.

"You know what I found this morning?"

"What?" Mamie asked.

"A picture of Jordan and Felecia at their kindergarten graduation.." Sister Brooks said, her voice laced with melancholy, "they made such a cute lil couple. Jordan had a smile a mile wide as he held Fe's hand."

"I remember that picture, Jordan had such a crush on your Felecia." Mamie remembered fondly.

"You know she's pregnant?!"

"Again, I mean, really?" Mamie said surprised. "I don't mean any harm, but she has seven children already!" Sister Brooks laughed at her friend's comment. "And this time we're talking twins."

"Twins!" Mamie said shocked at this new revelation. The women chatted for a while remembering the "good ole days."

"I had better get going, I don't want to wear out my welcome, ..."

"Francenia you could never do that... you were my first friend at the church."

"You remember?" Mamie asked.

"Chile, how could I forget! You walked in on your first Sunday there and we had on the same outfit."

"I wanted to die and strangle that sales clerk at Mangles..."

"Lucrecia Mickles, the devil's daughter..."

"She told me that no one had that suit." Mamie remembered.

"And she knew that I had bought it for the First Sunday!" Francenia chimed in, "And then she sat in the Number One Choir with that crooked grin on her face, waiting on the fire works." The two women giggled like two school girls at recess.

"But you played it off! You showed her! When it was time for remarks, you got up and announced that our outfits would be the new uniform for minister's wives and deaconesses. Her face fell so hard that I think that they're still picking up the pieces." Francenia said, laughing even more. The two women laughed so hard until tears fell from their eyes.

"Francenia, thank you..." Mamie said smiling at her friend.

"For what?"

"Just for being you, I needed to laugh. I have been crying so much in the past 24 hours..."

"Well, you know what the Bible says about a merry heart, even in times like these."

"And you know what?" Mamie asked.

"What?"

"I feel better, you were just what the doctor ordered." Mamie said patting her friend's hand.

"Reverend, you need anything?" Sister Brooks asked.

"Just your prayers my dear sister, just your prayers."

"You have those. Oh my heavens! Look at the time, I better run!" Sister Brooks said as she glanced at the pendant watch that the hung around her neck.

"Thank you again for coming..." Mamie said as she hugged her long time friend.

"Call me, if you need anything" she said as she departed. " My prayers are with you both, praise the Lord."

Mamie and Reverend Jacobs watched Sister Brooks walk down the hospital corridor and waved to her as she got on the elevator. Reverend Jacobs looked like he had aged ten years since Sunday, stubble was taking residence on his face and you could see the gray specs peeking amongst it. His face was consumed with worry and his heart was heavy. He and Jordan had left so many things unsaid and now he didn't know if he would have the chance to rectify them. "What if..." he asked himself, never being able to complete the sentence. He couldn't bear the thought of his son dying, even if he was gay. He wondered if Mamie blamed him for what was happening in that hospital room. After all, it was his sermon that had upset Jordan. It was his comments on the show that brought more attention to the burned building.

"This is all your fault," he told himself. The guilt was beating him down. He couldn't take much more. He bargained with God; he made promises to change. But would it be too much, too little, too late? He hoped not.

Rita stood in the door watching her son, it broke her heart seeing him in such pain. Equally, it troubled her to see Jordan laying there so helpless. All those machines helping him do something as simple as breathing. Simple. Nothing seemed to be simple anymore. All anyone wanted anymore was for Jordan to breathe on his own again. Before she knew it, tears were streaming down her cheeks. She tried to wipe them before Zander saw them. She told herself that she had to be strong.

"Zander.." Rita said softly choking back tears.

"Oh, hey Ma!" Zander said trying to muster up a smile for Rita.

"How's our boy doing?"

"No change..." Zander said taking a deep breath.

"You want to take a break? His mother said that she would sit with Jordan for a while and let you stretch your legs or get a bite to eat."

"Thanks Ma, but no, I think I'm going to stay here."

" Son, you really need to get something to eat, you're not going to do Jordan any good if you get sick, now are you?" Rita asked Zander.

"Ma! What if he wakes up and I'm not here?" Zander asked in protest.

"I'll tell his parents where you are and the nurse's station, so if anything changes they can come and get you." Rita assured.

" I don't know..." Zander said knowing that his mother was right, she always was.

"Zander, now listen to me... if you don't take a break, you are going to worry yourself sick and you'll both be here and then what..."

"Ma, you worry too much."

"I'm not worried, I'm right and you know it!"

"Okay ma, you win..." Zander said knowing that Rita wasn't going to let up. "I always do!" Rita said with a wink and a smile.

Mamie sat vigil with Jordan. Just like Zander, she talked to him, she hummed his favor hymn and rubbed his forehead. The tears rolled down her face as she looked at her pride and joy. She too thought of all the things that were unsaid.

"Jordan, it's mama... I love you son... come back to us. Zander is here and he misses you. So do I. Your daddy is worried about you, too. Jordan, it's time to wake son." Her voice trembled as she spoke.

The machines continued their rhythmic cadence.

She watched his body, lifeless, still and ironically peaceful even as the machines pumped breath into his body. She wondered if he knew what was going on around him. She hoped that he could hear her voice and that it would help lead him back to them.

"Jordan, it's time to wake up now.." She whispered fighting back the tears. She gently kissed him as she squeezed his hand. She whispered a prayer as she asked God to bring her child back to her.

"Lord, its me standing in the need of prayer, I need a blessing. Father, my son lies here and only you can revive him. He's not finished with his life. Bring him back from the brink. There are so many things that I need to say to him. I need to tell him how proud I am of him. I need him to hear the words 'I love you' uttered from my lips. Please Lord, don't rob me of that opportunity. Please give me the chance to be the mother, I haven't been. Please God, please..." she whispered as she rocked back and forth, whipping the tears from her eyes. She leaned over and kissed him on the forehead like she used to do as a child. It took her back to that time, a time when things were so simple. He was just Jordan, not the television personality, not the gay man, not the black gay man... just her little Jordie. She smiled as she remembered.

Rita watched as Zander played with his food. She hadn't been very successful in getting him to eat much, but at least he was putting a little something on his stomach.

"It's not going to jump on the fork," Rita said with smile.

"I'm really not hungry..."

"Son you got to eat!"

"Ma!..."

"Don't Ma, me.... *eat*!" Rita said motioning towards the food.

Zander took a couple of bites of the mashed potatoes and the sweet peas on his plate.

She tried to get his mind off Jordan for a while. She could tell that his brain was consumed with his partner's fate. She thought that his brain could use a break. No thinking, just relaxing.

"I called Oscar Lee.."

"You did? How is he doing?"

"He's fine, said he missed his angel," Rita said blushing.

"Alrighty then!" Zander said giving his mother a high five.

"Boy you so crazy!" Rita said laughing.

"His angel, huh? Maybe I had better have a talk with Mister Oscar Lee Thomas..." Zander said giving his mother a hard time.

"Zander Evan Eady, if you dare..."

"Relax, Ma! I wouldn't dream of interfering in your love life."

"That's right, don't meddle in grown folks bizness." Rita said shaking her finger at Zander.

"I guess you told me..."

"And you know this!"

"Look at ya, just stank... a woman in love!"

"Hush up, Zander! You're embarrassing me!" Rita said blushing.

" I'm sorry ma! It's just that I'm really happy for you. Mister Oscar Lee is a great man and if I had to choose a man for you he would be the one."

"He is a good man son..."

"So when am I gonna give you away..."

"Give me away?"

"Yeah, walk you down the aisle, throw you the wedding of the millennium, you know treat you to a shing-ding that your friends won't ever forget!"

"When and *if*, I marry Oscar Lee it be will a simple service in the Pastor's study or at the court house..."

"Oh no, it won't. Since I'll never have a daughter of my own, I want to throw you a wedding, something romantic, festive and..."

"Slow down son, I haven't even said yes yet!"

"And why is that Ma?"

"Why what?"

"Why haven't you said yes?"

"Because, I want to be sure that I am marrying Oscar Lee because I love him and not because I'm lonely."

"Oh, I see. So what does your heart say?"

"That I love him and that I could see spending the last of my days with Ozzie, I mean Oscar." Rita said, embarrassed that she had revealed her pet name for her beau.

"Ozzie?" Zander said trying not to laugh.

"Don't you start with me..." Rita said, letting Zander know that she was not to be played with.

"I wouldn't dream of it..." Zander said smiling.

"As I was saying..."

"Yes, ma'am."

"I just need to know in my heart of hearts that it's not because I miss your father that I am even thinking about marrying Oz... I mean Oscar. Lee."

"Ma, I think you deserve to be happy and you just told me that in your heart you love Mister Oscar Lee and that you could see yourself spending the rest of your life with him."

"Yes..."

"Then, I think you have your answer."

"I think I'm gonna pray just a little while longer."

"Okay.." Zander said smiling.

Rita sighed and closed her eyes, she just wanted to make sure that she was doing the right thing for all of the right reasons. She listened for the still voice within. No answer.

If you would like to order this or any other Ishai Book or a catalog, copy and fax or mail to:

Ishai Books
The Ishai Creative Group, Inc.
709 East Caracas Street
Tampa, Florida 33603-2328
813/234.6410 • Fax: 813/236.8809
E-Mail: IshaiBooks@aol.com

Name: ______________________________

Store/Company: ______________________________

Address: ______________________________

City, State: ______________________ Zip: __________

Phone: (   ) ______________ Fax: (   ) ______________

Ordered by: ______________________________

Ship to: ______________________________
(*If different*) ______________________________

Quantity	Description	Cost	Unit	Total
	Like Breathing • 1-892096-33-1 **Ricc Rollins** Retail: $14.00			
	Colorblind • 0-9669271-0-9 **Judy Candis** Retail $12.00			
	Detached • 1-892096-35-8 **Lorenzo C. Robertson** Ret. $14.00			
	The Best Man • 1-892096-01-3 **Dwayne Carter** Retail $ 14.00			

Sub-total	
S/H	$3.95
Total	

Method of Payment:

◯Cash ◯Check #:______ ◯Visa•MC•AMEX ◯C.O.D

• Minimums Apply•

Please Make Checks Payable to The Ishai Creative Group, Inc.